"Since you have two families coming, as well as the two newcomers who also probably wanted to bring support, it only makes sense," Della said.

Max nodded. "Yep. No reason to be nervous."

Confident Della had returned, thank goodness. "I'm not. I went to school with some of these people, you know. Since my boss, Sebastian, got engaged to your cousin Ruby, I'm sure he's going to be there. I've also worked with others at Crosswinds. And Malcom and I have done a couple of search and rescue operations before. So we're not all total strangers. It's inevitable that we'd know each other, especially in such a small town."

"True." As he watched her, his gaze darkened. "Damn, I'd like to kiss you right now. But I don't want to ruin your lipstick."

Heat flooded her. Taking a deep breath, she leaned forward, keeping her eyes locked on his. "I have the lipstick in my purse. I can always touch it up."

Instead of waiting for him to follow through, she pulled his face down to hers.

Dear Reader,

Once again, I was fortunate enough to return to writing about the Colton family. This time, the story combined several of my favorite things—mountains and dogs! I was thrilled to write a story about Della Winslow, a search and rescue volunteer and dog trainer in the beautiful state of Idaho. Pairing her with former playboy turned FBI agent Max Colton was a lot of fun! Throw in the huge Colton family, a small town and a serial killer on the loose, and what a story.

I truly hope you enjoy reading it as much as I did writing it.

Karen Whiddon

COLTON MOUNTAIN SEARCH

KAREN WHIDDON

HARLEQUIN
ROMANTIC
SUSPENSE

Special thanks and acknowledgment are given to Karen Whiddon for her contribution to The Coltons of Owl Creek miniseries.

HARLEQUIN®

ROMANTIC SUSPENSE™

Recycling programs for this product may not exist in your area.

ISBN-13: 978-1-335-59402-0

Colton Mountain Search

Copyright © 2024 by Harlequin Enterprises ULC

For questions and comments about the quality of this book, please contact us at CustomerService@Harlequin.com.

TM and ® are trademarks of Harlequin Enterprises ULC.

Harlequin Enterprises ULC
22 Adelaide St. West, 41st Floor
Toronto, Ontario M5H 4E3, Canada
www.Harlequin.com

Printed in Lithuania

MIX
Paper | Supporting responsible forestry
FSC® C021394

Karen Whiddon started weaving fanciful tales for her younger brothers at the age of eleven. Amid the gorgeous Catskill Mountains, then the majestic Rocky Mountains, she fueled her imagination with the natural beauty surrounding her. Karen now lives in north Texas, writes full-time and volunteers for a boxer dog rescue. She shares her life with her hero of a husband and four to five dogs, depending on if she is fostering. You can email Karen at kwhiddon1@aol.com. Fans can also check out her website, karenwhiddon.com.

Books by Karen Whiddon

Harlequin Romantic Suspense

The Coltons of Owl Creek

Colton Mountain Search

Visit the Author Profile page
at Harlequin.com for more titles.

Chapter 1

Even the light seemed different up in the mountains. Clearer, somehow. The sunshine and cloudless blue sky made this a perfect summer day. Della Winslow took a deep breath and smiled. She loved the crisp mountain air at this elevation, slightly cool even in August. Keeping a watchful eye on her surroundings, she whistled for her black Lab, Charlie. Though she usually kept him on leash, today she'd been allowing him to range ahead of her on the steep and rocky trail.

Since she'd trained him well, he immediately returned to her side, long black tail wagging. After praising him, she rewarded him with one of his favorite liver treats. This, she thought, was one of the reasons she loved her life choices. Not everyone got to work their passion. Hers had always been training dogs. Today she got to do that and work out as well, combining hiking in the Bitterroot Mountains along with schooling her already very talented search and rescue cadaver dog. She'd been working with him since she'd gotten him as a puppy at eight weeks old. Now two, he'd earned his certification and had accompanied her on several SAR missions, where he'd easily proved his skills.

Specifically, Charlie had been trained to smell decomposition. When working a scene, whether an accident of some sort or an act of nature, his job was to locate anything that had been left by a human body. This could be body parts, including tissue, blood and bone or fluids. He could also detect residue left by a scent, which meant he could tell if a body had been somewhere, even if it had been moved.

So far, she'd been working with him for eighteen months. Luckily, her job as a dog trainer at Crosswinds Training had made it easier for her to teach him, since he often needed to work up to eight hours a day. She'd also had to socialize and desensitize him, getting him used to sirens and flashing lights, since they'd commonly be requested at accident scenes. While she'd trained SAR dogs in the past, Charlie was her first cadaver dog. He'd already been an asset on the one accident scene they'd worked—a train derailment close to Boise.

These days, she spent as much of her time as she could fine-tuning his training. She'd known the instant she'd started with him that his hunt drive, confidence and unflappable nerve would serve him well in search and rescue work.

Today, though, they were mostly focused on fun. Every now and then, she'd call Charlie back to her before letting him roam again. Judging by the way he carried his tail curled over his back, he was thoroughly enjoying himself.

They entered a clearing. Charlie took off again, running in circles around her and panting happily. Smiling, Della watched him, her heart light.

Suddenly, her dog froze. He sat and barked once, looking back at her to see if she'd caught his cue.

Puzzled, she hurried toward him. Charlie had just given the signal that meant he'd found human remains.

As she got closer, she saw them. Bones. Large ones, unmistakably human, protruding from the dirt near the edge of the clearing.

Charlie stayed in place, watching as she circled the area. They both knew better than to disturb anything. Time to call in law enforcement.

Except this high up, her cell phone had no signal. She'd expected that since she'd been here before. A quarter mile back down the trail she could climb up on a few large boulders, and sometimes, if the conditions were just right, she could get a signal. Though the likelihood often ran fifty-fifty, she had to try. After all, the only other option would be to hike back to her vehicle and drive closer to civilization.

Before she left, she had to mark the scene. Digging in her backpack, she pulled out a strip of bright yellow cloth that she sometimes used for sight work. When she'd tied this around the nearest tree, she used her cell phone to take several photos of the area, including a couple of the bones themselves.

Then she whistled for Charlie, and they set off down the trail in the direction of the rock formation. Once there, she climbed up as far as she safely could and checked her cell. Two bars. Enough to call the Owl Creek Police Department and report her findings. If she was lucky, they'd send someone out to investigate right away.

It must have been a slow day in Owl Creek, because by the time Della reached the parking lot, two police cruisers were pulling up. Since the place where Charlie had located the body wasn't accessible by vehicle, all four of the uniformed officers had to hike back up along with Della and Charlie.

Luckily, they appeared to be in pretty good shape. Della kept her pace a little slower than usual, just in case.

By the time they reached the clearing, all four of the officers were only slightly out of breath. Charlie kept pace with Della, watching her every move. Since they had company, she'd given him the hand signal to stay by her side. Now he waited for her to signal him to search.

Once they'd stopped in the middle of the meadow, she pointed to the cloth she'd tied around the tree. "The bones are over there."

Next to her, Charlie quivered with impatience. "My dog is a search and rescue cadaver dog. He found them. And he really wants me to allow him to point them out again."

With a flick of her hand, she sent Charlie out again. He went to the bones he'd found earlier, sat and barked. Once she'd given him his verbal praise, he took off again.

Della stood back and watched while the police officers took photos of the scene. She kept an eye on Charlie, noticing the way he kept moving in circles around the field, almost as if he was actively working a crime scene.

She'd just had that thought when Charlie sat and barked, signaling he'd located something else. Dread coiling in her stomach, she walked over to him. As soon as she reached him, he began pawing at the dirt. She saw the gleam of another large bone and knew.

"Leave it," she commanded, gesturing him back into a sitting position. Then she turned. "He's found another body."

Immediately, all four men hurried over. One took a few more photographs while the other tried to call someone.

"There's no cell signal up here," she advised. "We'd have to walk about a quarter mile back and climb up on that stack of rocks. Even then, it's hit-or-miss."

The older officer, a man whose name tag read Handy, sighed. "I was afraid you'd say that. Now that we have more than one body, we're likely going to have to call in the FBI."

She frowned. "The FBI?"

"Just in case this might be the work of a serial killer," Handy explained. He turned to the others. "Larkins, you come with me. Santis, you and Kinney stay here and make sure nobody disturbs the scene until the FBI can send someone. Put out some crime scene tape or something. Once you're done, we'll all meet up at the squad cars."

"We're going to leave those bones unprotected?" Larkins asked. "What if wildlife comes along or something?"

Handy shook his head. "From the looks of them, they've been here a good while. I'm going to guess any animals have already gotten what they wanted." He glanced at Della. "Are you ready to go?"

"I am," she replied. "Charlie, come." Then, with her dog at her side, she led the way down.

When the call came in from the Owl Creek Police Department, the FBI switchboard operator passed the information to a supervisor, who immediately assigned the case to Max Colton. After all, Max had grown up in Owl Creek and everyone in the office knew his family all still lived there.

Human remains had been discovered by a woman training her SAR cadaver dog on a hiking trail. The police had been out, and the dog had promptly located another buried body, which might indicate a possible serial killer. Which was why the FBI and, now specifically, Max Colton had been asked to step in.

Naturally, Max agreed to take the assignment. Close to home meant he could fit in an extended visit to his family. Despite the fact that he worked about two hours away, with his busy career he found it more and more difficult to fit in a long visit home. With five siblings, he could usually manage to spend time with two or three of them. Maybe this trip, he could see all five.

Since he also had a special fondness for dogs, and in the past had been amazed by the supersmart, well-trained SAR canines, he figured this might be even more of a good fit for him.

Feeling excited and, as his assistant Jack liked to say, pumped, he headed out. In his line of work, he kept a go bag in his truck, so he didn't even need to stop at his apartment before hitting the road.

He made it to the Owl Creek city limits right after lunchtime. Because he hadn't taken the time to eat anything, he made a quick stop in the drive-through of a new burger joint on the outskirts of town. Eating while he drove, he went straight to the trails, wondering if they'd waited for him or if he'd need to round everyone back up.

Two squad cars and an older Jeep Cherokee were parked in the middle of the lot, which meant they'd waited. Several uniformed officers stood around talking to a slender woman with long brown hair that she wore in a thick braid down her back. A large black Lab stood next to her.

Parking, he killed the engine and got out. As he approached the group, he recognized all the officers. One of the benefits of growing up in a small town.

"Hey, Max!" Drew Handy greeted him with a smile. "I kind of figured they'd send you. That's the only reason we waited all this time. We knew you'd rush up here as soon as you got the case."

"Thanks," Max said. "I appreciate that." He glanced around. "I'm guessing they didn't send Fletcher." His cousin worked as a detective for the Owl Creek PD.

"He's off today," Handy replied. "Otherwise, I'm sure they would have."

The woman turned then, smiling, and Max lost all capacity for rational thought. He didn't know her—must not have ever met her, because he damn sure wouldn't forget a woman like her. Achingly beautiful in a natural kind of way, with large brown eyes and a lush mouth. Staring might be rude, but he couldn't seem to pull his gaze away.

Luckily, her dog stood and drew his attention. Long tail wagging furiously, the Lab quivered with eagerness. He was, Max thought, one hell of a good-looking animal. His black coat shone, and his eyes were clear and bright. The woman gave a quick hand signal and the dog sat back down, staying put at her side.

"Hey, there." Crouching to put himself at eye level, Max glanced up at the woman. "Is it okay if I pet him?"

Slowly, she nodded. "Charlie, free," she said, her expression reserved. Immediately, Charlie launched himself at Max, nearly bowling him over. Max laughed, fending off dog kisses and slobber while scratching the gleaming black fur.

"Charlie, heel," the woman said. Her clearly well-trained

dog returned to sit at her side. She waited until Max had gotten back on his feet before holding out a hand. "Della Winslow," she said. "My apologies. He's not usually so enthusiastic about strangers."

Shaking her hand, Max smiled. "No apology needed. I like most dogs and they like me. I'm Max Colton."

The wary look came back into her eyes. "I know who you are." She glanced at the officers, who were all watching with unabashed interest. "I've done some searches with your brother Malcolm. He's a nice guy."

Max nodded. His brother helped run the family ranch and did some volunteer SAR work on the side. "That he is," he replied.

She turned her attention back to the others. "Are you guys ready to hike back up to the site?"

"Yes, ma'am," they replied in unison, grinning as they looked from her to Max and back again. Her creamy skin became pink, but she turned and whistled for Charlie, striding ahead. Max shook his head at the officers and took off after her.

Over the years, with his aversion to any kind of permanent relationship, Max had managed to cultivate quite a reputation as a player. He knew the guys all thought they'd witnessed another hapless woman reacting to his supposed charm, but in fact it was the other way around. For the first time in his life, a woman had rendered Max Colton speechless. The sharp tug of attraction he'd felt had been something he'd never experienced, and he'd dated numerous beautiful women. He couldn't explain it and wasn't sure he even wanted to.

However, Max knew better than to mix business with pleasure. Della Winslow might be gorgeous, but while they were working together, he'd consider her strictly off-limits.

The hike up the path felt good after spending a couple of hours in the car. He'd put on his hiking boots earlier, aware reaching the site would require some effort. Years ago, when he'd lived in Owl Creek, he'd spent quite a bit of his adolescence on these very same trails.

Della led the way, her thick brown braid swinging. Charlie kept pace with her, occasionally ranging a bit ahead, though a single word from her brought him back to her side. They passed the outcrop of giant rocks Max remembered sitting on top of with friends and various dates. He'd felt like the king of the mountain, surveying the landscape and watching wildlife pass below.

"Not too much farther," Della said, glancing back over her shoulder at them.

"We've already taken a bunch of photos." Drew sounded out of breath. "And I'm guessing you'll want to use your own forensics?"

"We'll see." Noncommittal until he got a good idea what they were dealing with, Max shrugged. A lot depended on how old these burial sites turned out to be.

One more turn and they came out into a large clearing. Max spotted a bright yellow strip of cloth tied to a tree. "There?" he asked.

"Yes," Della answered. "Charlie found the first set of bones in that location."

Despite Drew having taken photos, Max pulled out his pocket camera and got to work. "I like to have my own," he explained, even though no one had asked.

As soon as he'd finished with the first grave, Della directed him to the second. He took the photos, careful not to disturb anything, and then met her again. Again, he felt a jolt straight to his midsection, which he managed once more to ignore. "Are you sure there aren't any more?"

The question appeared to startle her. She tilted her head, considering. "I guess we need to ask Charlie," she finally replied.

Hearing his name, the black Lab looked up at her, on instant alert. "Go out," she said, gesturing toward an area with her hand.

Tail curved high over his back, Charlie leaped forward, nose to the ground, intent on his work.

Everyone went silent and watched.

Max had watched search and rescue dogs work before, focused and unflappable in even the most horrific of circumstances. Most of them could, and would, do the same type of work as a cadaver dog if needed, but they specialized in finding signs of life rather than human remains. Cadaver dogs like Charlie received even more specialized training.

As alert as her dog, Della appeared to balance on the balls of her feet, ready to move the second Charlie gave an alert. Max honestly hoped he didn't, because if they found any additional bodies, this case would turn into a major investigation. Which, with four members of local law enforcement present, would be impossible to keep under wraps.

Charlie stopped, sat and barked once. Eyes wide, Della met Max's gaze and nodded. "He's found another one."

Damn it. "Stay put," Max ordered the Owl Creek police

crew. "This entire pasture is about to turn into a crime scene."

Following Della to where Charlie waited, Max looked around. This time, there were no visible signs of a body. "Let him dig," he told Della. "Just enough to unearth whatever he's found, not more."

"He knows his job," she shot back, her voice terse. One flip of her fingers and Charlie began digging.

It wasn't long before he unearthed a dirty and jagged bone. The instant he did, he sat and once again looked toward Della for cues.

Grim now, Max told Della they'd seen enough for now. "I'm going to have to call in a team," he said, speaking loud enough for the others to hear. "We'll bring in our own forensic people too. I'll need you to make sure to mark off as much of this area as you can."

"I doubt we have that much crime scene tape," Drew said. "But we'll do the best we can."

"I appreciate that." Returning his attention to Della, Max thanked her for her help. "Will you and Charlie be available to assist when I get my team in place?"

"Of course," she replied, scratching her dog behind his ears. "That's what we do."

"I'm going to need to hike down back to the rocks so I can make the call," he said. "Once I've done that, I've got a tent in my truck. I figure I might as well spend the night here so I can make sure nothing is disturbed."

Appearing unsurprised, she nodded. "Would you like Charlie and me to stay here with you? We have our own tent."

Of course she did. Working with SAR teams, Della would be prepared for anything. He had to admit, the prospect of spending some alone time with her so they could get to know each other had a lot of appeal. Probably more than it should have.

"I'll leave that up to you," he said. "I've got enough rations to get us through tonight and tomorrow morning. My team will bring more."

Her smile lit up her face. Again, he felt that tug. He swallowed hard, well aware he couldn't let her see how she affected him.

"I travel with rations too," she told him. "And dog food, so Charlie never has to miss a meal."

Aware of the others watching intently, Max turned to them. "The FBI will be taking the lead on this. I need you to keep this quiet for now. No media. Please just keep a lid on this until we figure out what we're dealing with."

All four men murmured their agreement. Though Max knew it would only be a matter of time until one of them told someone, hopefully this would buy him a little time.

"Good. Well, thank you for your assistance with this." He dismissed them with a smile. "I'll walk back with you as far as the boulders."

Della called Charlie to her side, and once again, the small group took off. This time, the hike was silent, everyone apparently lost in their own thoughts. Finding a mass burial ground tended to have that effect on people. And unfortunately, that was what this site was becoming. With the discovery of three bodies and who knew how many more, they likely had a serial killer on their hands.

As soon as they reached the towering rocks, Max and Della stopped. The policemen continued down to the parking lot. While Della gave Charlie some water, Max climbed to his former adolescent perch and checked his phone. Two and a half bars. Enough of a signal to make a call or two.

Once Max had outlined the situation to his supervisor, Brian Mahoney, and listed who and what he needed, he waited, watching Della interact with her dog below. A moment later, Brian returned to the line and informed Max that everyone would be on their way first thing in the morning. He'd have his entire team assembled by lunchtime. And yes, they'd all be prepared to camp as long as necessary.

Thanking the man, Max ended the call and climbed back down. Della looked up from her dog and smiled, her brown eyes bright. Mouth suddenly dry, Max wondered if he'd ever get accustomed to the gut punch of her beauty.

Della turned away, appearing completely unaware. "Let's go get our gear and establish a campsite."

Back on solid footing, he fell into step alongside her. "Yes, we've got to make sure we pitch our tents on safe ground." By which he meant not on top of any buried bodies.

"True." Nodding, Della smiled up at him again. This time he braced himself and, to his relief, was able to smile back. He counted it as a small victory. Once his team assembled, he knew he'd be too focused to pay much attention to a random physical attraction.

When they reached the lot, all the squad cars were gone.

"How long do you think you have before one of them alerts the media?" Della asked.

He grimaced. "I'm just hoping for enough time to get the full scope of the situation. The FBI will want to issue an official statement, but not until we have all the facts."

"People will panic once they know we have a serial killer in Owl Creek."

"I know." Pressing the key fob, he unlocked his truck and reached into the back seat, where he kept all his gear. He unloaded it all, looking up to see Della doing the same thing at her Jeep. Charlie sat quietly at her side, watching her.

"Are you sure you want to do this?" he asked, shouldering on his pack and grabbing his duffel. "You don't have to. You can always go home and come back tomorrow."

"It's all good." She loaded up quickly, clearly an expert in the art of packing. "If I'm on-site, Charlie and I can get an early start. Just in case there turn out to be more."

More. Damn, he hoped not. Finding three unmarked graves was bad enough. Any more than that and they'd have a potentially catastrophic situation on their hands. At least he knew his team would be busy getting data before coming this way. They'd look for reports of missing women, because most likely that was what these remains would turn out to be.

"Are you ready?" she asked. The question made Charlie stand, his tail wagging.

"Sure." Once she'd reached him, they went back to the trail. This time, he felt glad he'd packed a satellite phone in his gear. He even thought he might have remembered to charge it. At least with that, they'd have a way to communicate with the rest of the world.

Charlie led the way up, staying fairly close and glancing back often to make sure they followed. Once again, Max found himself enjoying the exercise, the fresh air and the company. He liked that Della apparently didn't feel the need to fill the silence with small talk.

"Do you have the resources for relatively quick identification?" she asked, after they'd passed the rocks. "I know sometimes that sort of thing can take time, especially when some of the bones have been there awhile."

"We do." He smiled. "It still takes longer than what you see on TV, but we're pretty fast. We're the FBI, after all."

Her eyes sparkled as she met his gaze. For a second, he could have sworn something arced between them. A kind of connection, almost as real as a physical touch. But then she looked away and the moment vanished. Which was a good thing, he supposed. He was about to be much too busy, and professional, to be making goo-goo eyes with the SAR handler.

They reached the clearing. The wind had picked up a little and even in August it carried a definite chill. Instinctively he eyed the sky for signs of a gathering storm, but the perfect blue dotted with fluffy white clouds allayed his fear. A peaceful summer afternoon with a breeze, nothing more.

Della had Charlie perform a search of the area where they'd decided to pitch their tents. Max watched, fascinated, as Della controlled exactly where she wanted Charlie to search. She used a combination of vocal cues and hand signals, all of which Charlie clearly understood.

After a few minutes with his nose to the ground, the talented dog returned to Della's side and sat.

"This means he didn't find anything," Della said. "So it's safe to get busy setting up camp."

They each tended to their own tents. They placed them side by side, almost touching. That way they'd have easy access to each other in case some sort of emergency arose. Standard protocol when in the wilderness, especially in small groups. It didn't help that all he could think of was how close she'd be sleeping in the tent next to him.

He gave himself a mental shake. This nonsense needed to stop. They were two professionals working a potential crime scene, nothing more.

"Firepit here?" she asked, already digging out a spot in the dirt. "I'm pretty sure we can gather enough rocks to make a perimeter."

"I can do that." He'd also noticed the rocks scattered around the edge of the clearing. Almost like markers… No, that was what they had Charlie for.

In a few minutes, he'd gathered enough good-sized rocks to ring their makeshift firepit. Despite the constant pull of physical attraction, he felt comfortable around Della and her dog. He actually looked forward to getting to know her better. In a purely work-colleague type of way.

Once they had the pit ready, they each went off to gather wood, making several trips. Since it hadn't rained in a good while, they found lots of dry timber in manageable sizes and hauled it back to the campsite.

"I have an old newspaper," she said. "I forgot to take it out of my duffel after my last rescue mission. I'm thinking we can use it to help get the fire started."

"That'll work," he replied, refraining from asking her

why she didn't read her news on her phone like everyone else. But then again, she likely went to remote locations like this one, where phone reception was spotty to nonexistent. So a physical newspaper made sense.

Watching him as if she could read his thoughts on his face, she shook her head and went into her tent to retrieve it. Handing it to him, she went to take care of her dog while he worked on the fire.

It wasn't long until he had a good-sized blaze going. Just in time, since the shadows were lengthening, and it would soon be dark.

This was one time where he was glad his reputation from the old days in Owl Creek apparently hadn't preceded him. Though they were alone in the woods, isolated from civilization, Della treated him like a work colleague. Nothing more, nothing less. Which was exactly as it should be.

If only he could get himself to regard her the exact same way.

Chapter 2

Della loved dogs more than people, as evidenced by the fact that she'd made training and working with them her life's work. Training search and rescue, drug detection and various other law enforcement canine officers had long been her passion. When Sebastian had added basic manners classes at Crosswinds, at first she had been ambivalent. Now she found she quite enjoyed it. Helping teach their owners how to communicate with their pets had also been unexpectedly rewarding. In all, she lived her life exactly the way she wanted to.

Her friends might be few, but the friendships were deep and long-lasting. When she dated, she made sure to keep things casual. She'd never been one to picture herself settled down and married with a couple of kids. In fact, she didn't really want that. She enjoyed the freedom of her current lifestyle and the opportunities for travel her work with SAR brought.

In short, she considered herself happy. Vibrantly alive even. The last thing she wanted or needed was to be attracted to Max Colton, a man everyone used to consider Owl Creek's major player.

Over the years, she'd heard the stories. He'd left swaths of brokenhearted women pining after him. *Love them and leave them* appeared to be Max Colton's mantra and Della had privately wondered how he'd managed to hook so many women. After all, his reputation surely preceded him. These chicks had to know what they were up against. Maybe they hadn't cared or they'd harbored some delusional belief that they'd be the one to change him.

She couldn't fault his choices. Like her, he appeared to live life exactly on his own terms. All the women throwing themselves after him had puzzled her. Perhaps they liked the challenge of pursuing the truly unattainable.

At any rate, Della had never understood why. Until today, when she'd come face-to-face with the man and felt a bone-deep longing the likes of which she hadn't believed was possible. She'd wanted to run, to hide, and she'd also wanted to jump his sexy-as-hell, bad-boy bones.

Quite the paradox and completely unlike her. Luckily, he didn't appear to feel the same tug of attraction as she did.

After he'd gathered the rocks, he went back for enough dry wood to use for kindling. Glad to be busy, she did the same.

While he worked on getting the fire going, she put out food and water for Charlie. Tail wagging, he gulped down his kibble, drank and then curled up on the ground near her.

Once Max had flames crackling, he dropped down to sit on the ground. She hesitated, even when he invited her to join him with a tilt of his head and a half smile.

She felt a moment of panic. What would they talk about? How much could they actually have in common, this wealthy playboy turned FBI agent and a free-spirited dog trainer?

In the end, she decided none of that mattered. At this moment in time, they were coworkers, nothing more.

As she lowered herself to the ground near, but not next to, him, he smiled again. "Tell me about what all goes into training a search and rescue dog."

So she did. She told him about how she'd begun working with Charlie as a puppy, the socialization work she'd done, taking him around fire stations and police stations so he'd get used to sirens and flashing lights. The obedience training they'd started on day one, all with the same positive reinforcement she taught in her classes at Crosswinds Training.

"That's my day job," she said, feeling relaxed and happy, and wondering if she'd prattled on for too long.

"I'm impressed." He sounded as if he meant it. "Not everyone gets to work doing something that they love."

While she'd talked, the fire had burned down to nearly embers. "I think it's time to turn in," he said.

Checking her watch, she was surprised to realize it was nearly eleven. "I agree." She pushed to her feet and stretched. Charlie eyed her but made no move to get up.

"Come on, boy," she said. "It's time to go to bed."

Charlie got up and came to her side. "See you in the morning," she told Max, and she and her dog went inside her tent.

She'd laid her sleeping bag out earlier. Crawling inside, she motioned to Charlie to join her.

As she settled into sleep, she found the sounds of wildlife comforting rather than frightening. Wolf howls, thankfully in the distance, made her tilt her head and listen. As long as they weren't visited by a bear, she'd be fine.

Sharing her sleeping bag, Charlie lifted his head a few times and sniffed the air, but he didn't appear worried. She laid her cheek against his head and gave him a gentle kiss. If he wasn't, she wasn't. She went to sleep with a smile on her face.

In the morning, she woke early and checked the time on her fitness tracker. Even at home, she made a habit out of watching the sunrise while sipping on her coffee. She signaled Charlie to be quiet and opened her tent flap. The sky had lightened enough that she could see, though the sun hadn't yet made an appearance over the horizon. Together, she and her dog went into the woods to make their morning toilet.

Back at camp, she added some wood to the still-smoldering embers, and once she had a decent-sized fire going, she washed her face with cleansing wipes and brushed her teeth. Then she got some water boiling to make coffee. While she waited, she glanced at Max's tent, which was still closed. Too bad, because she'd kind of wanted to watch the sunrise with him.

The instant the thought occurred to her, he popped his head out of his tent. With his tousled hair and early morning stubble, he looked even sexier than he had the day before. She swallowed hard. "Good morning," she said, her voice bright. "Are you a coffee drinker?"

"I am." Smiling lazily at her, which made her insides twitch, he stood. "I even brought my own cup. I'll be back in a moment," he said, before disappearing into the woods. Charlie watched him go, tail wagging lazily, but made no move to leave Della's side. It took every ounce of self-control she possessed not to keep her gaze locked on Max's very fine backside as he walked away.

Honestly. She rolled her eyes at herself. She wasn't sure what had gotten into her, but it was nothing that hard work wouldn't take care of. The FBI team would be there soon. That should be enough of a distraction to set her mind straight.

She had the coffee ready by the time he returned. He went to his tent and brought out his mug, and once she'd filled it, he sat down on the ground next to her.

Her first sip had her sighing in pleasure. Even instant coffee tasted amazing when made over a campfire. They sipped in silence while the sun colored the sky red, orange and pink. Charlie got up and circled a few times, before lying back down and heaving a contented sigh.

"Look at him," Max said. "I swear he looks like he's grinning."

"That's because he is." She laughed. "He's a very expressive dog."

"I should check in with my team." Max stood. "Much easier now that I have my sat phone."

While he did that, she fed Charlie and made herself a second cup of coffee, which she drank slowly. She needed to eat something too. She wasn't sure what kind of rations he'd brought, but she ate a protein granola bar and some of her favorite smoked beef jerky.

Emerging from his tent, Max appeared to be chowing down on his own protein bar or something.

"They're on their way," he announced, coming closer to use the last of the water to make himself a second cup of coffee. "ETA about ninety minutes."

Impressed, she checked her watch. It was barely seven thirty. "Wow, they sure got an early start."

He shrugged. "They're pretty fired up. It's not every day we get a case like this, and local too. That's the best part of the job. Assembling the evidence and using it to catch the bad guy."

"Are you going to meet them at the lot?" she asked.

"I am." He eyed her. "Are you okay with holding down the fort alone?"

His question made her laugh. "I am. Remember, Charlie and I were out here on a solo hike when we found the first set of remains. We'll be fine."

"Just don't get started without me."

She wiped out her cup and stowed it back in the tent. "Do you want to search a little more now?"

His gaze sharpened, but he shook his head. "Honestly, I do. But we'd better wait for the team."

"I understand." The proximity to him, the constant buzz of sexual tension and the prospect of the day that lay ahead of them had her practically vibrating with energy. Maybe she shouldn't have had that second cup of coffee.

Not wanting to stand around doing nothing for an hour and a half, she whistled for Charlie. "We're going to go for a walk."

"Can I come?" he asked. "It feels better to keep moving instead of just sitting here waiting."

"Sure."

They took off on the narrow, Charlie in the lead, with Max bringing up the rear. She knew exactly where she wanted to go. It had in fact been her intended destination yesterday, before Charlie had made his gruesome discovery.

"Do you have a route in mind?" Max asked from behind her.

"I do," she replied, without turning around. "I often come up here when I need to be reminded of my place in the universe. Have you ever been to Owl Falls?"

"I have." His voice sounded hushed, which told her the falls gave him the same feeling it did her. Reverence for the beautiful countryside in which they lived. A sense of peace and wonder and, often, simple joy at being alive.

The falls weren't easy to get to, which made for a challenging hike. She knew better than to come alone if there was even the slightest possibility of the weather changing, and considered walking here off-limits in the fall, winter and even spring. August with the higher temperatures seemed like the perfect time.

"Not many people hike up that far," he said. She liked that he didn't sound at all out of breath.

"I know. And it's best to go in teams, since some of the footing can be treacherous. But I've been hiking up there since I was a teenager, sometimes in groups and more and more often, alone. I'm always extremely careful."

"I believe you," he said.

Something in his voice made her turn to glance back at him. Because of this, she almost lost her footing, but after a stumble or two, she regained it. Luckily, without incident. Cussing her own carelessness, she resolved to not let him be such a distraction. She knew better.

Following the stream, they continued to climb. The physical exertion made talking difficult, which she liked.

As usual, Charlie led the way, carrying his tail curved over his back. He was such a happy dog.

They heard the roar of the waterfall before they saw it. She knew that around the next bend in the trail, it would come into view. Most people stopped there, admired the sight, took their photos and hiked back down. Not many continued to climb the rocky and sometimes slippery path to the top of the falls. She and Charlie had gone up there numerous times. She guessed she'd see what Max wanted to do.

They made the turn and she stopped, gazing up at the water cascading down. From here, the summit appeared unreachable, though she knew better.

Whistling for Charlie, she took a seat on one of the large rocks near the bank of the river. The sun felt warm on her skin. Charlie bounded back to her, then went carefully down to the edge of the water to get a drink.

"I could look at that all day," Max said, shading his eyes with his hand as he looked up at the falls.

"The view is even better from the top," she said, watching him to see his reaction.

"I imagine it is," he replied. "Unfortunately, I think we need to head back. By the time we get to camp, we'll need to hike to the parking lot to meet my team."

Surprised, she glanced at her watch. He was right. As usual, when she got out in nature, she tended to lose track of time.

Giving the waterfall one last look, she nodded. "I agree. I can always hike out here another time."

"Maybe I can go with you?" he asked. "I've never been up there. I'd really like to go."

She concealed her astonishment by turning her attention to Charlie and ruffling his fur. "Sure," she replied. "We'll have to do that sometime." Vague and noncommittal. That way neither of them had any expectations.

"Cool." Turning, he glanced at her. "Are you ready?"

"I am. Let's go."

They made it back to their camp without encountering any obstacles. Once there, Max checked in with his team via his sat phone before joining Della at her seat near the front of her tent. Apparently, all the exercise had worn Charlie out, because he'd gone inside and curled up to take a nap. Which was good, as she'd want him rested so he could work with the team once they arrived. In fact, she could go for a short nap herself.

"They should be here soon," Max said. "I'm going down to the parking lot to wait for them."

She nodded. "Charlie and I will be here when you all get back."

"Sounds good." Pushing to his feet with a fluid kind of grace that she again found attractive, he took a swig of water from the canteen. "Once we have everyone here, we'll get to work."

Staying seated, she watched until he disappeared out of sight. Then she crawled into her tent and joined her dog, figuring a quick nap would do her good.

Now that he knew who the Bureau had decided to send, Max felt really good about this team. Caroline Perrio, forensic pathologist and crime scene investigator, was one of the best in the business. Max had worked with her on a couple of cases before. The other two team members, Theo Darter and Chris Everitt, were both experienced agents. While on-site, Max would be designated special agent in charge, though that real title went to his boss, Brian Mahoney. Brian had elected to remain at the office in Boise. No one minded, as Brian wasn't a fan of nature or the outdoors. Max would provide daily reports as needed.

None of the team had worked with Della and Charlie before, though Caroline had heard of her work in SAR. They all seemed eager to meet Della and see Charlie in action.

Once at the lot, which was still empty except for his truck and Della's Jeep, he took the opportunity to sit in his vehicle and charge up his phone. Here, he got a half-way decent signal, so he was able to check his email and scroll through his social media feed.

By the time the team pulled up, he'd gotten thoroughly caught up and kind of wished he hadn't. There was something to be said for unplugging for a longer period of time.

Max helped unload their vehicle, a Bureau-issued white windowless van that looked like it belonged on the other side of the law. They were all excited and chattered happily, eager to start the investigation. While Max appreciated their enthusiasm, as they hiked up toward the campsite he found himself longing for the peace of Della's quietness.

"It's just up ahead," he said, when he could finally get a word in. And that seemed to only be because everyone except Caroline was out of breath.

"We don't hike much," Theo said when he caught Max eyeing him. "We'll be fine."

"As long as we can rest a little once we get there," Chris chimed in. Tall and lanky, he wore a Colorado

Rockies baseball cap that looked like it had seen better days.

"Rest?" Caroline teased. "I want to get right to work.
I can't wait to watch Della and her dog in action."

Again, Max appreciated Della. Clearly, she hiked
often. The two of them had kept up a brisk pace and
neither had seemed to mind.

"It's sure pretty out here," Theo said, gasping for
breath. "Do you mind if we take a break for a minute?"

"It's not too much farther," Max replied, reluctantly
slowing and then stopping. Slightly red in the face, Theo
bent over, hands on his knees, chest heaving. Next to him,
Chris gave his coworker a sympathetic smile, though he
also appeared grateful for the break.

Only Caroline looked visibly impatient. She shifted
her weight from foot to foot, making Max wonder if she
planned to forge on ahead without them. He wouldn't
blame her, but he wanted them all to arrive at camp at
the same time.

Five minutes dragged, but finally he made a show
of checking his watch. "Are you good to go?" he asked
Theo. "It really isn't too far away."

The other man nodded, and they took off again.

Another turn and they could make out the two tents
pitched at the edge of the meadow.

"It's pretty remote up here," Theo mused. "I'm guessing that's why the killer decided it would be a great place
to bury his bodies."

As they drew closer, there was no sign of Della or
Charlie, and Max felt a twinge of concern. He hoped they
hadn't gone off on another solo hike.

The others were chattering again, commenting on

everything from the size of the clearing to how close the tents had been pitched together. Theo, ever the practical one, had already begun laying things out in preparation for setting up two additional tents.

Caroline had already wandered over to look at the first set of bones, crouching on her haunches to study them. Despite all the photos they'd already taken, she had her camera in hand and was snapping some more.

Just then, Charlie bolted from the tent, barking an alert, though his tail wagged furiously. A moment later, Della peeked her head out and quieted him. "It's okay, boy," she said. "We're about to go to work." Judging by her tousled hair and sleepy eyes, she'd just awakened.

"Did you take a nap?" Max asked, smiling. The team went quiet, looking from Max to Della and her dog. Caroline pushed to her feet, smiling.

"I did." Covering her yawn with her hand, Della emerged. "It was supposed to be a short one, but clearly I overslept." She looked from one person to the next, her expression friendly. "I'm Della and this is my canine partner, Charlie."

"Hi! I'm Caroline Perrio." Hand outstretched, she approached Della. "Forensic pathologist and crime scene investigator."

After the two women shook hands, Max performed the rest of the introductions, unable to help but notice the way both Theo and Chris reacted to Della's beauty. Theo's pale skin flushed while Chris simply flashed Max a knowing grin.

Oblivious, Della told them the timeline of Charlie's discovery. "Max seems to think there might be more graves. I'm hoping he's wrong, but that's Charlie's area of expertise. Just let me know when you're ready for him to work."

"We will." Caroline glanced at Max. "I'd like to work on the three known graves. I'll need to prep them so they can be transported back to my lab." She pointed at Theo. "I'll need your help."

Theo nodded. "No problem."

"Perfect." Beaming, Caroline spun around and went back to the first set of bones. Theo trailed along after her.

"Okay, then." Max rubbed his hands together. "Why don't we see if Charlie can find anything else."

Eyes bright, the dog watched him, almost as if he understood everything Max said.

"We'll start over on this side." Della pointed. "And work our way back toward the areas where the first three graves were located."

Noting her phrasing, Max nodded. Like him, he suspected Della had a gut feeling they'd find more bodies hidden in this clearing.

"Are you ready?" Della asked. When he nodded, she quietly ordered Charlie to go to work. Even Caroline paused to watch the skilled dog work.

In less than five minutes, Charlie sat and gave his signal, a single bark. Della praised him, and she and her dog waited while Max and Chris hurried over.

The two men dug, using the small, blunt shovels the team had brought along for that purpose. Less than three inches under the topsoil, they found another set of bones.

"Damn it." Max shook his head. "I wonder how many more are out here."

Tongue lolling, Charlie watched him.

"Mark this one too," Max told Chris. "We might as well see how many more the dog finds."

"We're going to need more people," Caroline piped up. "And depending on the end total, another transport van or two. Three is about the maximum I can move in the single van we have."

Max rubbed his eyes. Expression grave, Della watched him. She knew, he realized. Somehow, just like him, she knew that they were going to find some sort of killing field here. What had formerly appeared to be an undisturbed, peaceful meadow would be forever tainted.

Uncharacteristically silent, the rest of the team suspected too. Their somber faces gave testimony to their feelings.

"Go ahead—send Charlie out," Max said.

In the next ten minutes, Charlie signaled twice more. Six bodies. Knowing he needed to make a report immediately, Max got out his cell phone and called his SAC.

"Are you effin' kidding me?" Brian asked. "Six?"

"Yes, sir. And there might be more." While Max fervently hoped they'd found all the graves, he had no idea how long the killer had been dumping his prey here. If not for Della taking a hike with her SAR dog, none of these would likely have ever been discovered.

"The media is going to have a field day. You know how they like to sensationalize serial killers." Brian exhaled loudly. "We need to keep a lid on this as long as we can. I'm going to have to bring in more people."

"And Caroline says she needs more transport vans. All these remains have to go back to her lab so she can ID them."

"I'll work on that." Brian sighed. "I'll give you a call once I have an ETA."

"Thanks." Max ended the call. "Brian's sending a couple more vans," he said. "He wants an update with the total once we're done."

"We'll need them for sure," Caroline replied, looking up.

Max walked over, checking out the fourth set of bones, which Chris still worked carefully to uncover. A gleam of something caught his eyes. "What's this?" he asked, pulling a bit of silver metal from the dirt. "It looks like a necklace. Some sort of wolf."

Several feet away, Della froze. "Let me see it," she said, hurrying over. "I need to know if there's an inscription on the back."

Max handed it over, noticing the way her hands trembled. She turned it to see the other side, and her expression crumpled. She let out a cry, so full of pain she might have been mortally wounded. "Angela," she said, gasping for air. "Oh, Angela."

Max took the necklace from her unresisting fingers. He turned it over and read the inscription carved into the back. *To Angela, from Della. Forever family.*

Della swayed. Afraid she might go down, Max pulled her close, supporting her with his arm.

"You knew this person?" he asked, frowning.

"Yes. Angela is…was…my cousin." Della's voice broke. Taking a deep breath, she leaned on Max and continued. "She went missing two years ago, in Kalispell, Montana. None of us ever gave up hope that we'd find her." She shuddered, her gaze unfocused, looking inward. "And now I have. She was killed."

As the enormity of the realization washed over her, Della seemed to shrink in upon herself. Shuddering, she turned away from the others, pressing her face into Max's chest. He held her close while she cried, great heaving sobs that she clearly tried to muffle.

Damn it. He hadn't expected this case to turn personal.

Wanting to give her some privacy, the rest of the team moved away. They gathered around one of the other graves and got busy working to clear dirt from the bones.

Standing motionless, Max tried to offer what comfort he could while poor Della mourned the loss of her cousin.

Though he'd only just met her, Max held her while she wept. Charlie, clearly worried about her, came over, sat down with his body pressed against her leg and whined. Despite her obvious pain, Della reached out blindly and laid her hand on the dog's head. This quieted him. Max wished he could do something similar for her.

After a few moments, Della seemed to get her emotions under control. Her shuddering quieted. She straightened and took the necklace out of Max's hands and moved away, avoiding eye contact. Charlie followed, sticking close to her side.

As if by mutual agreement, everyone stopped what they were doing and silently watched as Della and Charlie disappeared into her tent.

"That's awful," Caroline murmured. "What a horrible way to find out what happened to your cousin."

Max nodded. "It is. And even though she's tentatively identified the body, you'll still need to get a positive forensic ID."

"Of course." Caroline nodded. "Everyone, let's get back to work."

They worked for several hours, painstakingly unearthing the bones. During this time, Della did not emerge from her tent. When Max finally called for a break, Caroline came over and touched his arm. "Should you check on her?" she asked.

"Should I?" He shrugged. "She kind of seemed like she wanted to be left alone. Honestly, I can't blame her."

Caroline met his gaze. "I guess I was just thinking that since you two appear to be close, you'd be best able to offer her comfort."

"Close?" The description unsettled him. "I just met her yesterday."

"Oh. Wow." Now Caroline appeared flustered. "I'm sorry. I just assumed…"

For some reason this irritated him. Despite keeping his dating life low-key for the past several years, he couldn't escape his reputation. "Don't assume. The last thing I think Della would need or want right now would be me intruding on her personal grief."

"Maybe not." Caroline shrugged. "I know if it was me, I'd want to be left alone." Turning, she walked away.

This should have made him feel better. Truthfully, he'd been wishing he could figure out something to help Della. While it was true that he barely knew her, there'd been some sort of instant and intense connection between them. What that might lead to, if anything, he had no idea.

Naturally, he'd never admit such a thing to anyone, ever. Men like him—practical, grounded and focused on their career—weren't the type to experience more than a flash of sexual attraction. Lust, he could deal with. Anything more than that, and he'd always back the hell off. Relationships simply weren't his thing. Never had been.

He could—and would—concentrate on the case. After what had happened today, Della would likely ask for someone else to take her place if they needed any more search and rescue work. And he wouldn't blame her. When things became too personal, the professional aspect tended to fall by the wayside.

For now, he'd give her space, let her come to terms with what had happened to her cousin and, when she felt ready, figure out what she wanted to do going forward.

And most important of all, he'd keep his hands to himself from now on. No matter how tempting he found Della Winslow.

Chapter 3

Doubled over in grief inside, while trying to act normal on the outside, Della didn't know what to do with herself. She needed to scream, pound a pillow—something, anything—to release the awful pain building inside of her.

Charlie nudged her hand with his nose, intuitive as usual. She wrapped her arms around him, burying her face in his fur, and cried. Patient and loyal as always, he stood still and offered comfort the only way he knew how—by being there.

When she'd cried herself out, she wiped her eyes with the backs of her hands and kissed the top of Charlie's head. She felt slightly better. Instead of wanting to rage against the injustice of it all, she felt hollow. Drained. She needed to think.

The tent wasn't big enough to pace in and damned if she could go back out there and face the FBI agents just yet. They were all professionals, here to do a job. Meanwhile, she could hardly catch her breath. A hundred things ran through her mind as she struggled to process the information that her beloved cousin Angela had been murdered. When and how, of course she wanted to know that. But she also wondered how to find the words to tell her aunt and uncle, Angela's parents. Like Della, they'd refused to abandon hope that Angela would be found.

When they learned the truth about what had happened to her, they'd be devastated. And Della knew she had to be the one to tell them. News like this couldn't come from a stranger.

On top of all this, Della had to face the fact that she'd fallen apart while on the job. As someone who prided herself on her composure and professional demeanor, she'd found herself taking comfort from Max Colton, the stud of Owl Creek. Sure, he was a dedicated FBI agent, she reminded herself, but that didn't help. She figured she probably needed to apologize to the entire team.

Just not right now. Her emotions were too raw.

Charlie, the best dog ever, stayed close to her. She kept her hands tangled in his fur, stroking him. He snuggled close, offering comfort the only way he knew how.

Outside, the steady sound of the others working made her feel even worse. Briefly, she considered making a run for it, leaving her tent and heading for her Jeep in the parking lot with her dog. But she'd never do something like that. Not only did she have a reputation to consider, but she'd agreed to perform a service working with the FBI.

She owed Angela, and all the other nameless women buried here, to have their identities discovered and their killer found and brought to justice.

Oddly enough, it was this last thing that helped her the most. She might not have been able to save her cousin, but she sure as hell would play a part in finding out what had happened to her.

Aware she looked like a mess, she brushed her hair,

used a disposable wipe to clean her face and crawled out of her tent. She had to face the team sooner or later. Might as well get this over with.

From the looks of things, they were taking a break. Everyone sat together on the large rocks that ringed the edge of the clearing. They all had water and various snacks. Without exception, they went silent the instant they caught sight of her.

"Della." Caroline stood. "I was just about to come check on you and make sure you're okay."

"Thanks." From somewhere, Della summoned up what she hoped resembled a smile. "I'm still processing. I wanted to apologize for breaking down back there."

"Don't." Caroline shook her head. "We all understand and sympathize with you. Any of us would have had a similar reaction, making a discovery like that."

Nodding, Della took a deep breath. She desperately wanted to get back to normal, even if it was only temporary.

"Would you like some water or a snack?" Caroline asked. "We brought plenty of food."

Della gratefully accepted a bottled water and a small package of cheese crackers. She took a seat on a vacant rock, watching Charlie as he cozied up to Theo, hoping to score a handout for his own snack.

"Watch that one," Della called. "He'll take that chip right out of your hand if you let him get too close."

Theo laughed, but he moved his bag of chips a little farther away from Charlie. The others began talking among themselves again, and the warmth of the sunlight made Della feel a bit better.

A shadow blocked out the sun. Della looked up. Max.

He stood in front of her, gazing down at her with an inscrutable expression.

"Walk with me?" he asked. Despite everything, her heart skipped a beat.

Aware of everyone watching them while pretending not to, she nodded and stood.

Charlie, ever vigilant, immediately came to Della's side.

"He doesn't like to let you out of his sight, does he?" Max commented.

Swallowing past the lump in her throat, Della touched her dog's silky fur. "He's a good boy," she said.

When they'd gone far enough from the others that they could no longer be seen or heard, Max stopped. "Are you going to be all right to continue with this investigation?" he asked, the tone of his voice both concerned and businesslike. "None of us would blame you if you'd prefer we call in someone else."

Though it shouldn't have, it felt almost as if he'd slapped her. "I appreciate your concern, but I'm a professional," she replied, lifting her chin. "And Charlie's the best in the region. We started this case, and we'll finish it, thank you very much."

He watched her, unsmiling, that blue-eyed gaze of his searching her face. If he'd considered overriding her protests, he must have thought better of it, because he simply nodded. "Then let's get back to work. We've got several other agents joining us, so there'll be quite a few extra tents pitched here overnight."

Relieved, she whistled for Charlie. Once he'd rejoined her, she turned and made her way back to the others, without looking at Max again.

By the time she reached the clearing, everyone else had already started working again. Della found herself avoiding Angela's final resting place, helping Chris unearth a different set of bones.

"They're all female," Caroline said. "Which is not entirely unexpected, but in case any of you wondered. I'll know more once I examine them in the lab."

Della sent Charlie out to look again, working each part of the meadow in sections so they wouldn't miss anything. Never happier than when he was working, Charlie took his job seriously. He was very thorough and wouldn't move on until he'd finished.

Once she'd cleared one area, she marked it with a can of spray paint, putting large *X*s on each corner. Then she moved on to the next section.

When Charlie didn't find any more remains, Della breathed a sigh of relief. Six, then. Six was bad enough. But she was infinitely thankful there weren't more.

As she worked, both with and separate from the others, the sun felt warm upon her skin. The breeze picked up, coming down from higher elevations, which gave it a bit of a chill. All in all, if it had been under any other circumstances, it would have been perfect weather. Closing her eyes, Della put her head up and inhaled, hoping the fresh scent of the mountains could help cleanse some of the darkness clouding her soul. She couldn't believe her bright, vivacious cousin had been killed. Though distance had separated them once Angela moved to Montana, they'd managed to stay in touch. They'd joked that no matter how much time passed between conversations, they always picked up as if only a few minutes had passed.

When Angela disappeared, every time her phone rang, Della had always hoped it would be her. Saying she'd lost track of time, or she'd gone on a wonderful new adventure and just realized they needed to catch up.

Damn, Della was going to miss her. So, so much.

Tears pricked at her eyes. Her throat clogged and she choked back a sob. Not again, not here, not now. Later, she'd figure out a way to properly mourn. She squared her shoulders and sent Charlie out one more time, even though they'd already cleared every area.

"Are you all right?" Max asked. Somehow, he'd walked up behind her without her noticing.

She nodded. "I am. Thank you for asking." Inwardly wincing at how formal she sounded, she waved her hand at the field. "Charlie didn't find any more. So unless the killer has another burial ground somewhere else, six bodies appears to be it."

His gaze searched her face. "That's a relief." He took a deep breath. "Listen, I'm really sorry about your cousin."

As she looked up into his light blue eyes, everything else faded away. "Thank you."

Charlie came up and nudged her hand. Dizzy, she turned her attention to her dog. "Good boy, Charlie. Let's go get you some water."

And then, as if a simple glance hadn't rocked her to the core, she turned and walked away.

The rest of the crew arrived before dusk. Max and Theo went down to meet them. Aware they'd need a safe place to pitch their tents, she had Charlie do a search of the area on both sides of the existing three. He sniffed around but didn't signal, which was not unexpected but still came as a relief.

"Nothing, huh?" She scratched behind his ears in his favorite spot. "Good dog!" She tried to keep her voice cheerful, since Charlie reacted to her sorrow. Tail wagging, Charlie grinned up at her, though she suspected she didn't fool him. He knew her too well.

Caroline and Chris continued to work, talking quietly as they cleared dirt away from bones. Della went over to watch, Charlie close by her side. She took care not to venture too close so she wouldn't accidentally disturb anything.

"This is so sad," Caroline said, glancing up at Della.

"It is." Once again, Della found herself blinking back tears. "I'm sorry. I'm not usually so emotional."

"Don't apologize." Voice fierce, Caroline sat back on her heels. "I can't imagine how you must feel. If it had been me, I don't know what I would have done."

At a loss for words, Della nodded, hoping the simple gesture conveyed her thanks.

"I'm excellent at my job," Caroline continued. "So believe me when I say that I'll do everything in my power to make sure the killer is caught. Hopefully, that will give you some small measure of peace."

Retribution. "I want him brought to justice," Della said. "He needs to pay for what he's done. After he faces down the families of all his victims."

"Agreed." Caroline brushed a stray strand of hair away from her face. "Would you like to help me? I could use another set of hands."

Relieved to have something to do, Della immediately knelt in the dirt. Caroline handed her a pair of gloves and waited while Della put them on. Then Caroline showed her how to use a tool that looked like a miniature trowel to carefully unearth the bones from the earth and use a soft brush to clean them.

Normally, handling a deceased person's bones might have creeped Della out. But now all she could think about was that everything she did right in this investigation would bring the FBI that much closer to finding Angela's killer.

"Easy," Caroline cautioned, making Della realize she'd gotten a bit too impatient. "We don't want to break anything. I need the bones as intact as possible."

Nodding, Della slowed down. The work, the sheer physical act of digging in the earth, and then sifting dirt away carefully using a brush, helped time pass. At one point, she realized she kept watching the path, waiting for Max to return with the new members of the team.

"He's really a good agent," Caroline commented, making Della realize the other woman had noticed. "And easy on the eyes."

This last made Della smile. "There's a reason he's considered the playboy of Owl Creek."

Caroline's eyes widened. "He *is*?" she asked. "I had no idea."

"That must mean you're not from around these parts."

"True. I grew up in Denver. I moved here for this job." Caroline glanced back at the trail, as if she expected Max and the others to show at any moment. "But I've worked with Max on a couple of cases, and he's nothing but professional at work. People talk, though, and I know some of the guys envy him since he often is seen with beautiful women. He seems to do a lot of casual dating, and I've never gotten the sense that he goes around deliberately trying to break hearts."

Della considered Caroline's words. "You're right," she conceded. "I shouldn't have repeated old gossip. After all, it's been years since Max Colton lived in Owl Creek. I'm sure he's changed."

"Were you speaking from experience?" Caroline asked, watching Della closely.

Horrified, Della shook her head. "No, not at all. I'd never even met him before this case. Can we please pretend I never said anything?"

"Of course." Caroline got back to work. "And now I'm going to speak out of turn, so feel free to ignore me. I couldn't help but notice the way the two of you look at each other. Just remember, you can't always hold someone's past against them."

Max walked a few paces behind Jake and Ed. Without exception, both new male agents did a double take when they first caught sight of Della. She and Caroline both looked up and smiled when they approached, but immediately went back to working in the dirt. Either Della had gotten so used to men staring that she didn't react, or she was oblivious to her effect on them. She barely acknowledged their presence, though Caroline appeared to be having difficulty keeping from cracking up laughing.

Normally, Max would have found this sort of thing amusing. Now, though, he found himself clenching his teeth and biting back a sarcastic comment.

Since the light was fading, they decided to start fresh in the morning. Everyone gathered around while Jake and Ed pitched their tent.

"Somehow, I thought they'd send more people," Caroline commented.

"Two vans, two drivers," Jake shot back, clearly overhearing. "What more do you need?"

Caroline laughed. Theo and Chris joined in, ribbing the newcomers, claiming they'd gotten here late so they could avoid work. Even Max found himself smiling, glad that the team had developed an easy rapport.

Della kept to the edge of the group, quietly observing everyone. Charlie stayed close to her side. Ever since she'd discovered her cousin's body, her dog had seemed to sense she might need him. Max envied that. Many times over the course of his adult life he'd badly wanted to get a dog, but the long hours he spent working had always been a deterrent.

Once the tent had been pitched, the others gave Jake and Ed a quick tour of the site. While they did that, Max gathered more kindling for the fire. It didn't take long before he had a good-sized blaze going.

"Perfect for burgers," Jake announced. "Since Ed and I stopped at the store on the way up, I thought you all might like something a little better than the usual nonperishable rations."

"I could just hug you!" Caroline said, and then did exactly that. "Did you think to bring paper plates and buns and all of that?"

"We did." Grinning, Jake and Ed gave each other a high five. "We've been on several of these overnight cases before."

In addition to the meat, Ed had brought a cooler full of beer and soft drinks. The atmosphere lightened considerably as everyone relaxed. Jake started grilling the hamburger patties over the fire and people cracked open their drinks of choice.

Even Della appeared to perk up at the easy banter among the team. She didn't say much, though she accepted a diet cola. She looked up once and met Max's gaze, making him realize he might be watching her too closely.

He knew his team had noticed it too. He'd worked with all these agents before in some capacity or another. And, despite the fact that he did his damnedest to keep his personal life private, every single one of them had given him grief about his reputation as a player.

At least in this situation, they knew better than to say anything. Della had been through a lot, and everyone knew she'd be well within her rights to leave now that her dog had completed the search of the field. Then again, they'd only had time to partially excavate three of the graves. She might decide to stick around until they'd completed the task, but he doubted it.

In fact, he imagined she'd hightail it out of there at first light. And he wouldn't blame her. What he didn't understand was why the notion of her leaving made him feel so hollow. Likely because he felt responsible for everyone on his team, and despite the fact that she didn't work for the Bureau, she'd come in and assisted after finding the first grave.

Burgers were passed out and everyone ate. Darkness came as suddenly as if someone had flicked a switch, and stars looked like strands of diamonds in the cloudless night sky. Though the temperature had begun dropping, as it always did in the mountains after dark, it was still comfortable. If not for the circumstances, it would have been a perfect August evening.

"Where do you think the killer came from?" Della asked softly from beside him. "This isn't exactly an easy location to reach, especially dragging a dead body."

He braced himself for her reaction. "It's likely they were alive when he brought them here," he said.

Her eyes widened. "You're saying he killed them in this meadow?"

"Most likely." Noticing how she swayed, he reached out and grabbed her arm. "But we don't know that yet. Caroline will be able to tell us a lot more once she can examine the bones in her lab."

Ever respectful of Della's feelings, the team talked about everything but their findings. But finally, Caroline brought up her concerns. "There's another, smaller clearing just past that group of trees," she said, pointing. "It's too dark to see it right now, but I think we should have Charlie check that out too in the morning, just in case."

Della nodded. "We'll check it out at first light."

"Thanks." Caroline stood, stretching. "It's been a long day and it's likely going to be an even longer one tomorrow. I'm going to turn in."

After she disappeared into her tent, Theo and Chris made their excuses and did the same, followed by Jake and Ed. Which left Max and Della alone in front of the campfire, with Charlie stretched out close by.

Max wouldn't have minded getting some rest himself, but no way would he leave Della by herself. If she needed to talk, he'd provide an ear. If not, he could give her space too.

Staring into the fire, she didn't seem to be aware of his presence. They'd stopped adding wood and were letting it burn low, though the flames still provided enough light to make shadows dance around the darkness.

"Do you think he's still out there, killing women?" she asked, her voice low and intense.

Scooting closer, so they could talk without keeping everyone else awake, Max grimaced. "I think it's likely. However, a lot of that depends on what forensics reveals. If all these bones are pretty old, then whoever killed them might have moved on to another location."

"Will you be able to find out their identities?" she asked. The moonlight bathed her in soft silver, making her pale skin and long brown hair appear to glow. Again, he found himself marveling at her beauty, wondering how it was that she seemed completely unaware of it.

Realizing she'd asked him a question, he tore his gaze away and collected his thoughts. "As far as identifying them, I'd say yes. Caroline's really good at this sort of thing. And since we don't have any reports of missing women from Owl Creek, it'll likely turn out they came from somewhere else."

Like her cousin had. Though she didn't say this out loud, he could see it in her face. She looked away, stared at what remained of the fire, before directing her attention back to him.

"But he brought them here to kill them. Somehow, these women trusted him enough to travel to this remote location with their murderer."

Her tortured expression told him she was picturing her cousin.

"That's only a theory," he said, lightly touching her arm. "We're only at the beginning of this investigation. Lot of possibilities are going to get tossed around."

She turned to face him, her full lips slightly parted. Her gaze swung to his, the fire making flickers of gold in her eyes. At that moment, he would have given anything to chase the sadness from her face.

Somehow, they came together, mouth upon mouth. Kissing hungrily, urgently, with reckless abandon. He lost himself in the velvet sensation of her, desire searing his veins. Hands tangled in her hair, he crushed her to him.

Fully aroused, wanting her more than he'd ever wanted anyone, he forced himself to pull back. Inhaling the sweet scent of her, he brushed her brow with his lips. They were both breathing heavily and neither of them spoke.

After a moment, Della pushed to her feet, quietly called her dog and disappeared into her tent. Leaving him staring after her, aching with need and full of remorse.

Max sat by himself for a while, watching the fire burn down to embers, aware he'd need to apologize to Della in the morning. That kiss never should have happened. And he needed to make sure it never happened again.

That night, alone in his tent, he slept restlessly, tossing and turning on the uneven ground. It had been a long time since he'd burned for a woman like this. Usually, he was able to get it out of his system quickly so he could go on with his life. But none of the women he dated were like Della.

In the morning, he woke up to the sound of the others making breakfast. He got up, stiff and sore, and ambled out to greet everyone before going into the woods to take care of his morning toilet. When he returned, Theo handed him a large mug of coffee with a knowing smile, which Max ignored.

Della came sauntering up the path, Charlie close by her side. She smiled at everyone, including Max. "Good morning," she said.

Theo offered her coffee, but she lifted her mug to show him she already had some. "When did you even get up?" he asked.

"A little before sunrise." She wrinkled her nose. "You all were still asleep. Charlie and I walked to one of my favorite vantage points to watch the sun come up."

Among the food items that Jake and Ed had brought were doughnuts. "Carbs for energy," Ed chirped, passing them around.

Once everyone had eaten, Della announced she and Charlie were going to check out that smaller clearing now. "Hopefully, we won't find anything."

Whistling for her dog, who bounded over to her side immediately, she told him to heel.

"Do you mind if I come with you?" Max asked, keeping his voice casual.

Her gaze flashed to his. "Not at all."

With Charlie prancing between them, they walked toward the area.

Heart in his throat, he tried to find the right words. "I need to apologize for last night," he said, deciding he might as well be direct and up-front.

She glanced sideways at him. "No. You don't. You didn't take advantage of me, if that's what you're going to say. I'd honestly find that insulting. I participated equally. Was kissing on the job site inappropriate? Probably. And yes, we need to make sure it doesn't happen again."

All he could do was nod.

"There," she continued. "Have I covered everything you were going to say?"

He couldn't hide his amusement. "You have. And much more succinctly than I would have."

"Good. Then can we forget about it and get this area checked out?"

"Yes, we can."

Fascinated, Max watched while she gave Charlie the command to work. Nose to the ground, the Lab set off, carrying his tail in a happy curve over his back. Intent on her dog, Della seemed to be holding her breath. Hoping, Max guessed, that Charlie didn't find anything. After all, six bodies were more than enough.

A second after Max had that thought, Charlie sat and barked once. Max's heart sank.

Della glanced at Max, clearly stricken. "Another one," she said, her voice raspy.

Feeling grim himself, Max looked over at his team. Without exception, they'd all stopped what they were doing to watch Charlie work.

At Max's signal, Caroline got to her feet. She hurried over, followed by Theo. "I was afraid of that," she said. "Now we have seven."

"I don't understand." Della looked from one to the other. "Why over here? Why deviate from the other area?"

Max shrugged. "We can only guess." He hesitated, and then continued. "I'm thinking it's possible he started here. This one might have been his first victim."

"And then he realized he needed more room," Caroline finished for him.

Expression horrified, Della swallowed. "In my years volunteering for SAR, I've worked natural disasters. But never a murder scene with multiple bodies, all killed by a sick serial killer."

Max heard the part she didn't say. And never, ever with one of her loved ones being one of the victims. He watched as she squared her shoulders and took a deep breath. Then, praising Charlie, she sent him out to search again.

Luckily, the dog didn't turn up any more remains.

"I need to call this in," Max said. He hurried back to his tent, where he'd left the sat phone. Though it was still early, he knew Brian would want to be updated.

"Seven bodies?" Sounding nearly as horrified as Max felt, Brian cursed. "I've had people running reports on missing women from the area and have only turned up one. Not seven."

"I'd suggest expanding. Maybe make it statewide." Max thought for a second. "You might even do the tristate area."

Brian cursed again. "Tell Caroline I'm bringing in a couple more people to help her. We need to get ahead of this before the media does. The last thing we need is to start a widespread panic."

Max agreed. "We're hoping to start moving the bones out today," he said. "The only other people who know anything about this are the Owl Creek police officers who called us out. And at that time, there was only one body."

"Good. Let's try to keep a lid on this for as long as we can."

Promising to try, Max ended the call.

Chapter 4

With her work done, Della began packing up her things in preparation to head back to town. She had an afternoon and an evening dog training class to conduct at Crosswinds, so she needed to get home and shower.

Saying her goodbyes to the team, she smiled as they all thanked her and praised Charlie for his good work. Max offered to walk her to the parking lot and, ignoring the knowing looks of the others, she accepted. She resolved to keep things between them strictly businesslike.

Like the others, Max thanked her. "I really enjoyed working with you," he said, sounding sincere. Even though she doubted he was referring to the kiss they'd shared, Della felt her face heat.

"I enjoyed working with everyone too," she replied, purposely making generalities. "Please keep me posted on this case." She took a deep breath, then lifted her chin. "Also, I plan to notify my aunt and uncle of Angela's passing myself, so don't send someone official to do that, okay?"

"I'll make sure to notify the proper channels." He met her gaze. "That's going to be tough. Are you sure you don't want to wait until we have an official, positive ID?"

She grimaced. "I might. Just in case that's somehow

not her. Even if I think that I already know the truth, I don't want to give them wrong information. But they deserve to be told as soon as possible, once it's confirmed."

"I understand." The warmth of his gaze felt like a physical touch. "And I agree that you should wait. Just in case. And I'm just putting this out there, so you know. When the time comes, if you'd like me to go with you and lend you support, just say the word."

Touched, she wasn't sure how to respond. While this was a family matter, she knew she'd welcome his strong shoulder to lean on.

Except for one small thing. His reputation would precede him. If she showed up at her aunt and uncle's house with Max Colton, the playboy of Owl Creek, they'd think she'd lost her mind. Of course, once she delivered the awful news about Angela, whom she'd arrived with wouldn't matter.

She said none of this to Max, however. "I appreciate that," she replied simply. "You've been more than kind."

Which was the understatement of the year. She felt her face heat again. Luckily, Max wasn't watching her.

They'd reached the parking area. When they got to her Jeep, Max helped her load up. Panting, tail wagging happily, Charlie jumped up into the back seat, ready to go.

"Thank you again," she said, feeling awkward as she turned to face Max. "And I'd really like to remain as much in the loop as possible about this case."

"I'll make sure to do that." Expression intense, he met her gaze. "Della, I'm going to figure out who did this. I promise you that."

Believing him, she nodded. "If I can help in any way, feel free to reach out to me."

"I'll likely do that. I'm sure I'll have some questions about your cousin. I'll definitely be in touch." Reaching into his pocket, he pulled out a business card and handed it to her. "Here's my number if you need me for anything. Please don't hesitate to call."

"I won't." Since there was nothing more to say, she pocketed the card, smiled and got into her Jeep. "Take care," she said, waving as she started the engine and drove away.

Now she understood, she thought, eyeing Max in her rearview mirror until she made a turn and could no longer see him. For as long as she could remember, she'd heard stories of the legions of brokenhearted women Max Colton left in his wake. Until this very moment, she'd wondered what could make someone abandon all reason and set themselves up for heartbreak. Now she knew.

When she pulled into her driveway, she felt a sense of relief at the sight of her familiar home. She'd grown up in this house, the only child of a single mother. After a brief stint in Boise, Della had returned to help care for her mother through her long battle with pancreatic cancer. A fight her mom had ultimately lost.

Having Aunt Mary and Uncle Alex, and of course Angela, next door had been a lifesaver through it all. Now, as she looked at the house next door, the knowledge that she had to go over there and tear apart her family's world sat like a lead weight in her stomach.

Maybe, she thought, she should do as Max had suggested and wait until they had a definitive medical ID. After all, what if some other woman had stolen Angela's necklace?

Hefting her backpack and duffel bag out of the Jeep, she called Charlie, and they went into the house. She was well aware she might be indulging in a bit of self-delusion. Nonetheless, her decision made her feel slightly better.

Once she'd received official notification, she'd break the news to her aunt and uncle. Until then, she'd keep it to herself.

A hot shower and a change of clothes made her feel better. She had back-to-back classes to teach tonight, the first one a basic manners class and the second, advanced manners. Now that Crosswinds' owner, Sebastian Cross, was about to become a family man, he'd decided to branch out and offer classes to the general public. Before, Crosswinds had only focused on training search and rescue dogs. Now they'd expanded, with Della teaching most of the classes. She'd learned only the most dedicated dog owners who completed the first class followed up by taking the second.

But for those who did, the possibilities were endless. They could train their dog in obedience, agility or rally, among other things. Sebastian had hired a couple more trainers who specialized in various dog sports, even bringing in one from Denver. Crosswinds had a well-respected name among law enforcement agencies for their SAR dogs. Soon, if Della had her way, they'd also have a presence in the competitive world of dog sports. Watching her manners clients go on to other things and succeed made Della truly happy. She honestly loved her job, and there was nothing else, besides search and rescue work, that she'd rather do.

Since she had a little bit of time before she had to go

to work, she went ahead and made lunch, saving half of it to eat for dinner later. Charlie had curled up in his dog bed and gone to sleep, clearly exhausted after his busy couple of days.

Della puttered around the house, doing a load of laundry and tidying up. To her dismay, her thoughts kept returning to Max Colton and that amazing, sensual kiss.

She couldn't wait to go to work. Keeping busy should help her get her thoughts back on track.

Though she usually brought Charlie to work with her, tonight she decided to leave him home. He'd definitely earned a night off. Her first class would all be people and dogs new to the training center, so while she covered the basics and assessed each pair, she wouldn't need Charlie to demonstrate anything.

When she entered Crosswinds Training, Pepper greeted her. One of the employees who worked in the retail store, Pepper also handled registration. "You've got a full class tonight," Pepper said. "Nine dogs and owners."

"Awesome. I'd better go get set up. They should start arriving soon."

As the dog training area filled, Della saw she had a good mixture of breeds and ages. She'd worked with some of the younger dogs in puppy kindergarten a few weeks ago.

In the first class, she went over the curriculum, passing out worksheets for what she expected them to do at home and a list of supplies they were going to need. "Get some high-quality dog treats," she advised. "Something that's just a step above what they get at home. Personally, I like to use liver treats."

She then had each client walk their dog around the

middle of the ring to give her an idea of what, if any, training they might already have received. As usual, she made detailed notes.

A few of the clients lingered after she'd dismissed the class, which wasn't unusual, especially since she'd told them to come to her with any questions.

The first one, a young woman whose dog wouldn't stop jumping on her, asked for advice about how to stop that. Della gave her some exercises to try at home.

The second man had attended her puppy class with his bloodhound, Rolo. He just wanted to tell Della how well Rolo had been doing, and that he was hoping to move on to obedience trials. She smiled, petted the adorable droopy-eyed dog and told him she'd see him next time.

The last individual, a man with a young Rottweiler, hung back until everyone else had left. During the class, Della had noticed him staring at her, which she'd found slightly off-putting, but she put it down to first-class nerves. In dog training, they all knew they were actually teaching the humans, not the dogs. Once the people knew what to do, their pets learned how to follow.

"I'm Hal," he said, holding out his hand. "Hal Murcheson." After they shook hands, he continued holding on for a heartbeat too long, which forced her to tug her fingers away. Meanwhile, his Rottie kept pulling on the leash, clearly anxious to leave.

"What can I help you with, Hal?" she asked, keeping her voice pleasant.

"I was wondering if you'd like to go out and have a drink sometime." His friendly smile didn't match up with the way he focused his gaze intently on her chest.

"Oh, that's so nice of you," she replied, on familiar

ground since this happened occasionally. "But I don't date clients."

Almost on cue, the Rottweiler barked and made another lunge toward the door. Hal yanked him back and told him no, before refocusing his attention on Della.

"Then maybe I'll have to drop out of your class," he teased. "Though Marco here could use some training."

"That's what I'm here for." Checking her phone, she glanced toward the retail area. "Now, if you don't have a training-related question, I have another class starting in fifteen minutes. I need to get ready for it."

"Do you mind if I watch?"

"I'm going to have to say yes, I do mind. For these types of classes, especially on the first night, I don't want any distractions. I suggest you take Marco home and start working on some of the things I touched on in class."

For a moment, she thought he might continue to push, but to her relief he nodded and left, Marco pulling hard all the way.

"You all right, hon?" Pepper asked. "I couldn't help but notice what happened."

"I'm fine." Della shook her head. "He wanted a date, but I'm hoping now that I turned him down, he'll focus on training his dog."

"He's new to Owl Creek, he said. Just moved here for work." Worry still shone in Pepper's eyes. "I'll watch and make sure he doesn't come back. I'd hate for him to try and follow you home."

"Aww, I appreciate that, but I'm sure it'll be fine." Della touched Pepper's arm to reassure her. "Every now and then, I get a client who's a bit overly enthusiastic. It's been a while, but I know how to handle it."

"I'm still going to keep an eye out," Pepper replied.

The next class, Advanced Manners, contained people and their dogs who had recently passed the previous Basic Manners class. Many of them were eager to show Della what they'd been working on and how far they'd come.

"I'm proud of you all," Della said, meaning it. One of her greatest joys was seeing how far her students and their owners could go if they tried. She passed out the new curriculum for the next six weeks, and then they got started.

By the time she'd finished up with that class, Della was more than ready to go home and rest. After the last client had left, she wandered into the store to purchase some treats for Charlie.

"You look tired," Pepper chided.

Since Max had asked Della to keep the investigation under wraps, she couldn't share details about what she and Charlie had been doing for the past couple of days. "I've been busy," she responded. "I'm sure I'll feel better once I get some sleep. I need to check the schedule while I'm here." The two Manners classes were only held once a week, but if enrollment warranted, she'd sometimes have another on Wednesdays. They must have gotten a lot of sign-ups, because she had a full class for Wednesday evening. She'd only be working those twice a week for the next six weeks, which was a good thing. Well-trained humans made for well-behaved dogs.

"Looks like you'll have lots of time to train Charlie along with the other six you've been assigned," Pepper said, reading over her shoulder. "Speaking of Charlie, why didn't you bring him tonight?"

"He got a lot of exercise this weekend." Della smiled. "We hiked up to Owl Falls."

"Oh, fun." Another customer came in, pulling Pepper's attention away from Della. "See you later."

As a precaution, Della scanned the parking lot before walking outside. Not that she thought Hal would have returned to try to press his luck, but better safe than sorry. After all, Angela had always seen the good in everyone, and she'd lost her life.

Grief slammed into her, making her gasp for breath. *Not yet*, she reminded herself. Not until she had an official, positive ID. Until then, she'd simply hope the grave belonged to some other unfortunate soul.

After Della left, Max had hiked back up to the crime scene, using the alone time to try to figure out why he felt so attuned to her. No, he'd decided, he'd call his feelings *protective* instead. That had to be it. One of the reasons he'd gone into law enforcement had been a deep-seated desire to protect the public. And watching Della, a capable and confident woman, discover the body of her own beloved cousin had stirred up every protective instinct he possessed and then some.

Did that explain why he'd kissed her? If he really wanted to mess with his head, he could convince himself of that too. But he'd never been in the habit of indulging in self-delusion, so why start now?

Della's beauty attracted him. Plain and simple. But since she clearly wasn't the type of woman willing to settle for what little he had to offer, he'd need to rein himself in.

When he reached the site, he found everyone hard

at work. Entire skeletons had been carefully unearthed and Caroline had begun preparing them for transit back to her lab.

"We should have most of them out of here by tomorrow afternoon," she said cheerfully. "I've got my two best assistants on standby, and I've heard they're sending me a few more people to help out in the lab."

"How long do you think before you're able to start getting IDs on them?" he asked.

She shrugged. "It depends what I find on each victim and also what's in the database. Some of them were disturbed by animals and, quite frankly, we're lucky it wasn't worse."

Caroline took a deep breath. "But I'm going to start with Della's cousin first. I want to be able to confirm for her that this is actually Angela Hobbs."

"I appreciate that. She's decided to wait until she has official confirmation before telling her family."

"I agree." Caroline shook her head. "I've been working for the Bureau for nearly twenty years. This is the first time I've ever been involved in a case where one of the team found a murder victim who was a member of their own family."

Remembering the stark pain in Della's beautiful eyes, the jagged control she'd tried—and failed—to exert over her emotions, he grimaced. "Definitely a tough time," he said, meaning it. "Even more reason to catch this guy."

They worked until dusk and then ate another meal around a smaller campfire. This time, they ate out of cans. The mood was more somber, the knowledge of the seven shallow graves weighing heavy on their minds.

They all retired early, planning to rise with the sun.

One more night in the tent. Bright and early the next morning, Max helped as the team carefully transported the remains down the path to the vans, one by one.

By the time they'd gotten the seventh victim securely loaded up, it was early afternoon. "Let's get the camp broken down and head out," Max decided. "We can grab something for lunch on the road."

Perspiring, grateful for the slight breeze stirring the trees, everyone packed up their tents. Max made sure the fire was completely out, pouring water just in case any embers still smoldered.

They debated whether or not to leave the crime scene tape. Since Charlie had made it clear they'd found all the graves that were there, Max didn't want to provide an easy target for the media to photograph.

"What about the killer?" Theo asked. "If we leave it, he'll know we're on to him. But if we take it, he might just bury another victim after we're gone."

Max gestured around the field. "All of his graves have been disturbed. He's likely going to figure that out whether there's crime scene tape or not. Let's take it down."

After making sure they hadn't left anything in the clearing, they hiked again back down to the vehicles. Caroline had decided to wait, watching over everything, she'd said.

By the time Max put his truck in Drive, following the vans down the mountain, a bone-deep sort of weariness had set in. The others would go back to Boise, but Max had to head out to Owl Creek. His family owned Colton Ranch. It had been started by his father, Buck, and managed by him along with Max's two older brothers, Greg and Malcolm. Their sister, Lizzy, lived in town and worked as a graphic artist.

In addition to them, Max had six cousins who also lived in Owl Creek. His uncle Robert and Robert's oldest son, Chase, had founded Colton Properties. Fletcher had gone into law enforcement, and Wade was Special Forces in the Marines. Ruby had gone to veterinary school and started her own veterinary practice in town, Hannah had a catering business, and Frannie, the youngest, owned and managed a bookstore/café.

With such a large family, the only way they could all get together when Max happened to be in town was to schedule a sit-down dinner. Mama Jen, Max's aunt, usually organized something.

This week, they were all meeting at a restaurant in town. Everyone had agreed to attend because in addition to catching up with each other, they were meeting their half siblings for the first time.

The story could have been a soap opera. Max's mother, Jessie, had left her husband, Buck, and had an affair with his brother, Robert. The two of them had built a house near Boise and together they'd had two more children, Nathan and Sarah.

Robert hadn't completely abandoned his wife, Jenny, along with their six children, not in the same way Jessie had ditched her entire family. But Robert had been a distant and often absent husband and father. Buck had helped Jenny with her brood of six, and Jenny had helped him with his four, and as a result the kids were more like siblings than cousins. Ten. A huge family, by any standards.

And now there were two more. Once Robert had

passed away, the rest of the story had come to light after his funeral. Max and his siblings had wondered if their mother, Jessie, would actually make an appearance at the service. They weren't even sure they'd recognize her if she did, they hadn't seen her in so long. And like Max, the others felt a lot of resentment and simmering anger at her for what she did. Nothing like a mother abandoning her children to instill a deflated sense of self-worth.

His father had tried to bolster their self-esteem, but Buck was a cowboy through and through, and not much good with emotional stuff. If not for Mama Jen and their extended family of cousins, Max suspected they'd likely all have amounted to nothing. As it was, Max himself shied away from commitment. He blamed his demanding career, but part of him never wanted to risk feeling abandoned again.

Shaking off the past and the unsettling memories, he thought about the case. He'd never worked a full-on serial killer case before, though of course he'd studied all the big ones during his time at Quantico. He knew enough to understand that seven bodies might only be the tip of the iceberg. A very real possibility existed that the murderer might have other burial grounds in different locations. He hoped not, but couldn't discount the notion altogether.

As he continued to drive north, the landscape flattened, the craggy peaks and evergreen trees giving way to rolling hills of fertile grass. When the first herds of cattle came into view, the part of Max that would always be a rancher came to life. One more turn and then the ranch spread out ahead of him. The red-and-white wooden house matched the large barn. In the distance he could see the bunkhouse where the ranch hands lived. A smaller guesthouse, barely visible past the private garden, was where Max's oldest brother, Greg, lived.

Home. A rush of happiness filled him. Visiting Colton Ranch helped put the rest of his life in perspective. Eight hundred fertile acres filled with cattle and horses brought the kind of peace city life couldn't buy. At least as far as Max was concerned. He suspected his father and brothers might think otherwise, since keeping the place running was their job.

Driving through the gates, Max parked in front of the garage. Though he'd called his dad to let him know about his visit, he knew no one would be inside the house at this time of day. Too much to be done. He remembered it well.

Once inside, Max carried his stuff upstairs into his old bedroom and immediately jumped into the shower. He figured his father and brothers were likely out working cattle, so they wouldn't be back at the house until later.

After his shower, he toyed with the idea of taking a nap, but felt too keyed up to possibly sleep. He couldn't stop thinking about Della Winslow. He wondered what she was doing, how she was holding up. He couldn't forget how soft her lips had felt when they'd kissed. In fact, he found himself almost wishing he had a dog so he could sign up for one of her classes.

Ridiculous. And unlike him. They'd worked together on a case. He'd promised to keep her posted. He'd offered support when she'd suffered a horrific loss and experienced unimaginable pain. True, she might be gorgeous, but he knew lots of beautiful women. He'd touch base with her soon.

Taking a seat at the huge handmade oak kitchen table, he opened his laptop and logged in to Wi-Fi. Within minutes, he began filling out his initial report. Tedious and time-consuming, the task made him lose track of time. When the creak of the back door made him raise his head, the sight of his aunt made him grin.

"Mama Jen!" Jumping to his feet, he rushed over and wrapped the older woman in a hug, lifting her off her feet. "I'm so happy to see you."

Once he'd set her down, she beamed back at him. "I heard you were coming for a visit. Buck asked me to come over and make a special dinner, just for you."

Hearing her say that made him feel like a kid again. Despite often seeming emotionally distant, Mama Jen had been more of a mother to him than his own ever had. Just thinking of her cooking made his stomach growl.

"What are you making?" he asked, letting his eagerness show. "I could really go for some smothered steak."

"That's exactly what I was thinking! With mashed potatoes, gravy and green beans. And those biscuits you love so much."

He hugged her again. "Thank you. I can't wait. Who all's coming?" Usually when Mama Jen cooked, he knew to expect a crowd.

"Just you, your dad, Greg and Malcolm. Lizzy couldn't make it."

"What about the cousins?" Her children.

She tried for a laugh but ended up frowning instead. "I invited them. Chase claims he's too busy, Fletcher too. Wade is working. Ruby says she's too tired. Hannah and Frannie made plans with Lizzy. Girls' night out, they say.

They all said to tell you hello and that they'll see you at that dinner when you meet your new half siblings."

Since no one had communicated a date, time or place for that to him, he was surprised. When he said as much to Jenny, she shook her head.

"Thursday night," she said. "At that new barbecue place in town. Back Forty, I think it's called. Seven o'clock."

"Wow." He shouldn't have been surprised that Jenny knew all the details. After all, she was the glue that held the entire family together. "Are you coming?" he asked.

"Me?" She snorted. "So I could meet the children of my cheating husband and my own sister? Hard pass."

He couldn't blame her. "I get it. I'm not even sure I want to go myself."

Though she shook her head, she refrained from commenting. "I'd better get to cooking," she said instead. "Buck and the boys are always starving when they come in from working cattle." Despite working part-time as a nurse, Jenny always enjoyed making the family a good meal.

"What can I do to help?" he asked.

"Nothing." Like she always did, she shooed him out of the kitchen. Jenny didn't like anyone getting in her space when she created her masterpieces. Though she wasn't a gourmet cook, everyone in the Colton family considered her comfort food better than anything made by a fancy chef.

While she puttered around doing her prep work, Max continued filling out reports, which he despised. Although he knew they were a necessity, he always found the paperwork time-consuming and tedious. Somehow, working on them in his family home made them feel less like work.

He'd just finished the last report and closed his computer when the back door opened, and his father and brothers came stomping into the kitchen. They smelled like cattle and horses and sweat, the aroma of Max's childhood. Bickering lightly among themselves, they stopped short when they caught sight of Max and Jenny.

"Damn, I forgot," Buck said, rushing forward and sweeping Max up in a bear hug. "Good to see you, son."

"It's good to be here." Max barely got the words out before his dad released him and Greg and Malcolm tag-team hugged him. Of the three of them, Malcolm was the tallest, but only by an inch.

"Been too long," Greg said. "Let's go get cleaned up and then we'll catch up over dinner."

While the boys took off for the showers, Buck went into the kitchen and spoke quietly to Jenny. The two of them had been close for years. When Max had been younger, he'd wished his dad would marry Jenny, so they could all be one big happy family. It would have been a sort of poetic justice, since the two brothers had clearly married the wrong sister.

These days, Max had a different philosophy. Buck and Jenny seemed happy with things the way they were. And if they were good, so was Max.

Greg returned first, his hair still damp from the shower. Breaking off his conversation with Jenny, Buck excused himself and went off to clean himself up. Jenny watched him go and then returned to cooking.

A few minutes later, Malcolm joined them. "How do

you two feel about meeting Mom's other two kids?" he asked, cutting right to the chase.

Max and Greg exchanged glances. "I'm not looking forward to it," Max admitted. "How about you?"

"I think it'll be fun," Malcolm replied, his eyes twinkling. "I mean, it's always been kind of a Colton thing, having such a big family. I like the idea of adding a couple more."

Greg eyed him. "I wonder if our mother actually stuck around for them. It kind of sounds like she did. Which might not actually be a good thing, you know?"

Max did know. They all did. It hadn't been easy for any of them to get over having their own mother abandon them. If not for Jenny stepping in and trying to fill in the gap, he often thought the family would have fallen apart.

"The past is the past," Malcolm pointed out, as if he knew what Max had been thinking. "All we can do is move forward."

"We know." Greg and Max spoke in unison.

"Dinner is almost ready," Jenny chimed in. "Would one of you boys go check on your father?"

"No need—I'm here." Buck grinned. "Let's eat."

Chapter 5

The next morning, Della woke shortly after sunrise. She'd slept deeply and felt well rested, ready to take on a new day. With a new attitude. Though she suspected she might be giving in to self-delusion, until she got the official notice that the body in the grave definitely belonged to Angela, she'd decided she wouldn't allow herself to dwell in the deep, dark recesses of grief. All these years, she hadn't given up hope, and while finding the necklace she'd given her cousin was certainly damning, she'd simply move in a place of hope until she knew differently.

That decided, she had a leisurely breakfast and then she and Charlie went for a walk. The cloudless sky and light breeze made for perfect walking weather, and she let Charlie sniff to his canine heart's content.

When they returned, Charlie went and got his favorite toy and amused himself by tossing it around in the living room. With the entire day free, Della decided to take him out to Crosswinds and work on more training.

Not many people realized how many hours of work went into training a search and rescue dog. She'd started Charlie young, taking him everywhere she went and working on his socialization skills. She also had to get him desensitized to loud noises, so they made trips to the police station, the fire department and anywhere they heard sirens. In addition to that, they'd begun work on basic training. Charlie had been around more dogs and more people than any other dog she'd owned.

Taking him into work on her day off was one of her favorite things to do.

Putting a well-trained canine through his paces was one of the great pleasures of Della's life. Over the years, she'd worked with lots of dogs, some belonging to others, and some to her. She'd met good ones, bad ones and many in between. And there'd never been a dog like Charlie. The instant she'd met the young black Lab in the shelter, they'd locked eyes and she'd known he was meant to be hers. They shared such a close bond instantly, which made working with him a thing of beauty.

Even her coworkers at Crosswinds remarked on it. The owner of the dog training facility, Sebastian Cross, often used her and Charlie for advertising videos and promotional material. And in an environment of accomplished and certified dog trainers, she and Charlie had become minor celebrities. Sometimes, when she was putting her dog through his paces, she'd look up to find a small crowd had gathered to watch.

Today was no exception. For fun, she was letting Charlie run the Agility course, one of his absolute favorite nonwork activities next to Dock Diving. Everything had been set up for a level one class later that afternoon, so Della put her dog through the course. He loved running through the tunnel, up the ramp and back down, but most of all, he adored jumping over jumps. His movements were poetry in action. He soared over the obstacle, his tail curved high over his back. As soon as he'd run the course, he came trotting over to her, panting happily.

When they finished, she looked up and saw a couple of her coworkers admiring Charlie. Then she noticed Max Colton standing near the doorway, watching her intently.

As before, her first glimpse of him sent a jolt through her system. More than merely handsome, he radiated a kind of quiet confidence that she found more than attractive. In fact, she'd venture to view it as dangerous.

Mentally shaking her head, she took a deep breath and tried to act normal. "Hey!" She greeted him with a friendly smile and walked over. Ignoring the wide stares of the others, she watched as he bent over to pet Charlie. "What brings you out this way?"

Meeting her gaze, he appeared to lose his train of thought. She thought about teasing him, but then, as she realized he might be here on official business, her smile faded. "Did you get confirmation of identity? Is that why you've come?"

"No, it's too soon for that." Lightly touching her arm, he shook his head. "I'm sorry. I didn't mean to make you think…"

"It's okay." Now she felt awkward. "You will let me know as soon as you find out, right?"

"Yes, I will." He took a deep breath. "Actually, I came by to see if you wanted to have lunch."

He couldn't have shocked her more. "Lunch? With you?"

One corner of his mouth kicked up in amusement, sending another jab to her stomach. "Yes. Grab a sandwich or something? You know, that thing friends sometimes do."

Friends. Right. She wasn't sure whether to be flattered or insulted. But since she truly had no interest in becoming romantically involved with a man like him, she thought they actually might be able to become friends. Once she got past this ridiculous attraction, that was.

She looked down at her dog to give herself time to gather her thoughts.

"We'd need a dog-friendly patio," she said, stroking Charlie's head. "Which means we'll have to go to Tap Out Brewery."

"I love that place," he replied. "Are you able to leave now?"

"As a matter of fact, I am." Since her coworkers' stares felt like they were burning holes into her back, the sooner, the better. "Charlie and I just finished up and I'm done for the day."

"Great." They walked outside together. He'd parked his truck next to her Jeep. "Want to ride together? I can bring you back to pick up your vehicle."

"I'll just follow you," she said. "That way I can go home after we eat."

Driving into town with Charlie sitting happily in the back seat, she tried to quash a buzz of unfamiliar excitement. She hadn't really thought this through, she realized. Once people saw her and Max Colton together, the rumor mill would go into overdrive. And since they couldn't yet discuss the case, they'd have no choice but to let people think whatever they liked.

Maybe people would realize Della wasn't Max's type. Over the years, he'd been linked up with a number of beautiful women, all of them with blond hair and blue eyes. Della's light brown hair and ordinary brown eyes were about as far as one could get from that.

Oddly enough, this made her feel better. Surely anyone with a propensity to gossip would take one look at her and realize she wasn't in Max Colton's league.

As they pulled into the parking lot, she supposed she should be glad it was nearly one, toward the end of the noon lunch rush. A popular place to have lunch or an early dinner, Tap Out would be quiet from about two until five. After eight at night, and during any kind of sporting event, the brewpub was packed, with a rowdy atmosphere.

"They have the best chicken tenders," Max said, taking her arm. This startled her and she gave him a quick glance, which made him let go.

"Sorry," he muttered. "Old habits."

Instead of going in the front door, they went directly to the patio. There were quite a few patrons enjoying the nice weather, and even a couple of other dogs. Charlie wagged his tail happily, but ever obedient, he stayed by Della's side.

The waitress came to take their drink order, bringing Charlie his own bowl of water. They both ordered a Tap Out Lager, smiling at each other over their menus.

Their beers came quickly, and they both ordered lunch. Max went with the chicken fingers and Della got a flatbread pizza. The waitress promised to bring the food out as soon as it was cooked and disappeared.

Della took a sip of her beer and sat back in her chair.

"Tell me about Angela," Max asked. "What was she like?"

Della sighed. "You would have loved her. Everyone

did. She was bright and funny and beautiful, from the inside out. Let me show you." Reaching into her purse, she pulled out a wallet, opened it and extracted a photo. "This was taken the last time she visited Owl Creek. Maybe two months before she disappeared."

In the picture, Della stood side by side with Angela, a taller woman with purple-and-blond hair. Arms around each other, they beamed at the camera, the affection between them clear and vivid. Looking at it made Della's throat ache. Swallowing, she handed it over to him. "Isn't she beautiful?" she asked.

He studied it a moment in silence. "She's pretty," he replied, handing the photo back. "You know, in my opinion, I've never met another woman who could hold a candle to you. But I have to admit your cousin comes close."

Blinking, Della tried to process what he'd just said. Then she realized he had to be acting from habit. Once a playboy, always a playboy.

When she didn't respond, he took a sip of his beer. "What was Angela doing in Kalispell?"

Relieved to be back on familiar ground, she put the photo carefully back into her wallet. "She went there to start her own hair salon with one of her friends from cosmetology school. They'd had their grand opening and seemed to be doing well."

"Did she go to cosmetology school here in Idaho?"

"Yes, in Boise." She sighed. "Angela had a real talent with hair. She could make anyone look good, no matter how old or how young. I always intended on making the trip there to see her in action and get my hair done. Now I wish I had."

Max must've seen her blink back tears, so he gave her

a moment. Composing herself, she took a sip of her drink and shook her head. "Damn, I'm going to miss her. I kept hoping she'd simply gone off on one of her epic adventures and lost track of time. Though it wasn't like her not to keep in touch, none of us knew what else to think."

"Did you notify the authorities?"

"Yes. Her parents filed a missing person report. Her business partner did too. Because Angela was dedicated to her work and to the business." Della's voice broke. To cover, she took another sip of her drink. Despite vowing not to give up hope until Caroline weighed in, she wasn't in the habit of living under delusions.

"Her apartment looked like she intended to return," Della continued. "Her parents—my aunt and uncle— went out there. There wasn't anything missing. Even her luggage was still in the closet, which kind of negated the whole gone-on-a-trip theory."

Again, Max gave her a minute, which she appreciated.

She refused to cry in front of him again, so she blinked several times and then grimaced. "The family all went into panic mode. Except me, because I knew that wouldn't help her. I helped contact every friend she'd ever had— at least the ones that I could reach or that I knew about. I made sure to be there for my aunt and uncle. And I refused to give up hope. They did too."

She bowed her head, lost in emotion. "Thanks for listening to me," she said.

"No thanks necessary. I'm really sorry everything played out the way it did."

On the patio at Della's feet, Charlie stretched out, clearly enjoying basking in the sun. Every now and then, he'd raise his head and look up at her, as if wanting to make sure she was okay.

"You're a good boy, Charlie Black," Della said. "The best dog ever."

The waitress arrived with their food just then, a welcome relief. Concentrating on her lunch gave her time to collect her emotions and regain some of her composure.

They ate in a kind of companionable silence. She liked that Max didn't feel the need to fill the quiet with small talk or seem to expect her to.

She glanced up at him, only to find him watching her, his expression intense.

"Are you okay?" he asked.

Considering his words, she finally nodded. "I think I will be. But I'm really going to miss Angela." She pushed her plate away. She'd managed to eat about half of her pizza and would take the rest home to eat later.

"When was the last time the two of you spoke?" he asked. He'd demolished his meal and leaned back in his chair, his eyes locked on hers.

Something in his light blue eyes made her yearn to lean across the table and touch him. Instead, she focused on his question. "She and I spoke a couple of days before she disappeared. She'd recently joined a new church and seemed excited about the new friends she'd made."

"A church?" His gaze sharpened, though his tone remained casual. "Were you able to reach out to them and see if they knew anything?"

She grimaced. "That's just it. We couldn't. Angela was pretty vague when she talked about them and none of us knew to press her. Even Karyn, her business partner, didn't know much about Angela joining a church.

We didn't even know the name of it or where it was located."

"That's odd," he mused. "Though it might not mean anything. Then again, I've learned the hard way that sometimes the smallest clue could be the missing link."

"We told the police about it when we filed the missing person report," she said. "They didn't seem too concerned."

"Probably because there isn't any real reason to be. It's just another clue. She might have met someone at this church, though, maybe a friend who might know something that might help."

"I thought of that," Della admitted. "But since Angela didn't give me very much information and she'd just started going there, I didn't think much would come of it."

"You're probably right," Max replied. "For now, I'll just add that information to my file."

"Do you mind if we change the subject?" she asked. "I still am dreading the moment when I have to go let Angela's parents know." Pushing to her feet, she handed him Charlie's leash. "Would you mind watching him while I go to the ladies' room?"

"Not at all," he responded. Charlie sat up when she walked away, but when she gave him the hand signal to stay, he didn't follow.

Forcing himself to tear his gaze away from Della as she walked away, Max managed to smile when the waitress walked up. He took care of the bill and left a generous tip.

While waiting for Della to return, he petted Charlie.

The black Lab seemed to like the attention, leaning into Max's touch. As Della strolled across the room toward them, Max realized he didn't want the afternoon to end yet. He wondered if she'd be willing to continue hanging out on the patio, enjoying the nice weather. Since the restaurant wasn't crowded, he knew they wouldn't mind.

She sat down and took a sip of her half-finished beer. "Are you ready to go?" she asked.

"Not until you are," he replied. "I'm actually liking getting to pet your dog."

As if he understood, Charlie whined, making Della laugh.

"I've got nowhere urgent to be," she said, surprising him. "As long as we can talk about something other than the case."

"I can do that." He found himself telling her about his mother carrying on an affair with his uncle.

"She deserted her children?" she asked, her eyes wide. "That's unreal."

"I know. And my uncle basically deserted his family too. But my aunt Jenny and my dad pitched in and worked together to make sure we all had good childhoods. When we all get together, it's like one huge family." He smiled. "My cousins are more like siblings than anything else."

"I'd heard the stories," she admitted. "Your family kind of owns most of Owl Creek. I went to school with some of your cousins, and your sister, Lizzy, was a couple years ahead of me."

Della finished her beer and shifted in her seat. Max had emptied his glass too. The waitress noticed and reappeared, asking if they wanted another.

"Oh, no, thank you," Della said.

Max declined also and the waitress moved away.

Afraid Della would push to her feet and start to leave, Max continued talking. "It gets even more bizarre," he said. "As I'm sure you've heard, my uncle Robert recently passed away."

She nodded. "Yes, the funeral was a big deal in town. It's all everyone talked about." She took a deep breath. "I'm sorry for your loss."

"Thanks." Watching her closely, Max grimaced. "I know how people in Owl Creek gossip about my family. So even though we tried to keep it quiet, I'm guessing you heard about what happened after the will was read."

"No." She shook her head. "Whatever you did must have worked, because no one's said anything."

Glancing around to make sure no one was close enough to overhear, he leaned toward her. "We've all just learned we have a couple of half siblings."

Della's mouth dropped open in shock. "What?"

"Yes, two more Coltons. A brother and a sister. All the rest of us kids are supposed to have dinner Thursday night at that new barbecue place in town and meet them."

"Back Forty? I've been wanting to try that," she said, clearly still mulling over what he'd said.

She had other questions, he could tell. He saw it in her face. And he also realized that as distractions went, this particular topic of conversation obviously did the trick. The sadness had receded from her eyes, replaced by curiosity. He liked the way her brown eyes glowed.

In fact, he liked everything about this woman.

"Would you go with me?" he asked, surprising himself. "I really could use the support."

Head tilted, she studied him. "Are you sure you want to bring a friend to something like this? It seems more like it should be a family matter, don't you think?"

"Maybe." He shrugged. "Maybe not. I'm sure some of the others will bring friends. It's all going to be very informal."

Since she still didn't appear convinced, he admitted the truth. "I'm not sure I even want to go, to be honest."

She caught on right away. "It's not their fault, you know. Whatever your mother did to you and your brothers and sister, it had nothing to do with them."

"I'm aware. It's just we didn't even find out about them until after the funeral, after the will was read."

"They didn't come?" She gaped at him. "To their own father's funeral?"

Now he wanted to change the subject. Instead, he tried to steer the conversation back on track. "Will you come with me? Or at least think about it? I really could use the support of a friend."

"Friend? Is that what we are?"

Her directness was refreshing. Another thing to like about her.

"I'd like to think so," he answered. He didn't feel like he had to give his "I'm not looking for a relationship" speech, because other than that one accidental kiss, he hadn't given her any indication he'd be romantically interested.

Even if he was.

The second the thought occurred to him, he shut it right down.

She laughed, the light sound easing some of the tightness in his chest. "I like that. Friends. And you know what? I think I will. It might do me good to get out and be around people who don't know me. What time do you want to pick me up? Or would you rather I meet you there?"

"I'll pick you up at six thirty."

"Okay." Her eyes sparkled as she got to her feet. "I'll text you my address." She typed and his phone pinged. "There. It's a bit out of town, but not too far from Crosswinds."

Tamping down his regret that the afternoon had ended, he stood. Following her and Charlie outside, he watched while she loaded the dog up in her Jeep and turned to face him.

"Thanks for lunch," she said. "I enjoyed it."

"Me too." He would not kiss her upturned face. He absolutely would not. Because he suspected if he did, she wouldn't go to dinner with him Thursday. And he realized he desperately wanted to see her again.

He stood outside his truck and watched until her taillights had disappeared. Then, shaking his head at himself, he got in, started the ignition and drove back to the ranch.

Once there, he set up his laptop in the large dining room. He had two back-to-back online meetings scheduled for that afternoon. Both were about the serial killer case. The first call would be between Max and Brian, discussing how to manage the media. The FBI would soon be releasing an official statement. They didn't want to cause a mass panic, but they had a duty to let the public know.

Caroline would be conducting the second one, briefing the team on her findings. He strongly doubted she'd be able to positively ID Della's cousin's remains. Even if she did, the official statement by the Bureau wouldn't identify any-one, pending official notification of the victims' families.

The family he was most concerned about was Della's. The anguish he'd seen in her expressive brown eyes would haunt him for a long time. Actually, he wished he could be with her when she learned the truth, though he suspected deep down she already knew.

Since Caroline had promised to call Della as soon as she knew, he decided he'd try to check in with Della later, to see if there was anything he could do to help. For now, he had work to attend to, for which he was deeply grateful. He needed to get his mind off Della Winslow and back where it belonged. On his job. This case.

Brian sent the link for the meeting and Max clicked on it. A moment later, his boss's face filled the laptop screen.

"Good afternoon," Brian said, his expression unchar-acteristically grim. "I've had my assistant busy drafting the press release. I thought we could go through it and get everything fine-tuned. I'm going to have a tentative story 'leaked' to the press later today."

Which meant that would give the media time to have a feeding frenzy, complete with various possible scenarios and speculation. The local Owl Creek police would direct all questions to the FBI. Eventually, Brian would sched-ule a press conference and release the official statement.

Max and Brian tossed phrases back and forth, using previous statements made by other state FBI divisions when addressing their own serial killer investigations. Finally, they settled on something both of them liked and ended the call.

With thirty minutes to go until his second meeting, Max used the time to make a glass of iced tea and grab a couple of the homemade chocolate chip cookies Mama Jen had left behind. His dad and his brothers were still out working the ranch, so he had the house to himself.

Growing up, he'd been required to help out around the place. After he got home from school, he'd had to come home, change and head to the barn, to help muck out stalls, exercise horses or help with the feedings. He hadn't minded, though even then he'd known that he wanted something different than a life spent tending horses or cattle.

With two older sons already committed, Buck had been much more lenient with the younger two kids, Max and his sister, Lizzy. They'd been allowed to pursue their own interests and Buck had given them his enthusiastic support over their choices. When Max had gone to Quantico, Buck and Jenny had even thrown him a going-away-slash-celebratory party.

Checking his watch, Max took a seat and opened his laptop. A moment later, he found the meeting invite and clicked on it.

The second Zoom call brought the entire team back together. Though Brian had scheduled the meeting, he quickly turned it over to Caroline to brief them on her findings.

"I've successfully been able to identify four of the remains," she announced. "Using DNA and cross-referencing missing person reports with a narrow focus on females between the ages of eighteen and thirty, we had a resounding success. As for the other three, my forensic team is still working on those."

A series of photos appeared on the screen. "These are the victims, along with their name, age and last-known address at the time of their disappearance. We have not yet been successful in finding anything that might link them together."

Everyone fell silent as they studied the photos. All young, all pretty. Max focused in on the first one. Angela Hobbs. Della's cousin.

Though his throat had briefly closed, Max managed to find his voice. "I assume you've started the process of locating and notifying next of kin?"

Caroline eyed him, her expression sympathetic. "Yes. I'll be doing that once we finish this meeting."

And Della was by herself. Then and there, Max knew he'd be heading out to her place as soon as he could. Locating her text from earlier, he put her address into his GPS. Twenty minutes, if he drove fast. He toyed with asking Caroline to wait, to give him a head start, but didn't want the gossip mill to go into overdrive.

For now, he needed to force himself to pay attention to the rest of the meeting.

"These young women are from all over the tristate area," Caroline was saying. "Though Angela Hobbs grew up here in Owl Creek, at the time of her disappearance, she was living in Kalispell, Montana." Caroline used a pointer to highlight each woman's profile. "The others came from Idaho, Wyoming and Utah."

"Idaho?" Max asked. "But not Owl Creek?"

"No. Pocatello." Caroline shook her head. "The question is, what did they have in common?"

That was what they needed to look for. The single

common denominator that might lead them to the reason the killer had targeted these particular women.

Unfortunately, at this moment they had nothing.

"Theo, you and Chris start working on the ones from Wyoming and Utah," Brian ordered. "Jake and Ed, help them. Max, I want you to check out the two from Idaho, especially the one who grew up in your hometown. I want each of you to dig into their backgrounds, talk to their friends and family, learn their hobbies. There has to be something similar that each of these women did or knew."

"And I'll continue to work to identify the others," Caroline said. "Once I have more information on them, I'll get with you all again."

Now that the assignments had been passed out, the meeting ended. Max immediately grabbed his truck keys and headed out the door. He needed to get to Della as soon as possible. He hated that she'd be alone when she learned the news about her cousin.

Chapter 6

By the time Della got home from lunch with Max, she'd received individual text messages from four different coworkers, every single one of them wanting the dirt on how she knew Max Colton and what might be going on between them. Since his reputation preceded him, she supposed she couldn't blame them. After all, she'd worked with most of them for years and they all knew her to be a steady, low-key and down-to-earth woman. Not the type to be taken in by a man who was known for loving and leaving women.

Instead of responding individually, she made a group text and sent out a two-word response. We're friends!

In response, she received a few emojis, exclamation points, and one flat-out declaration that said, When you're up here next, we want details. Again, no more than she'd expected. Heck, she'd have done the same if she'd spotted any of her coworkers hanging around with Max.

The thought caused a twinge of unease, which shocked her. Jealousy? Or just that she didn't like the thought of what—*sharing Max Colton with anyone*? As if he belonged to her or some such nonsense.

Shaking her head at her own foolishness, Della decided to keep busy with some housework and laundry.

As she puttered around the house, Charlie watched from the comfort of his oversize dog bed. He'd had a busy couple of days and had earned his rest. Speaking of rest, she wouldn't mind taking a short nap herself. With one load of clothes in the washer and another in the dryer, now might be the perfect time to do that.

On her way to the bedroom, her cell phone rang. Caroline's number was displayed on the screen, which sent Della's heart rate into overdrive. Taking a deep breath, she answered.

"Good afternoon," Caroline said, her voice soft. "I just finished briefing the team. As promised, I'm calling you to let you know I've identified four of the bodies."

Though she'd expected this, for a moment Della's world spun. She put out a hand to steady herself, gripping the side of her dresser. "Was one of them Angela?" she croaked, suspecting she already knew the answer.

"Yes. I'm very sorry."

"Thank you." Blinking back tears, Della raised her chin and took a deep breath. "Have you determined her cause of death yet?"

"We're still working on that. It's much more difficult at this stage."

When there were only bones. Though Caroline didn't say that out loud, Della knew what she meant. "When and if you figure that out, will you also let me know?"

"Of course," Caroline replied. "Again, I'm really sorry for your loss."

After murmuring her thanks, Della ended the call. Numb, she sat down at her kitchen table. Through the window over the sink, she could see the house next door, where Angela had grown up and where Della had spent as much time as at her own home. Her aunt and uncle still lived there. Now Della had to summon up the strength to go over there and break both of their hearts.

She didn't know how long she sat there, staring into space, lost in her memories and thoughts. But when Charlie nudged her hand with his nose, she blinked and pushed to her feet. Charlie whined, then gave a short bark and hurried over to the front door, his tail wagging.

A moment later, her doorbell rang.

Not really sure she wanted to deal with anyone, she looked through the peephole. Max Colton stood on her doorstep, dragging a hand through his hair, his expression concerned.

At the sight of his handsome face, her heartbeat skipped. Though she wasn't sure why he'd come or even how he'd found her house, she opened the door.

"Max…" she began.

Without speaking, he stepped forward, closing the door shut behind him, and pulled her into his arms. "I'm here," he told her.

Face against his chest, she froze. And then, as the warmth of his strong body seeped into her bones, she heaved a giant sob and began to weep.

He offered her comfort, a silent rock of a man, saying nothing. She didn't know how it was that he'd come to comfort her, but right this moment, she didn't care. He'd understood that some things shouldn't have to be dealt with alone.

Finally, she had no more tears, having cried herself out. Eyes swollen, she stepped away and disappeared into her bathroom to blow her nose and wash her face. She still wasn't entirely sure why Max had come and she half suspected he might be gone when she emerged. Either way, she owed him a debt of gratitude for his unwavering support. She appreciated that he hadn't asked for anything in return.

Instead, he waited for her in the kitchen, one hip resting against the counter. Charlie had taken a seat right next to him, leaning himself against Max's leg for pets. Even her dog loved this man. She eyed him, one part of her thinking he looked too damn sexy for her peace of mind.

Friends, she reminded herself. She needed to remember that.

"Caroline told me she was going to let you know she'd identified the remains," he said. "I wanted to make sure you were all right."

Blinking, she stared at him, her words of gratitude stuck in her throat. Needing a second to compose herself, she went to the fridge and poured herself a glass of lemonade. Without thinking, she got one for Max too. Handing it to him, she sighed. "Thank you. Though deep down inside, I knew this was coming, it's still hard." She glanced at the house next door. "Now I've got to fill my aunt and uncle in."

"My offer to go with you still stands," he said, his sympathetic expression making her ache for another hug. "I'm here if you need me."

Briefly, she considered. "I think it's best if I go by myself. They wouldn't appreciate me bringing a stranger."

"Maybe not." He drew himself up. "But I'm an FBI agent. Eventually, I'll have to speak to them. I can go in my official capacity. It might help."

He had a point. Charlie nudged him and Max bent down to continue scratching behind the dog's ears.

Restless, she went to the kitchen window again to look at the house next door. Two vehicles were in the driveway, which meant both her aunt and uncle were home.

"I want to tell them now," she said, deciding. "And yes, I'd like you to come with me, in an official capacity."

Straightening, he gave a wordless nod.

She marched to the front door, gathering up every ounce of strength she possessed. Though she knew it might be best to call first to let them know she was coming, she felt strongly that they'd hear something in her voice and know. No way she wanted them to learn their daughter's fate on the telephone. They deserved better than that.

With Max right behind her, she crossed the distance between the two houses. Stepping up onto the front porch, she rang the bell. A moment later, her aunt answered the door, her expression puzzled.

"Della?" Her gaze swung from Della to Max.

"Aunt Mary, this is Max Colton with the FBI," Della said, her voice trembling only slightly. "May we come in?"

At first, her aunt appeared puzzled. But then she jerked her head in a quick nod and motioned them past her. "Let me call your uncle," she said. "Please, wait in the den."

Instead of dropping down onto the sofa as she would normally, Della stood, twisting her hands nervously.

"Do you want me to tell them?" Max offered. "In my official capacity, of course."

Tempting as the offer might be, Della had never been a coward. "I'll do it."

"Just stick to the facts," he advised. "It'll be easier on them that way."

"What's going on?" Uncle Alex demanded as he entered the room. "Mary tells me you brought an FBI agent here? Do you have news of Angela?"

Could she do this? Trying to speak past the ache in her throat, she nodded. "I do. And I'm afraid it's not good."

Somehow, she managed to relay what Caroline had told her. She left out the fact that she and Charlie had been the ones to find the body, or even that they'd found six more unmarked graves.

"But who killed her?" Aunt Mary asked, seemingly unaware of the tears streaking down her face. Uncle Alex had covered his face with his hands to hide his emotions but lifted his head at the question.

At a complete loss for words, Della looked toward Max for help.

"We're working on finding that out," Max replied. "As soon as we know anything, I promise we will inform you." He took a deep breath. "For now, I'm afraid I have to ask you to keep this quiet. We'll be holding a press conference about the entire situation soon. Until then, if you could keep this under wraps, we'd appreciate it."

Uncle Alex's gaze narrowed. For a moment, Della thought he'd protest, but instead he simply bowed his head. "We've got to notify our family and her friends. Can we do that?"

"Yes, of course," Max responded.

"Thank you for letting us know." Voice wooden, Mary turned and walked out of the room. A moment later, her husband followed.

Aching, Della wished there was something she could say, something she could do, to help ease their pain. Instead, she knew she'd have to let them deal with it however they chose.

"Come on," she said quietly, touching Max's arm. "We can show ourselves out."

Back in her own kitchen, Della realized she had no memory of how she'd gotten there. Charlie rushed over, tail wagging, and she dropped to the floor and buried her face in his fur.

She didn't cry. She had no more tears left inside of her to shed. Instead, she held her beloved dog and took comfort from his unwavering devotion.

Instead of leaving, Max took a seat at the kitchen table. He waited quietly, both giving her space and lending his support, if she needed it.

She appreciated him more than she could say.

Finally, she got up and went to let Charlie outside. As if he understood, the dog took care of his business quickly, bounding back to the door to indicate he was ready to go in.

When they returned to the kitchen, Max still waited.

Eyeing him, she admired his patience, the way he managed to emit both an aura of stillness and a readiness to spring into action if needed. Now she finally understood why so many other women had been willing to throw themselves at him.

As she approached, he stood. "Della," he began. The intensity in his gaze was her undoing.

Somehow, she wound up in his arms, her mouth on his. Hungry—so, so hungry. His hand tangled in her hair, they devoured each other. This kiss took their first one to another level. Smoldering, intense, almost overwhelming. Each kiss, every touch, set her ablaze with longing. Their tongues tangled, breath intertwined, and she couldn't get enough.

With their clothing an unwelcome barrier between their skin, they tore at each other's shirts, pants and, finally, undergarments. As he stepped out of his boxers, his arousal free, she couldn't stop herself from stroking the physical demonstration of his need for her.

As he pushed into her hands, desire clawed at her.

"Are you sure?" he asked. When she nodded, he bent over and retrieved a condom from his jeans. She helped him tug it on, each movement arousing her to a fevered pitch.

When they'd finished, they kissed again. Body tingling, she throbbed with an ache to take him inside of her. Somehow, they made it to the living room and fell naked onto the sofa. Limbs entangled, wrapped around each other, she pushed him back and climbed on top. As she took him deep inside, his body filled her velvet softness, and she arched back and let out a moan. All the superlatives applied—eroticism brought to vibrant, immediate life with every movement.

Nothing gentle about this. She demanded and he gave. Everything, all at once. Electrified, the tension built in her. She burned. And yet she needed more.

Then, just as she almost reached the apex, he rolled, pinning her beneath him. "Not yet," he rasped, even as she bucked against him. "Just. Give me a minute."

She could feel his heart thudding against her skin. Somehow, shivering, she held herself still. When he began to move again, each slow stroke an exquisite form of torture, she writhed beneath him. Using her body, she tried to urge him to go faster. She burned for him. When he finally let go of his restraint, she met him stroke for stroke. Raw possession. And this time, when she reached the peak, she toppled over it. Explosive pleasure clawed through her, like nothing she'd ever felt before.

A moment later, he shuddered and let go. They held on to each other while his body bucked and hers clenched.

He slid his hand along the curve of her hip, tucking her body into his. They lay together while their heart rates slowed and their breathing got back to normal.

Finally, he raised himself up on one elbow and smoothed her hair away from her face. "You're so beautiful," he said.

She made a face. "So are you."

"I'm serious." He kissed her neck, right below her jaw, which made her shiver.

"As am I." Because she knew she ought to move, she shifted away and began gathering up her clothes from the floor. He watched her for a moment while she got dressed, then sighed and did the same.

"No regrets." She hadn't meant to say that out loud, but when she saw his startled expression, she realized she had.

"Right," he replied. He frowned and then took a deep breath. "Listen, we can still be friends, right?"

Chest aching, she slowly nodded. "Of course."

Silently thanking him for the reminder, she walked to the front door and held it open. "Give me a call when you hear something on the case."

"I will," he replied. "And don't forget dinner Thursday."

As friends. No way was she going to allow this man to break her heart. She had too much sense for that. "Of course."

Head spinning, his entire body buzzing, Max hurried to his truck. Instead of feeling sated after that amazing round of lovemaking, he craved more. He'd successfully fought the urge to ask her if he could stay. For the first time in forever, he'd longed to spend the night with a woman tucked up against his body.

Not just any woman. Della.

What the hell was wrong with him? Not only would getting involved with her be the height of unprofessionalism, but her personal involvement with one of the victims could jeopardize the entire case.

Also, if he were completely honest, with his reputation as a player, he didn't want the folks of Owl Creek to make wrong judgments about Della's character. She didn't deserve that. All the other women he'd dated had known up front what they were getting into. The rules had been agreed to by both parties. He and Della had never discussed anything other than the fact that they were friends.

Friends. Most people might find that insulting. Normally he would, especially around a woman as sexy as her. But he genuinely *liked* Della Winslow. Sure, he also desired her, but from past experience he knew finding a woman he enjoyed being around outweighed any rush of passion. He'd also learned it never worked out trying to have both.

As he started the truck and drove home, he wondered what the hell he was going to do. He hadn't meant for this to happen, and clearly, neither had she. But damn, he refused to regret it. Because no matter how he tried to spin it, he'd never experienced this kind of connection with another woman. He kind of doubted he ever would again.

Snorting at his own uncharacteristic train of thought, instead of driving directly back to the ranch, he decided to stop in town for a drink. By now, Tap Out Brewery ought to be hopping. He figured he'd see if he could snag a seat at the bar, have a beer and do some people-watching. Maybe that would help clear his head.

Briefly, he considered calling one of his cousins, like Fletcher, who worked as a detective for the Owl Creek Police Department. But then Fletcher would want to discuss the case, and Max wasn't in the mood for that. No, it would be better to go alone, have his drink and try to unwind.

He had to circle the packed parking lot several times before he lucked out into a space when someone left.

Once inside, he had to shoulder his way through people to get to the packed bar. Surprised to see a couple of empty stools, he took one. The bartender caught his eye and motioned that he'd be over as soon as he could. Since there were only two behind the bar, Max figured he might be in for a bit of a wait. However, he had his beer in less than five minutes. Grateful, Max took a long drink and then surveyed the room. He always found people-watching entertaining.

"I hear we're having a news conference tomorrow." One of the cops who'd originally been at the meadow dropped into the seat next to him. "To talk about that mass grave site up in the mountains."

Max eyed him, drawing a blank when he tried to remember the guy's name. Luckily, he'd spoken quietly, and no one else appeared to have heard.

Apparently realizing this, the man stuck out his hand and Max shook it. "Ryan Larkins," he said. "Owl Creek PD. I work with your cousin Fletcher. We've been getting calls all day about a potential serial killer and were told to refer all of them to the FBI. Everyone says the FBI is going to talk about it officially tomorrow."

Max didn't bother to say his own name since Ryan clearly remembered it. Since the story would have just been leaked to the press, Max wondered if Ryan knew this for a fact or was simply fishing for info.

"Are we?" he asked casually, taking a long drink of his beer. "I haven't been informed if that's the case. But then again, I'm not part of the PR department, so I'm not involved."

Larkins nodded and ordered his own beer. While he waited for it to arrive, he turned and eyed Max. "What did you all find in that meadow? Must have been something interesting, if there's a need to brief the general public. I heard there were several more bodies."

Beginning to regret his impulsive decision to stop here, Max shook his head. "I'm sorry, but I can't discuss an ongoing investigation. You'll have to wait for the news conference, like everyone else."

Ryan's eyes narrowed. "Come on, Max. I'm not just a citizen. What's the big secret?"

He should have called Fletcher. If his cousin had been sitting here with him, he bet this guy wouldn't have been so inquisitive. "Sorry. I seriously am not at liberty to give you any information. I would if I could."

Though Ryan didn't appear convinced, he nodded. His beer arrived and he took a huge gulp, wiping his mouth with the back of his hand. "You can tell me," he finally said, his beefy face reddening. "We're both in law enforcement."

"I really can't." Infusing his voice with regret, Max drained the rest of his beer. He motioned to the bartender and closed out his tab. "Sorry," he told Ryan. "I've got to run."

Ryan's eyes narrowed further, and for a moment, Max thought there might be a fight. To his surprise, he clenched his fists, realizing he'd actually welcome that. Clearly, he needed to blow off some steam.

Instead, the other man backed down. "Have a good night."

Max nodded. There were lots of other ways to blow off steam. He kept a workout bag in his trunk. He could head to the gym, change and lift weights plus do some cardio. Breaking a good sweat would definitely help him release some of his pent-up tension. But then again, having mind-blowing sex usually took care of that too. Since he'd definitely just done that, he didn't understand his current mood.

Fletcher called when Max was getting into his truck. "Want to meet up for a beer?" Fletcher asked.

"I'm just leaving Tap Out," Max replied. "I ran into one of your officers. Ryan Larkins."

Laughing, Fletcher took a moment to speak. "Did he try to interrogate you? He's been bugging the heck out of me to find out what's going on in the investigation."

"Yep," Max admitted. "I barely stopped myself from getting into a bar fight with him."

"I can imagine. And I'm guessing you don't want to go back inside and wait for me."

"Nope," Max replied. "Sorry, but I'm heading back to the ranch."

"Are you going to be at the presser tomorrow?" Fletcher asked. "They've requested that I appear and stand near the police chief and the mayor to represent Owl Creek PD."

"I haven't been asked to be there," Max replied. "At least not yet. I didn't even know there was anything scheduled for tomorrow. I'm guessing my boss must be driving up to do it."

"Isn't that kind of weird?" Fletcher asked. "You're already in town since you're actively working the case. I'd think they'd want you involved."

"I'm just glad they don't. Giving public speeches has never been one of my favorite activities."

Fletcher laughed again. "I hear you. See you Thursday?"

"I'll be there. I'm looking forward to trying a half rack of ribs."

Once the call ended, Max eyed his phone and realized he'd missed several calls and had a couple of voice mails. All from his SAC Brian. With all the noise inside the bar, he hadn't been able to hear it ring. There was even a text from Brian, asking Max to call him ASAP.

Max had a sinking feeling that this would be regarding the press conference tomorrow. Though there was always the chance that they'd learned something new regarding the investigation. Before he even got a chance to return the call, his phone rang again.

"Brian," Max began. "Sorry I missed you. What's going on?"

"I'm driving out to Owl Creek in the morning," Brian said. "We're holding a joint press conference with OCPD. I've shared my PowerPoint presentation with you. I need you to take a look at it and let me know if there's anything you'd like to add or change."

Relieved, Max agreed to do so as soon as he got back to the ranch.

"Also," Brian continued, "I'm going to need you to meet me at the police department headquarters tomorrow around ten. The presser is at eleven."

"I'll be there," Max promised. He should have seen this coming. Since Brian had placed Max in charge while in Owl Creek, there was no way Brian would brief the media without him.

Back at the ranch, he walked inside the house and realized he'd interrupted dinner. His father and two brothers were in the middle of their meal, which consisted of leftovers from what Jenny had cooked the previous evening.

Max made himself a plate and sat down to eat. Luckily, his family wasn't into small talk, so he was able to finish his meal and head up to his room. He heard the television come on downstairs, which was good. It meant no one would be disturbing him.

The next morning, Max put on his best suit and tie. Glad his father and brothers were already out working on the ranch, he eyed himself in the mirror. Sometimes, FBI agents got to wear their Bureau windbreakers over slacks and a shirt. Brian had decided this was not one of those times.

Driving into town, Max arrived at the police station thirty minutes early. Despite that, Brian was waiting for him on a metal bench out front, drinking a large to-go cup of coffee. The various news crews had already started setting up out front. In addition to the local stations, Max recognized a couple of reporters from national news. Luckily, no one knew him or Brian, so they were left alone. For now, at least. That would definitely change once the presser started.

"Morning," Max said, dropping on the bench next

to his boss. Brian also wore a dark suit along with sunglasses that screamed *federal agent.*

"Nice town," Brian commented. "I've never made it out this way before."

"It's a popular tourist destination," Max pointed out. He pulled his own sunglasses from his pocket and put them on. "Are we having this thing outside?" he asked.

"We are." Brian nodded. "That way there's more room for both the news crews and the citizens. The mayor tells me he's posted notices all around town, in shop windows, as well as on the city's social media. He expects a large turnout."

Sure enough, people were already filling up the lot and parking in the street. Since Max recognized many of them, he was especially glad he'd put on the sunglasses. They may not completely hide him, but at least they'd give people pause while they tried to figure out his identity. Of course, once everything started, they'd recognize him for certain.

Finally, the police chief emerged, accompanied by the mayor, Skipper Carlson. Though Chief Stanton wore his uniform, the mayor had chosen a dark suit as well. A retired ski instructor, Skipper usually went around town in jeans, a T-shirt and motorcycle boots. Max thought he cleaned up well. A couple of junior staffers came out with them, also dressed up. They carried a microphone, speakers and a wooden podium that had seen better days. They got all this set up and did a couple of "Testing, 1-2-3"s on the mic.

Meanwhile, the crowd of townspeople continued to grow. Max recognized Angela's parents, though he saw no sign of Della. Too bad. He should have asked Brian to have Della and Charlie there to represent the SAR team who'd made the initial discovery. Too late now.

Several other police officers emerged from the building, most of them in uniform. Max's cousin Fletcher came with them. There was no sign of Ryan Larkins, which made Max smile.

Brian took one last deep gulp of his coffee and stood. "Showtime," he murmured. "Let's go."

Joining him, Max kept his gaze fixed straight ahead. Since it seemed half of Owl Creek was here, not to mention all the news teams, he needed to project the stereotypical image people associated with an FBI agent. "Let's do this," he said.

Chapter 7

Della watched the press conference on her television, along with everyone else in town who didn't attend in person. Gossip had run rampant through all the shops and restaurants. Crosswinds hadn't been immune. Since no one knew exactly what the topic would be, imaginations ran high. Her aunt and uncle apparently hadn't discussed Angela's death with any of their friends or acquaintances in town, because no one came up to Della with expressions of sympathy.

The FBI had decided to hold the news conference with very short notice, likely to keep gossip from reaching a fevered pitch. It had only been announced yesterday afternoon. She imagined some of the major news outlets had done a bit of scrambling to get their reporters into town on time.

Della had briefly considered making the drive into town to see everything in person, but in the end, she'd decided against it. If they mentioned anything about Angela, she'd likely lose her composure. The last thing she wanted was to have a meltdown on live TV.

Plus, since it was Wednesday, she'd be working at Crosswinds tonight. Her coworkers would already have too many questions because they'd have figured out that she and Charlie had been the ones to find the graves.

And since the identities of some of the victims had been released, they'd know her cousin Angela had been one of them.

Her aunt and uncle had called her the minute they learned of the news conference. "Is it true?" Aunt Mary had asked. "There were other women killed? Angela wasn't the only one?"

"Yes. There were six others," Della had replied softly. "That's why the FBI has taken over. They're working the case as a probable serial killer."

Aunt Mary had gasped. "Why didn't you mention this before, when you told us about Angela?"

"Because the FBI asked me not to." Della's gut had clenched. "They've promised to find the killer."

"They'd better." For a moment, her aunt had sounded furious. "Before Alex gathers up all his friends in this town and they go out and find him themselves."

The mingled anger and pain in her aunt Mary's usually calm voice had made Della's chest hurt. She stared at the TV, wondering if she'd be able to see them.

As the camera panned out over the crowd, Della spotted her aunt and uncle, standing front and center. Uncle Alex had his arm around Aunt Mary, almost holding her up. Several of their friends surrounded them, clearly there to offer their support.

It looked like a large portion of the town had turned out for this event. Judging by the variety of the rumors being bandied about, Della wasn't surprised. They'd flown fast and furious, beginning the moment the press conference had been announced. No doubt everyone wanted to find out which of those rumors were true. Della couldn't blame them, though she knew everyone would be shocked once they knew the truth.

When the camera returned to the group near the podium, Della spotted Max, wearing a dark suit and sunglasses. He stood next to another, shorter man similarly attired. If someone had asked for a couple of actors to portray FBI agents, the two of them would have made the cut.

The mayor stepped forward and spoke into the mic. He too had dressed with care, forgoing his usual casual Western attire for a suit and tie, though he still wore a black cowboy hat. He began by welcoming everyone, though he wished it was for a better reason. He then introduced chief of police Kevin Stanton and turned the microphone over to him.

Clearly working from a script, the police chief read from a paper. He detailed how a search and rescue canine and handler had happened across remains buried in a shallow grave while hiking. He didn't mention Della and Charlie by name, though she knew everyone in town would guess it was her.

"We called in the FBI," Kevin said. "And now Special Agent in Charge Brian Mahoney will discuss what they've found."

While the SAC spoke, Della watched Max. He stood ramrod straight, staring directly ahead, his handsome face expressionless. When several in the crowd gasped at the words *serial killer*, he didn't physically react. Inwardly, she suspected he was wincing.

Ending the speech with the usual platitudes, Brian told the crowd that they had no reason to panic. They were currently working all leads and this killer *would* be apprehended.

She wondered if he'd take questions from the townspeople or the reporters. Apparently not, as he'd already turned away. Several reporters shouted out to him, though he didn't acknowledge any of their requests. Along with the mayor, police chief and Max, he disappeared inside the police station. The camera followed them until the doors closed behind them.

A reporter appeared on the screen, her blue eyes sparking with excitement. When she began talking, Della grabbed the remote and clicked the television off. She'd seen enough.

When her aunt and uncle arrived home next door, she saw them pull up in the driveway out her kitchen window. Watching as they got out of the car, she realized they both looked like they'd aged twenty years since she'd given them the awful news.

They'd also been avoiding her. As if they felt she was somehow responsible.

Shaking off the thought, she waited until they'd gone into the house before calling Charlie. Another new Manners class tonight. This time, she'd bring her dog to work with her and let him demonstrate.

Once she got to Crosswinds, she managed to dodge people until right before her class started. Sebastian, the owner, even popped into her work area, but once he saw her students had already arrived, he left. Della figured he was just as curious as everyone else.

She was busy with back-to-back classes, and the time flew. The students were all focused and respectful, which was good since she didn't have to deal with another Hal.

She dreaded seeing him again at the next class and actually found herself hoping he wouldn't show up. Sometimes students dropped out after one or two classes, deciding training their dog was too much work.

As soon as her second class ended, she and Charlie hurried out to her Jeep. By some miracle, no one stopped her. With Charlie in the back seat, she pulled out of the parking lot and headed home.

A few miles in and she began to suspect someone might be following her. A black Honda with black rims. Hoping she was wrong, she made an abrupt right turn without signaling. The Honda did the same.

Maybe just coincidence. However, until she knew for sure, she wasn't going home.

Another right turn. The Honda followed. Now heading back the way she'd come, she passed the turnoff to Crosswinds and kept going toward downtown Owl Creek. She could either pull into the police station parking lot or one of the well-lit gas stations. She'd decide once she got there.

As she drove, she kept checking her rearview mirror, hoping the other vehicle would turn off and disappear. No such luck. She had no idea why anyone would want to follow her, unless it was some overzealous reporter in search of a story. Which made no sense. She hadn't been mentioned by name in the press conference. No one would have any reason to wish to interview her.

Ahead, she saw the sign for the Chevron station. Impulsively, she turned in, pulling up to one of the pumps like she meant to fill her tank. To her shock, the Honda did the same, parking at the pump right behind her.

She swore under her breath. Instead of getting out of

her vehicle, she pulled forward into one of the parking spaces near the entrance. Then she hopped out, grabbing Charlie's leash and bringing him with her. She hurried into the store, where she could ask for help.

As she yanked open the glass door, someone called her name.

Turning, she saw Hal Murcheson getting out of the black Honda and waving at her.

Jaw clenched, she continued on inside the store. At least there were several other customers, plus two cashiers behind the counter. The pumps were busy and people were buying snacks or drinks. She found a spot close to the exit, near the cashiers, and turned to face the door.

Undeterred, Hal followed her inside. "Hey, Della," he said. "I thought I saw you leaving Crosswinds. I've been trying to flag you down since then."

"Flag me down?" she asked, crossing her arms. "No, you weren't. I'd like you to explain why you've been following me."

She'd spoken in a loud enough voice to draw the attention of several customers. Hal noticed this too. He came closer. Too close, which forced her to take a couple of steps back to escape him.

"I just wanted to say hello," he said, smiling. "I actually waited for you to finish up at Crosswinds, but you didn't see me. That's why I had to follow you."

"You didn't *have* to follow me," she insisted. "Do you have any idea how badly you frightened me?"

Right then, Charlie growled. She looked at her dog, the one who loved everyone, and realized he'd gotten to his feet. Hackles up, he'd bared his teeth, clearly intent on protecting her.

"I swear, I didn't mean—"

"Go away, Hal." Interrupting him, she tried for her most intimidating stare. "If you don't leave right now, I'm going to have to call the police."

A large college-age kid stepped up, accompanied by one of his friends. Both of them towered over Hal and Della. "Ma'am, is this man bothering you?" the kid asked.

"Yes, he is," Della replied.

"Back off," Hal said, sneering at the kid. "This doesn't concern you."

Della whipped out her phone. "I'm calling 911," she warned.

"Why?" Hal asked quickly. "Just because one of your students happened to run into you at a gas station? That's a little ridiculous, don't you think?"

"You just admitted that you were following me," she replied. "Either you leave, or I'm calling the police."

"Fine." He threw up his hands. "I'm going. I'll see you next week in class."

"No, you won't. You're not welcome back at Crosswinds. I'll make sure you get a full refund of whatever you paid."

Eyes narrowed, he glared at her. "You can't do that. I'm a paying customer. I haven't done anything wrong."

"You're stalking and harassing me. I don't have to put up with that."

By now, a small crowd had gathered. The two teenagers who'd originally sprung to her rescue appeared ready to escort Hal out if needed.

The front door opened and a uniformed police officer came inside. "I got a call about a disturbance here."

Relieved to see it was one of the men who'd initially responded to her discovery up in the meadow, Della quickly filled him in on the situation. Even if she couldn't remember his name, she knew he recognized her. As she explained, Hal tried several times to interrupt her. Each time, the officer asked him to be quiet.

When she finally finished, both the teenage boys and several other customers backed her up.

"I didn't do anything illegal," Hal said, his sullen expression matching his voice. "I'm taking one of Della's dog training classes and I got a little excited to see her outside of the school."

The policeman shook his head and she finally caught sight of his badge. *Santis*. "I'll need to see some identification," he said. "Your driver's license, please."

Though Hal appeared as if he wanted to protest, he finally reached into his back pocket, extracted his wallet and his ID, and handed them over. Santis studied the ID for a moment, and then, instead of giving it back, he asked Hal to come with him out to his cruiser. "I need to put this into our system and make sure you don't have any outstanding warrants or anything," Santis said. "Shouldn't take too long."

"Is this really necessary?" Hal asked. By now, the bystanders had wandered off to pay for their own purchases or go home.

"Yes, it is. Please come with me, sir." Officer Santis then turned to Della. "You can go ahead and leave now, Della. I'll make sure this man doesn't follow you."

Della thanked him and hurried back out to her Jeep and loaded Charlie up. She got in and backed out of her space, but when she reached the road and turned in the direction of home, she realized she'd started shaking so hard she could barely grip the wheel. Even though she knew Officer Santis would still be detaining Hal, she couldn't stop looking in her rearview mirror.

By the time she pulled into her driveway, with her heart trying to pound its way out of her chest, she was on the verge of a full-out panic attack.

Telling herself she'd be safe once she got inside, she opened her door, got out and grabbed Charlie's lead. Together, they rushed for her house. Though her shaking hands fumbled with the key, finally they made it inside. She closed and locked the door behind her. Then she pulled out her phone and dialed Max's number.

Max had started researching churches in Kalispell when his phone rang. Seeing Della's number come up on his screen made his heart skip a beat. Figuring she was calling to discuss the press conference earlier that day, he answered.

"Max, I need your help." Voice flat and shaky, Della didn't sound at all like herself.

Alarmed, he asked her if she was all right.

After a long silent pause, she exhaled. "No. Is there any way you can come over? I can text you my address if you don't remember it."

He didn't even hesitate. "I've got it. Sit tight. I'm on my way."

Closing his laptop, he snatched his keys up off the dresser and rushed through the living room, where his father had some old Western movie on. "I'll be back later," Max said.

Buck simply grunted, barely looking away from the TV.

Though he drove safely and carefully, Max broke every speed limit between the ranch and Della's house.

When he pulled up and parked, he felt relieved to see her Jeep was the only vehicle in the driveway. He wasn't sure what he'd expected—reporters harassing her, maybe—but since that didn't appear to be the case, his worry ratcheted up a notch.

As he sprinted up the sidewalk, the front door opened. He rushed inside, pulling her into his arms as soon as she shut the door.

"Della?" Cradling her, he realized her entire body trembled. He kissed the top of her head and held on to her, wishing he could give her his warmth or his strength or whatever it might be that she needed. "What the hell happened?"

Haltingly, she explained, her voice muffled since her face was still pressed against his chest. As she told him about the man named Hal, his shock turned to fury.

When she finally finished, most of her tremors seemed to have subsided. Gently, he steered her over to the couch. When she sat down, he went with her. Hip to hip, one arm still around her shoulders, she leaned into him. He tamped down his rage since none of that was directed at her. It was a good thing this Hal person wasn't here right now, because Max didn't entirely trust himself not to inflict some serious bodily harm. Which, as an FBI agent on assignment, would not be a good thing to do.

Charlie, viewing this as an invitation to join them, jumped up next to Max and nudged him with his head.

"Not now, Charlie," Della said. "Get down."

A good dog, Charlie instantly complied, tail wagging.

Seeing the bond between Della and her dog made Max want one of his own. If only he didn't spend such long hours at work, he would have gotten a dog years ago. Maybe someday.

"Charlie was with me in the Jeep," Della continued. "If anything happened to him because some guy decided to stalk me, I could never live with myself."

"I assume you've talked to Sebastian and made sure that person is banned from Crosswinds permanently?" Max asked.

"Not yet." She swallowed. "But I will. I'm not as worried about what might happen while I'm at work. He followed me after I left. I think he's trying to find out where I live. I can't be afraid to be alone in my own home."

He agreed. "Would you like me to have a word with him? Or with Fletcher, since he's a detective with OCPD?"

"Officer Santis was called out and had a talk with him already," she replied. "Honestly, I don't think any of that will make a difference with this guy. He seriously doesn't seem to think what he's doing is stalking or even wrong. And since he hasn't made an actual threat, I don't have enough to request a restraining order."

"Which might be a good thing, even though it might not seem like it," Max said. "Restraining orders don't always work. Sometimes they have the effect of enraging the person they're taken out against. I've seen it happen."

She groaned. "Great, just great." She went quiet for a moment and then sat bolt upright. "What if Hal's the one who killed all those women?"

Pulling her back to him, he kissed her cheek. "I promise we'll check him out, okay?"

"But you don't think it's likely. I can tell by the tone of your voice."

Surprised that she could read him so well, he nodded. "Whoever this killer is, he's been stashing bodies up there for a good while. Your cousin disappeared two years ago. Caroline said some of the remains have been there even longer. A guy like that isn't going to risk drawing attention to himself like Hal did."

Her gaze locked on his, she finally nodded. "Then why is Hal bothering me? I don't get it."

Unable to pull his gaze away, he grimaced. "Probably because of the way you look. You're beautiful, you know. Hal's probably never seen anyone who looks quite like you."

To her credit, she didn't disparage her looks or try to pretend she had no idea what he meant. "I've been told that before," she said. "But honestly, that sort of thing is subjective. I don't care about how I look. What should matter is the fact that I've worked hard to get to do what I do. I've gotten every dog training certification possible. I'm good."

Her confidence made him grin. He liked seeing this side of her.

She took a deep breath before continuing. "Actually, you know what? Without bragging, I have to say I'm excellent. I like helping people with their dogs, almost as much as I enjoy training for search and rescue work."

"I can tell you do," he said. "You're an actual example of someone working their dream job."

This comment made her go still. "Thank you," she said. "But if you can see that, why can't people like Hal? How I look should have no bearing on anything. I wear very little makeup on purpose and I keep my hair in a ponytail ninety-nine percent of the time. Just because someone might think I'm pretty doesn't give him the right to harass me."

"Agreed," he told her. "Men like him have no concept of how women should be treated."

"Exactly! It shocks me that someone with a dog could come to my class, supposedly to help them both learn how to communicate better, and then act like that."

"I'm sorry this happened to you," he said. "Hopefully, he'll have realized you're not interested and will leave you alone."

"Possibly." She didn't sound convinced. "I feel sorry for his poor dog."

Of course she did. He had to say, he'd never met a woman like Della Winslow. Again, he felt that tug of attraction, so much more than mere sexual desire.

Something must have shown on his face.

"What?" she asked. "Why are you looking at me like that?"

"Like what?" he countered, though he knew.

"As if I just spilled something all over myself."

He laughed. That did it. He could no more stop himself from kissing her than he could keep from breathing. The instant his mouth touched hers, she wrapped her arms around him and kissed him back.

"This," she breathed, her lips still against his. "I needed this."

Addictive, he thought, and he was powerless to stop himself from drowning. Reckless now, he didn't care about anything other than her.

They made it to her bedroom this time, shedding their

clothing as they went. He managed to put on his condom, though his hands shook so badly she had to help him. Her mischievous grin only aroused him more.

Kisses again, urgent and open-mouthed. And hot. So damn hot. Wrapped around each other, they fell onto her bed, she laughing, he trying to keep from losing control too soon. No other woman had ever affected him this way. Never.

Raw and powerful, his naked need fed off hers. And when they came together, their lovemaking was every bit as electrifying as it had been the first time. Maybe even more.

Della. Moving together, her body tightly sheathing him, he called out her name right before he fell into the abyss. She, clenching around him, pulled him back out and into the light. They came together, all at once, and collapsed at the same time. He held her while their breathing and heart rates slowed. She curled into him, drowsy and content, and he kissed the top of her head. Her scent, vanilla and peaches, enveloped him. He felt as if he could lie there and hold her forever.

In the other room, Charlie barked, reminding them that reality still waited. Della stirred, turning in his arms to smile up at him. With her drowsy eyes and tousled hair, her beauty awed and humbled him.

Damned if he wasn't about to get himself into deep, deep trouble. He needed to change his way of thinking. Because once this case was over, he'd be going back to his sterile apartment in Boise and living his life like he had before. Without her.

The thought shouldn't have brought him pain. He

hadn't known her long enough to get too attached. Especially since he didn't do relationships. At all.

But yet again, as he got up off the bed and out of her arms, got dressed and prepared to leave her, instead of feeling sated, he only wanted more.

Yep. Definitely deep, deep trouble.

Unaware of his thoughts, she propped herself up on one elbow and watched as he dressed. The sexy little smile on her beautiful face had him aching to gather her close again. He managed to resist. Even when she stood, the sheet falling from her delectable curves, and wore her clothes with her gaze trained on him, he didn't move.

She showed him out, standing on her toes to press one last kiss on his mouth, before locking the door behind him. Dazed, he walked to his truck, climbed in and started the engine.

All the way home, he tried reasoning with himself. Temporary infatuation, that was what this had to be. Nothing more. Eventually, he'd get Della Winslow out of his system and both their lives would return to normal.

Or would they?

When he got back to the ranch, the last thing he felt like doing was talking to his dad and brothers. Instead of going into the main house, he headed out back to the shed where he stored his woodworking tools. His workshop, the one place on the sprawling ranch that belonged only to him. When he needed to think, whether about a case or something more personal, he'd found the best way to get through his unsettled emotions was to work with wood. He loved everything about the process, from the designing to the carving, the sanding and building and staining. Over the last several years, as he'd honed his skills, he'd gotten really good. He'd made quite a bit of furniture, well enough that one of the shops on Main Street allowed him to display several pieces for sale. He liked to have a decent inventory so he could keep them restocked when they sold, which they did quite often. Every time he came back home, he made time to work on a few things.

Today, he'd work on his favorite—and bestselling—piece. His oversize rocking chairs. He had several in various stages and decided to focus on the ones that were basically finished, except for needing paint or stain. Painting always soothed his soul, which was exactly the kind of thing he needed right now.

The white ones were the most popular. He'd made the chairs in several styles, from modern farmhouse to rustic and sleek modern, to round things out.

He'd also made a few side items, small tables to go alongside the chairs. He'd started work on an ambitious new piece, an outdoor sectional that he'd only just begun putting together.

Grabbing a can of white paint, he got busy. Anytime his thoughts strayed to Della, he redirected them to the case. While the killer had apparently been getting away with this for several years, now that they were on to him, he'd eventually make a mistake.

Also, Max couldn't shake the seemingly random information that Angela had joined a new church right before her death. Once interviews were complete with some of the other victims' family members, they'd know if there was a connection.

For several years, there had been rumors around Owl Creek about some kind of church called the Ever After

Church. Since there wasn't any kind of actual church building, Max guessed maybe they met in individual homes. Which would mean their congregation remained relatively small. At one point, Sebastian Cross, the owner of Crosswinds Training, had been approached by a member of the Ever After Church. This man, Bob, apparently quite wealthy, had tried to buy Crosswinds and the land around it for the church. Sebastian had turned him down, the same way he'd refused to sell to other interested parties over the years.

Since then, Max hadn't heard of any other attempts by the church to purchase land or buildings. Which meant there was one more thing he needed to look into. Tomorrow he'd check property tax records for the county. While the connection might currently seem tenuous, it wouldn't hurt to have all the information in case something developed.

Naturally, thinking of Crosswinds brought Della to mind. Again. He shook his head, wondering why he couldn't seem to get her out of his system. He wasn't even sure he wanted to.

That thought shocked him. While he couldn't deny the strength of the attraction between them, he wasn't in any kind of a position to even attempt to begin a relationship.

But then again, wasn't that what he'd done?

After that thought, no amount of painting could settle him down. Disgusted, Max finished painting the chair he'd started and cleaned everything up. He'd better start worrying about the family dinner tomorrow night. While he was glad he'd invited Della, bringing her with him to something like this meant he'd have to convince his entire family that they were just friends.

Even worse, he'd need to convince himself.

Chapter 8

After Max left, Della went to the front window and watched as he got into his truck. She stood there until his taillights faded into the night. Then she turned and smiled at her dog, who watched her with his head tilted, his tail wagging slowly.

"You like him too, don't you, Charlie?" she asked. "Come on, boy. Let's go outside and then we'll get on the couch and watch some TV."

Charlie barked as if he understood.

A mess of conflicting emotions, Della hoped getting back to routine might help her feel…normal. Once she'd taken care of her dog, the two of them settled onto the sofa and she turned on the television. A crime drama had just come on, one that she normally watched, so hopefully she could get lost in the show.

But she couldn't shut off her mind. She couldn't stop thinking about everything.

Her joy at the burgeoning feelings Max brought was overlaid by her ever-present grief at the loss of her cousin. There was the mystery of who'd killed Angela and wondering if Owl Creek had a serial killer walking among them. Add in the fact that she now had a stalker, and she felt overwhelmed. It was too much. Part of her wanted to run; the other part knew she had to stand her ground and fight for justice for her cousin. And possibly reach out and grab a chance at happiness for herself.

She must have fallen asleep on the couch, because the next thing she knew, she woke up to the sound of Charlie snoring, his furry face a foot or so away. Chuckling, she shook her head and checked the time: 1:00 a.m. She grabbed the remote, turned off the television and whistled for Charlie. Then she and her dog went to bed.

Thursday morning dawned bright and sunny. Sunlight streaming through her bedroom window woke her. She got up, carried her coffee out to the back porch and settled gingerly into her ancient patio chair to watch Charlie play in the yard.

The sun on her skin felt warm, the coffee tasted delightful, and her dog had always been all the company she needed. But she couldn't stop thinking about Max. Not only the explosive and passionate lovemaking they'd shared once again, but the other connection they seemed to have. She didn't think it was all one-sided, but then again, his reputation preceded him.

And tonight, she'd agreed to accompany him to a family dinner. As his *friend*. What the heck had she been thinking?

But hearing him talk about his family and the circumstances behind their meeting tonight, she'd known he needed her support. And she'd be there to give it, no matter how anyone else might view her being in attendance.

Finishing her coffee, she called Charlie inside and made herself an egg-white omelet. After breakfast, she showered and got dressed. Still feeling unsettled and restless, Della decided to go into town and do a little retail therapy. Though she wasn't a big shopper, every now and then she liked to buy a few small items to spruce up her house or something new to wear. Since tonight she'd be meeting Max for dinner with his family, she felt like a new outfit might be in order. At the very least, maybe a new pair of earrings or a necklace.

As she got ready to go, Charlie waited, watching her. When she'd finished, he went to the front door and barked. Tail wagging, panting eagerly, he clearly expected her to take him to Crosswinds to train, like they did most days.

"Not today, boy," she said, petting him. "It's going to be a day off for both of us. But if you're a good boy while I'm gone, I just might bring you something from that dog bakery in that pet store downtown."

Charlie barked again, as if he understood. He went and curled up in his oversize dog bed and watched her as she made herself a large cup of coffee to go.

There were only a couple of stores downtown that sold clothing. She decided she'd check all of them out before stopping at her favorite place, a resale shop tucked away on a back street where she'd found some fabulous clothes in the past.

Walking down the sidewalk on Main Street, she skipped all the stores where she usually shopped for things for her home. Today would be one of the rare days where she concentrated only on herself.

She found a beautiful pair of silver earrings in one of the tourist shops. A good start. She purchased them and browsed through the clothing racks, which consisted mostly of souvenir T-shirts. Not what she needed.

The next shop was a place she'd purchased clothes from before. Since she'd decided to wear jeans tonight, she needed a new shirt. However, the instant she walked inside, she caught sight of a soft pale green dress in a baby-doll style that she knew would be flattering. The first thing she noticed when she picked it up was the pockets. And it was in her size. Even better, the price seemed reasonable. Though she didn't need it for the barbecue dinner tonight, surely there'd be another occasion where she could wear it.

Max came instantly to mind, which made her blush. Shaking her head at her own foolishness, she carried the dress over to the changing room to try it on.

It fit exactly the way she'd known it would. Twirling in front of the full-length mirror, she felt pretty in a way she had never felt before.

He'd called her beautiful. Over the years, other men had paid her compliments. She'd paid them no mind, certain they'd all had ulterior motives. But Max, who admittedly was one of the most handsome men she'd ever met, had meant it. As corny as it might sound, she'd seen his reaction to her appearance in the depths of his light blue eyes.

She took off the dress and put her own clothes back on. Then, before she could talk herself out of it, she went to the counter and paid.

After that, she went to the resale shop, but nothing there caught her eye. Surely, she could find something in her closet to wear along with her favorite pair of jeans. Max had said the dinner would be casual, after all.

Back at the house, Charlie greeted her and then, after a quick trip outside, curled up in his bed to resume his nap. Nerves still humming, Della did some housework, wishing she could stop feeling so nervous. This wasn't a big deal. Just dinner with a friend and his family. But for whatever reason, it felt like more.

That afternoon, she must have changed her outfit six times, trying for the right mixture of casual but not too much so. Since the dinner would be held at a barbecue place, she'd decided on jeans and boots. It was deciding on the right top and accessories that had her wavering between frustration and indecision. Worse, she didn't know why she cared so much. Max would definitely make sure his family knew that she was just his friend, not a date.

Except this felt like a date. More than a date. A take-your-girlfriend-to-meet-your-family kind of thing. She wasn't Max's girlfriend, though, no matter how much it felt like she was.

Finally, she chose a pretty black shoulder-less top, her new dangly silver earrings and several silver bracelets. That done, she took care with her makeup. Usually, she went with the bare minimum, going for a natural look. Tonight, she tried for more of a glam look, using the eye-shadow techniques one of her girlfriends in college had taught her. When she'd finished, she peered at herself in the mirror, added some neutral lipstick and smiled.

Then she got dressed, choosing a pair of black boots with a slight heel. She'd barely finished adding her jewelry when the doorbell rang.

The sound made her heart stutter in her chest. Though she knew she shouldn't, she secretly hoped her appearance would knock Max Colton's socks off. This despite the fact that they'd agreed they were only friends and occasional coworkers. Who'd made love twice now and probably would again. She knew that she shouldn't harbor this secret desire to wow him, but she did.

Hurrying to get the door, her boot heels clicking on the hardwood floors, she took a deep breath before turning the handle. Charlie, who'd heard the doorbell, pranced around her in excitement, his tail wagging furiously.

She opened the door, and her heart stuttered as she took in Max, his broad shoulders filling her doorway. Tonight, he'd gone with a Western shirt and jeans, along with a pair of brown ostrich-skin boots.

"Come on in," she said, stepping aside so Max could enter. Next to her, Charlie sat waiting, panting happily as he waited for Max to notice him.

But Max didn't budge. Instead, he stood frozen, staring at her as if she'd suddenly grown two heads.

Sudden insecurity grabbed her. Maybe she'd overdone it. Perhaps she wasn't as great at putting on makeup as she'd thought. Could her outfit be too much, or too little, or...?

"You look gorgeous," Max said, his voice raspy. He finally stepped inside, closing the door behind him, all without taking his eyes off her. Charlie barked happily, butting Max with his head so he'd pet him. Absently, Max reached down and scratched her dog behind the ears, still staring at Della.

She stared back. Her entire body felt warm and tingly. He'd said *gorgeous*. Better than *beautiful*. Though she'd never really cared what she looked like, tonight she did. She'd take it.

More grateful for the compliment than she should have been, and wondering where the weird insecurity had come from, she finally managed to break her trance. Looking away, she smiled and thanked him. Max smiled back and ruffled Charlie's fur, continuing to scratch him behind his ears. Charlie leaned into him, clearly in canine heaven.

Warmth spread through her, watching as her beloved dog thoroughly enjoyed Max's attention. Charlie liked him, and if there was ever a good judge of character, it was Charlie. Prior reputation or not, her instincts said Max was a good man, a kind man and, more importantly, her friend. Charlie's approval simply confirmed it.

Time to reclaim her sense of self and stop all this nonsense clattering around inside of her head. Charlie glanced at her as if he agreed, his long tail still wagging.

"Are you ready?" she asked, once Max straightened. "I've been dying to try that barbecue. When they first opened, it was so crowded, with over an hour's wait. I decided to try it later, once the novelty had worn off, but I haven't managed to make it in yet."

Still staring at her, he finally blinked. "I haven't been there either. Honestly, a barbecue place seems like an odd choice to meet two new half siblings, but what do I know?"

She kind of agreed with him there. "I'm thinking whoever chose it is trying to go with a casual atmosphere."

"Maybe so." He held the door open for her and then waited while she locked it. When they reached his truck, he did the same.

Once he'd started the engine, he turned and looked at her. "We reserved an entire section of the restaurant," he said. "Even so, it'll likely be crowded. I just wanted to warn you."

"Thanks. I figured. Since you have two families coming, one with six siblings, one with four, plus add in their spouses or dates or whatever, as well as the two newcomers, who also probably wanted to bring support, it only makes sense."

He nodded. "Yep. No reason to be nervous."

Confident Della had returned, thank goodness. "I'm not. I went to school with some of these people, you know. Since my boss, Sebastian, got engaged to your cousin Ruby, I'm sure he's going to be there. I've also worked with others at Crosswinds. And Malcolm and I have done a couple of search and rescue operations before. So we're not all total strangers. It's inevitable that we'd know each other, especially in such a small town."

"True." As he watched her, his gaze had darkened. "Damn, I'd like to kiss you right now. But I don't want to ruin your lipstick."

Heat flooded her. Taking a deep breath, she leaned forward, keeping her eyes locked on his. "I have the lipstick in my purse. I can always touch it up."

Instead of waiting for him to follow through, she pulled his face down to hers. If she'd needed a reason to question why she felt they were more than merely friends, this would be it. This soul-searching electricity that flared between them every time they touched. And the instant their lips met, neither of them seemed to be very good at maintaining control.

The realization that her aunt and uncle next door could walk out at any moment and see her making out with the notorious playboy Max Colton was the only thing that made Della pull back. Heart racing, desire turning her body to a puddle of need, she sat back in her seat and stared at him.

Chest heaving, pupils dilated, Max seemed to be having just as much difficulty reining himself in. "Damn," he managed. "If this dinner wasn't so important to my family, I'd say forget about it and take you back inside to finish what we just started."

She gave a strangled laugh. "None of that," she said, though she secretly wanted to do the same. "Plus, there's always afterward."

Since making out with Della like a randy teenager in the front seat of his truck had damn near decimated him, Max knew he had to get his arousal under control before walking into the restaurant and facing his family. He glanced sideways at Della. Her swollen lips and tousled hair gave her the appearance of a woman who'd been thoroughly kissed.

Then she mentioned what they might do after the dinner, and now making love to her was all he could think about. Judging by her flushed complexion and dilated pupils, she felt the same.

They'd need a little bit of time to get their composure together. While he didn't want to be late, he also didn't want anyone in his family to know he and Della had been kissing. If they figured it out, the teasing would be unmerciful.

"Are you okay?" Della asked, her voice a little unsteady. "Maybe we should drive around a few minutes before we go in?"

Her comment, oddly enough, helped defuse some of his tension. "My thoughts exactly," he replied. "We've just got to clear our heads."

"I know what would help. Classic rock," she said. Reaching for his radio dial, she glanced at him. "Do you mind if I change the station?"

Curious, he shrugged. "Do your thing."

With a few turns of the knob, she put the radio on 96.9 The Eagle, Boise's classic rock station. The Rolling Stones came on, singing about "Satisfaction." Without hesitation, Della turned up the volume and began singing along, slightly off-key.

"Come on," she urged, elbowing him. "It'll help get your mind off other things."

What could he do but join her?

To his surprise, by the time they reached the restaurant, his almost painful arousal had subsided, and he felt…normal. Happy even. He didn't even feel the need to drive around the block a couple more times.

Pulling into the parking lot, he turned the volume down. "Thank you," he told her. "That really helped."

Her infectious grin had him smiling back. "Music helps almost anything."

He found a spot next to a sleek Mercedes and parked. They were only ten minutes late. Perfect timing, since he hadn't wanted to be the first one there nor the last. By now, he figured about half of the group would have arrived, with the rest of them straggling in over the next ten or fifteen minutes.

"Let's go," he said. Jumping out, he hurried over to the passenger side so he could help her down.

She took his arm and lifted her face to sniff the air. "That smells absolutely amazing. Nothing like some good smoked brisket."

Leave it to her to focus on the food. And she was right—the aroma coming from the place made his mouth water.

Side by side, they walked to the door. Once he opened

it for her and they were in, she slipped her hand into his. Enchanted way more than he should have been, he followed the sign toward the back part of the restaurant where his family had reserved a private room.

A quick scan of the people there told him his new half siblings weren't yet in attendance.

The first people he spotted were his cousin Ruby and Della's boss, Sebastian Cross, standing very close to each other. Max had never seen a couple more meant for each other than those two. Ruby gazed up into Sebastian's rugged face with an adoring look, totally engrossed in whatever he had to say.

Grinning, Della dragged Max over. "Sebastian! And Ruby! It's so good to see you. Have you eaten here before?"

The two turned, Sebastian smiling. "Della! I didn't know you'd be here." And then, as he realized she and Max were holding hands, his smile faltered, and he frowned. "May I have a word with you privately?"

Though Della's smile wavered, she agreed. "Excuse me one minute," she told Max. "I'll be right back."

When she and her boss moved away, Ruby crossed her arms and glared at him. "I went to school with Della Winslow," she said. "She's a good person. I like her."

Pretending not to understand the warning note in her voice, Max nodded. "I like her too."

"You know what I mean," Ruby continued. "She's not your usual type. If you think you can treat her the same way you have the others, you can't. You'll break her heart."

With that, she spun on her heel and stormed off, back to where Sebastian appeared to be lecturing Della.

When Ruby reached them, Della made her escape, hurrying back over to Max.

"Whew." Shaking her head, she took his arm. "Ruby looked pretty intense. What was that all about?"

"Ruby wanted to warn me not to hurt you," he replied. "And judging from the way Sebastian is glowering at me, he said something similar to you."

"He did. He's like family to me. He's always been a little overprotective, but he acts like he's really worried about me being with you. I tried to tell him that we're only friends, but he didn't seem convinced."

Likely because they'd been holding hands. Though tempted to reach for her hand again, he didn't. Instead, he kept her arm tucked into his.

"Well, let's not let those two ruin our evening," Max said. "Come on. Let me introduce you to the rest of my family."

Though he should have known it was coming, the way his family gave him and Della strange looks hurt Max's feelings. Sure, she wasn't his usual type of date. Those women had been placeholders, he realized. He'd purposely dated women who didn't expect anything but a good time, and once he gave them that, they went their separate ways.

But Della… They were *friends*, he reminded himself. Not dating. Because he definitely didn't want to think about why being with her felt a million times better than any other woman.

His cousin Fletcher had his arm around Kiki Shelton, a vibrant, dark-haired woman who was the perfect counterpoint for the more serious Fletcher. Kiki and Della appeared to hit it off right from the start, chattering happily together while more and more family members arrived. Listening in, Max realized Kiki had a foster dog named Fancy and she'd been training her at Crosswinds. Since talking about dogs was one of Della's passions, the two women had lots to discuss.

The restaurant had set up three long tables each with about ten chairs. Patrons had to go up to the front counter, grab a plastic tray and order their meal. Their choices were sliced and dished up right in front of them and placed on a plate. Once they'd paid and gotten their drink, they carried the tray to the table to eat. Someone went around with a basket full of rolls. If it tasted as good as it smelled, they were in for a treat.

Max ordered the brisket, and after a moment's hesitation, Della did the same. For his two sides, he chose potato salad and pinto beans. Della got macaroni and cheese and green beans. They both got iced tea.

As soon as they'd taken their seats and unloaded their trays, a strange hush came over the room. Max glanced up and realized Nathan and Sarah Colton, his mother and Uncle Robert's other two children, had arrived. Though he'd suspected his mother wouldn't come, nonetheless he was relieved when he didn't see her. Since Jessie hadn't bothered to make contact with any of her other children for years, why would she suddenly care to do so now?

"Welcome!" Since she hadn't yet gotten her food or taken a seat, Max's sister, Lizzy, greeted them. She'd come alone and, smiling, led Nathan and Sarah around the room, introducing them to their half siblings. Max had a moment to consider how strange they must feel, knowing some were related to their mother and others to their father.

When Lizzy reached Max and Della, she eyed Max. "Are you here with Della?" she asked, her brows raised.

"I am." Keeping his smile firmly in place, Max turned to Nathan and Sarah. Nathan towered over his sister, but they both had the exact same smile. "I swear I've seen you before," Max commented to Sarah.

"You probably have," she replied, her green eyes twinkling. "I'm a librarian. I work in the main branch of the Boise Public Library."

"That must be where. I live in Boise." Max shook her hand before eyeing her brother. "And I understand you're in law enforcement."

"That's correct." Unlike his sister, Nathan Colton appeared slightly uneasy. "I've heard you're with the FBI?"

"I am."

Lizzy tugged Sarah away, leaving Nathan to follow.

"We'll talk more later," Max said, watching as Lizzy introduced the two to more of his family members.

"That didn't seem so awkward," Della mused. She picked up her fork and dug in.

A moment later, Max did the same. Though the meal had cooled slightly, the tender brisket had a wonderful smoky flavor. "This is really good," he said.

"Yes, it is." She nodded. "You sound surprised."

Since he'd just taken another bite, he chewed and swallowed before answering. "I wasn't sure what to expect. Idaho isn't exactly known for good barbecue."

They finished their meal, talking in between bites. All of Max's earlier apprehension had vanished, mostly due to how comfortable Della seemed. Anytime one of his cousins stopped by, she seemed to instinctively know exactly the right thing to say.

Max couldn't help but notice his oldest brother stayed far on the other side of the room. Greg seemed intent on inhaling his food. Malcolm walked in, spotted Della and made a beeline toward her.

"Hey, Max," he said, then turned his attention to Della. "I heard you and Charlie were the ones who made the discovery up on the hiking trail."

"We were." Smiling up at him, she stabbed the last bit of her green beans and popped them in her mouth.

Suddenly, Malcolm seemed to realize Della had come with Max. Eyes narrowed, he looked from one to the other. "How do you two know each other?" he asked. Then, before either of them could respond, he answered his own question. "Let me guess. This is the case that brought Max home."

"Bingo," Max replied. He fought the urge to put his arm around Della's shoulders, aware he had no right to feel so possessive. However, watching her smile at his brother brought on a flash of jealousy so strong he frowned.

Malcolm, somehow seeming to sense this, grinned. "Take good care of her, little brother," he teased. "Della is pretty damn special."

Then, before Max could respond, Malcolm walked away.

Expression bemused, Della watched him go. "What was that all about?" she asked. "I get that you have a reputation, but why is everyone so worried about me? Not only can I take care of myself, but we've told them all that we're just friends."

He managed a casual shrug, pretending to be wounded. "I don't know what you've heard about me, but it's likely not true."

This made her laugh. "You forget, I've lived in Owl Creek my entire life. And while you graduated high school the year before I started, your reputation precedes you."

For the first time in his life, he found himself regretting the way he'd avoided any kind of long-term relationship. But then again, maybe there'd been a reason. He doubted he could have gotten to this point in his career if he'd allowed himself to get bogged down. Now he had to wonder if any of it had been worth it.

"Hey, Max, do you have a minute?" His cousin Chase, CEO of Colton Properties, dropped into the seat across from him. Chase glanced at Della and smiled. "In private, if you don't mind."

Della stood. "That's my hint to make a trip to the ladies' room. Gentlemen, please excuse me."

Max watched her as she walked away. When he looked back at Chase, the other man shook his head. "Man, you really have it bad."

Since he suspected his cousin was right, instead of responding to this, Max asked what Chase needed.

"I have some issues going on with Colton Properties," Chase said. "I don't really want to go into detail, but I'd like to have a security team take a look at my system. Since you're with the FBI, I figured you might have a recommendation."

"SecuritKey is the best in the industry," Max replied. "They're pretty exclusive. They don't even advertise, but I can put you in touch with the owner. Her name is Sloan Presley."

"Thank you." Chase looked past Max and smiled. "Della's coming back. She's a keeper, you know." With that, he stood, clapped Max on the shoulder and rejoined the small group at one of the tables.

"Is everything okay?" Della asked, sliding back into her chair.

Instantly, the annoyance he'd felt from Chase's last comment vanished. "Never been better," he replied. "Let's go talk to Nathan and Sarah one last time and then we can go."

Smiling, Della came with him, though this time she didn't hold his hand. He couldn't help but wish she would.

Standing close to his sister, Nathan looked up when the two of them approached. Sarah's smile faltered around the edges. She looked exhausted. Even Nathan had a bit of fatigue around his blue eyes. Initially, Max hadn't wanted to like either, but Sarah pulled on his heartstrings and Nate seemed like an upstanding guy.

"We'll have to get together again sometime," he said, clapping his new half brother on the back. "Like you can probably tell, we're all open to expanding our family. The only stipulation is you should know I have no intention of meeting with our mother."

At the mention of Jessie, Nathan's smile vanished. "That's good, because I doubt she wants to meet with you either," he said, grimacing.

Despite everything, hearing that hurt more than it should.

As if she sensed this, Della slipped her hand into his.

Chapter 9

"That was something else," Della said. Never had she been so glad to leave a restaurant. She hadn't known she could feel so protective toward Max, but she did. Though he hadn't outwardly reacted to his half brother's statement, she'd seen the flash of pain in his eyes. When she'd taken his hand and squeezed, he'd held on tightly as if she was some kind of lifeline.

No matter how awful they might be, she suspected no one ever outgrew the need for their mother. Even Nathan and Sarah had looked pained when they'd talked about their mother.

"I left home as soon as I could," Nathan had continued, apparently oblivious. "She's always been pretty awful, as I'm sure you know."

"I do," Max had agreed, still clutching Della's hand. He gestured around the room. "We all do."

"Well, she's gotten worse ever since she joined that weird church," Sarah had interjected. "You can't even talk to her now."

At the word *church*, Max had tensed. He'd asked a few more questions, but as soon as he learned Jessie had joined the Ever After Church, he'd been ready to go.

He was unusually quiet as he drove her home, and

Della figured he needed time lost in his own head. When they finally pulled up into her driveway, he leaned over and kissed her on the cheek, clearly distracted. "Thanks for coming with me," he said. "I really appreciate it."

"Did you want to come in?" she offered, even though she felt pretty sure he didn't.

"Not this time." He shook his head. "I can't help but feel there's something I'm overlooking. I need to investigate how far that church has reached."

"The Ever After Church?" For years, fringe members had been hanging around town. There'd been rumors they wanted to build an actual physical building, maybe even some sort of compound, but nothing had ever come of it. At least not that she knew of.

"Yes." His clipped answer made her study him. As she realized what he might mean, she sat up straight.

"Are you thinking they might have had something to do with Angela's—and others'—murder?" she asked.

"I don't know. But I'm sure as hell going to look into it." Meeting her gaze, he grimaced. "Any other time, you know I'd come in. But I'm looking at several hours of computer work, and you are way too much of a distraction."

This made her smile. She leaned over and kissed him softly. "Another time, then."

"Definitely." He checked out his fitness tracker watch. "I've got to go. I'd like to get started on it right away."

She opened her door. "Thanks for inviting me," she said. "I had a nice evening. I'll talk to you later. Please, if you learn anything interesting, let me know."

"I will," he said, waiting until she'd reached her front door and unlocked it before putting his truck in Reverse.

After watching him drive away, she went inside. Charlie danced around, greeting her as if she'd been gone for days instead of hours. She got down on the floor with him, returning his affection as effusively as he gave it.

Once she'd let him out and back in, she went to change into her pajamas and wash off her makeup. She'd enjoyed the evening more than she'd thought she would, at least right up until the end, when Nathan had made that offhand comment to Max. Growing up in Owl Creek, she knew most of the Colton family by sight. Despite being legends around town, especially because of Colton Properties, she found them surprisingly down-to-earth.

And while there definitely had been a bit of dysfunction there, relating to Jessie and Robert Colton, she couldn't exactly blame them. Anyone would be bitter after being ditched by a parent. Parents weren't supposed to abandon their children. The one thing kids should be able to count on was their mother or father's unconditional love.

Though she was enough of a realist to understand this wasn't always the case, it tore at her heartstrings to know Max and his siblings had never known what she had. She missed her mother still, with every fiber of her being, and she'd always be grateful to have had that kind of maternal love.

She and Charlie settled on the couch to watch a movie. Charlie was one of the few dogs who watched television with her. Snuggling into her side, he kept his eyes fixed on the TV until he finally grew tired and dozed off.

Though tempted to text Max since she couldn't stop thinking about him, she didn't. Instead, she finished the movie, took Charlie out once again and went to bed.

The next morning, she had a full day scheduled at Crosswinds. She wanted to get in there early, since she needed to fit all six of her charges in, plus make time to train Charlie.

When she woke, the first thing she did was check her phone. No message from Max or anyone else. Chiding herself for acting like a teenager with a crush, she drank her coffee while she got ready. She made herself a protein smoothie to go, and she and Charlie got on the road shortly after sunrise.

The orange-and-pink sky lightened her heart. She arrived at Crosswinds, parked and hurried inside with Charlie.

After placing Charlie in a sit-stay, Della went back to get one of the newer dogs she'd started training, a Belgian Malinois named Beth. Beth was young, barely nine months old, but she'd been started on basic obedience training and the myriad of desensitizing and socialization work required of a good SAR dog.

Beth had a bit of a reactive personality, but once she settled down and got to work, Della was able to get her to focus.

She'd been training in the ring thirty minutes when she looked up to find Sebastian standing near the entrance to the ring, watching her.

"Do you have a minute?" he asked. "When you're all done, of course."

Hoping he wasn't going to lecture her on Max Colton again, she nodded. "I'm just about finished with Beth here. Let me take her outside and I'll be right with you."

Clearly tired, Beth had just started to pant. Della knew

if she had pressed her too much longer, the young dog would shut down.

After taking Beth outside, Della returned her to the kennel. Of the ten dogs currently on the property, she worked with six while Sebastian took the other four. Between those and her new classes for the general public, she kept busy. Of course, if she got called out on a SAR mission, her boss would have to take over everything until she got back.

When she returned, Sebastian had taken a seat in the small office they both used for paperwork. "Pull up a chair," he said. "I'm wondering how you've been holding up since your cousin's death."

Unbidden tears filled her eyes. Blinking them away, she dropped into a seat. "I'm doing okay," she replied. "The FBI has promised to keep in touch with any new info regarding the case."

"FBI being Max Colton?"

Deliberately holding his gaze, she nodded. "He's a good guy, Sebastian. I promise."

"I never doubted that. He's just not your type."

Della bit back a retort and nodded instead.

"I'm aware it's not any of my business," Sebastian continued. "But you're like a sister to me and I'd hate to see you get hurt."

"I know." She smiled. "And I appreciate that. But since we've already had this discussion, do you mind if we don't do it again?"

This made him chuckle. "Point made." He took a deep breath. "I also wanted to ask how the classes are going. I heard there was an incident with one of the clients?"

"I can't believe I forgot to tell you." She relayed everything that had happened with Hal. "While I feel bad for his dog, I don't want him back on the property."

Grim-faced, he nodded. "I one hundred percent agree. I'll take care of it. And, please, let me know if this man bothers you again."

"I will. Since I have classes again tonight, I'm hoping he doesn't show up. Pepper did call him and let him know his class fee would be refunded since he's now banned from the premises."

Sebastian nodded. "All I can say is after what happened before, we are definitely prepared to deal with someone like him this time."

Della knew he referred to a few months ago, when it seemed like Crosswinds had been under attack almost constantly. "Thank you."

"One of my dogs is being picked up by his new handler later today," Sebastian said. "I'll be spending the afternoon working with them before they head back to Denver. I can take over one of your dogs once Silver is gone."

"That would be great," she said. "If you don't mind, would you take Chadwick? He's the newest and I've barely started training him." She laughed. "There aren't enough hours in the day sometimes."

"I'll take him," Sebastian said. "As a matter of fact, I can start working with him right now."

Thanking him, Della went to get her next dog. She knew her limitations and tried to stick to four dogs before lunch, and if she felt up to it, she did a little light work with some of her new ones.

After an hour of ring work with her next dog, Della decided to take an early, and long, lunch. She took Charlie home and scarfed down a quick sandwich. Then, with a little extra time on her hands, she decided to go into town and do some purposeful shopping.

Though her budget didn't allow for many extravagances, she usually allowed herself to buy one decorative or household item each season. For summer, she'd planned to purchase a few pieces of outdoor furniture, specifically chairs and possibly a small table to put in between them.

Now here it was actually August, and she hadn't been able to find anything she liked that she could afford. "Champagne tastes," she told herself. She hadn't been able to stop thinking about the handmade rocking chairs she'd seen for sale in a shop downtown called Angus's Whatnots. The sign on the display only said they'd been crafted by a local artist, which actually endeared them to her even more.

What she liked best about them was their quirkiness. They were big and clunky, yet sleek and well-made. The ones she wanted had been stained a dark mahogany and she could just picture one on her back porch.

Since they were a bit pricey, she told herself one was all she needed for right now. Once she had it, she could sit out on her back patio and rock while she drank her coffee. And she could finally get rid of the beat-up old chair she'd gotten at a garage sale.

Decision made, she hopped into her Jeep and drove into town. She could only hope the one she wanted would still be there, because the salesperson she'd talked to had mentioned the chairs were extremely popular.

To her relief, it appeared several of the white painted chairs had sold but the two dark-stained ones were still there, along with a small table clearly built to sit in between them.

Exhaling, she checked the price tag again, just in case they'd gone on sale. Nope. Still the same price, just high enough to make her feel a teeny bit nauseated. "You get what you pay for," she muttered under her breath and turned to head up to the counter to make her purchase.

The teenager working the register grinned when she told him she wanted to buy one of the chairs. "They're pretty popular," he agreed. "How many do you want?"

About to say just the one, she considered. "How often does the person who makes them bring in new inventory?"

"When stock gets low," he answered. "My dad owns the store and he likes to keep more of the white ones around, since people seem to want those the most."

"I want the dark brown," she said. "Just one. And I'll take the little table too." The last had been an impulse, but it felt right.

"Only one?" the kid asked, clearly dismayed. "Most people buy two."

"I just need one, thank you."

He shrugged and rang her up.

She managed not to wince when she heard the total. "Here you go," she said, counting out cash and handing it over.

Brows raised, he recounted it before putting it into his register and giving her the change. "Not many people pay with cash these days," he commented.

"It's how I roll." She only used credit cards in an emergency.

"Do you need some help loading it up?" he asked.

"Yes, please." She hadn't thought about what she'd do once she got home. Hopefully, she could manage to wrestle the thing from her Jeep and onto her back porch. She wasn't sure about navigating the stairs, though. Maybe she'd call Max and see if he could help her.

Once he'd carried the chair and small table out for her and loaded them into the back of her Jeep, she realized she could actually fit the other chair if she wanted to buy it. For whatever reason, she kept picturing sitting out on the back porch with Max, each of them in their own chair. She had enough cash with her to cover it.

"You know what?" she said. "I just decided. I'll take the other matching chair too."

Instead of reacting with surprise, the kid fist-bumped the air. "Yessss! I knew it. Come on back inside and let me ring you up, and then I'll bring it out for you."

Once everything had been loaded up into her Jeep, Della thanked her helper and got in to drive home. She didn't want to think about how she'd get all this unloaded and up to her porch. While she supposed she could always call Max, part of her wanted to surprise him with the chairs. After all, she'd bought the second one because she could so easily picture the two of them sitting out there with their morning coffee.

Since the furniture took up so much space and blocked her view out the back window, Della didn't notice the vehicle following her until she turned into her driveway and it did too. Parking right behind her, it blocked her in. A black Honda with black rims. Hal's car.

Heart pounding, she made sure her doors were locked and got out her phone in case she needed to call 911.

Hal got out and sauntered over. Expression amused,

he motioned for her to roll down her window. When she shook her head, his gaze narrowed, and his smile vanished.

"Get out of the car," he ordered. "Now."

"Go away," she responded, desperately trying to figure out what to do now. She couldn't help hoping when he saw she wasn't receptive, he'd simply leave.

When he turned and went back to his vehicle, she held her breath. But instead of getting in and driving off, he retrieved what looked like a metal baseball bat and came back. He rapped sharply on the driver's-side glass.

"Don't make me have to break your window," he said, his confident smile chilling her to the bone.

Even so, a flash of anger mixed in with her fear. "And then what?" she asked, speaking loud enough so he could hear her. "Once you take out your frustration on my Jeep, what are you planning to do?"

"What I should have done the first day that I met you," he answered. "Make you mine."

Heart pounding, fingers shaking, she dialed 911. As she did, he raised the bat and shattered her window.

The night before, Max had gone down a rabbit hole with the Ever After Church. After leaving Della's house, he'd driven straight to the ranch and holed himself up in his room. After hours scouring the internet as well as accessing FBI data on the church, he hadn't come up with anything concrete that might have tied them to the serial killer.

He'd gone to bed with a headache and his eyes burning. When he got up in the morning, later than he usually did, all he could think of was Della and the way he'd brushed her off the night before.

The house had been empty, since no self-respecting rancher ever wasted a sunrise.

Since he had a Zoom meeting scheduled with the team at ten, he had enough time to grab a shower and down a couple of cups of strong black coffee before sitting down with his laptop and logging in to the meeting.

First, Caroline gave her report on her efforts to identify the last three bodies. So far, she hadn't met with any success. She'd even scoured missing person databases looking for anything that might be close enough.

"What about you, Max?" Brian asked. "Any new leads on your end?"

"Della said Angela had mentioned joining a new church," Max said. "But no one seems to have any concrete information on it. We don't know what it was called or where it was located. I've kind of wondered if there was any connection with the other victims, though the distance might rule that out."

"With Angela in Montana and the others from other places in the tristate area, the possibility of them all belonging to the same church is a long shot," Brian mused.

Max took a deep breath and then told them about the Ever After Church. "It seems to bear a lot of similarities with a cult."

Brian nodded. "Continue to dig on that one. It's all we've got right now, and the media is really putting the pressure on us. I even took a call from Senator McCutchin the other day, wondering how close we are to catching this guy."

Everyone looked grim.

"Caroline, have you found any other possible connections?" Brian asked.

"Other than the various physical similarities—age, gender and build—no," Caroline replied. "We've got all of them but those three identified and next of kin has been notified. I'll email you all the list and last-known locations."

"Thank you," Brian said. "As soon as we have that, the team can begin the interview process. I'll be assigning each of you some to work on."

Max cleared his throat. "I'd like to deal with all the ones who lived close to Owl Creek," he said. "Since I'm already here."

Brian nodded. "Done. I'll give everyone their assignments once I review Caroline's information." He took a deep breath. "I don't have to remind you all that we have a ticking clock on this case. We need to catch this killer as soon as possible."

They went over statistics, discussed the various missing person databases and the ongoing search for various police reports mentioning attacks on women by unrelated men. Brian had assigned Theo and Chris to sift through those.

After nearly ninety minutes, the meeting wrapped up. As soon as he clicked *Exit*, Max closed his laptop and phoned Della. When she didn't answer, he left her a message, asking her to call him. Just in case, he also sent a text. He figured she was working at Crosswinds, and it would make sense for her to mute her phone when training dogs.

He stood and stretched, checking his phone one more time, even though barely a minute had passed. He wasn't usually so impatient, but he found himself longing to see her.

As a matter of fact, he might as well just head on over there. Ever since she'd told him about that former client stalking her, he'd been uneasy. A bit worried too, though hopefully the guy had taken the hint and would now leave her alone. Still, it wouldn't hurt for Max to check on her. Maybe he could take her to lunch so he could explain his abrupt departure last night. Just the thought of seeing her again immediately lightened his mood.

On the way, Max even considered stopping in town and getting Della flowers. Damn, he had it bad. He ended up shelving this idea. If he were to show up at Crosswinds with a bouquet for her, that would certainly start the gossip mill up again.

When he pulled up in the parking lot, he didn't see Della's Jeep. Parking, he tried calling her again. Still no answer. He sent another quick text just in case, but nothing.

As he was debating whether to go inside and ask, Sebastian walked out. Max got out of his truck and met the other man halfway. "Any idea where I might find Della?" he asked.

Sebastian smiled. "She said she was going to take a long lunch and maybe do some shopping. I'd check town first. Have you tried calling her?"

"I have, but she's not answering. She also hasn't responded to my texts." He shrugged. "I can't help but worry. She told me about that former client who was stalking her."

Now Sebastian's smile turned into a frown. "Yeah, I called that guy and banned him from Crosswinds. To make sure there's no misunderstanding, I even refunded his class fee."

"Thank you." Max nodded. "I guess I'll head into town and see if I can meet up with her."

"Knock yourself out," Sebastian said. "Listen, Ruby says you're a good guy. But I want you to know that I consider Della family. Don't do anything to hurt her, or you'll be answering to me."

Solemnly, Max nodded. "I won't. And I appreciate you for saying that. It's good to know she has so many people in her corner."

The two men shook hands. Then Max got into his truck and drove into town, hoping he'd be lucky enough to find Della.

Up and down Main Street, looking for her Jeep, he began to feel a little bit stalkerish himself. Still, he couldn't seem to shake the feeling that something might be wrong.

After making one final pass by the shops, he decided to head to her house. Maybe she'd done some whirlwind shopping and gone home to take a nap. Though that didn't explain why she wasn't answering her phone or his texts.

On the way to Della's place, two Owl Creek cruisers came up behind him, lights flashing and sirens blaring. He pulled over and they blasted on past.

Were they heading to her house? Heart pounding, Max pulled back onto the road. Stomping the accelerator to the floor, he followed the flashing lights all the way to Della's house.

Sure enough, both police cars pulled up in front of her place. Max parked right behind them and jumped out, flashing his FBI badge so they wouldn't attempt to make him leave. Her Jeep sat in the driveway, blocked in by a black Honda. Then he saw the glass on the pavement and realized the driver's-side window had been shattered.

His heart stuttered in his chest. He wanted to bellow her name but knew better. All he could think about with every ragged breath was that Della had to be okay.

"We received a 911 call from this location," one of the uniformed officers informed him. "The caller didn't identify herself, only started screaming."

Max cursed. "Anything else I need to know?"

"That's all we have."

Drawing his gun, Max gestured at them to do the same. "This is a personal friend of mine. A man has been stalking her and I suspect that might be his vehicle back there."

They approached the front door with their weapons drawn. One of the officers broke away and headed around toward the back. The fence gate was locked, however, so he didn't get very far.

Taking the lead, Max tried the front door. Unlocked. As he stepped into the foyer, he heard Charlie. The dog seemed to be alternating between growling and snarling.

"FBI," Max called out. "Della, it's me. If you can, let me know you're safe."

A second later, Della came around the corner. Disheveled, with darkening bruises around her throat, but alive. She was carrying a metal baseball bat.

"He's in there." She pointed toward her living room. "Charlie's keeping him down."

Max motioned to the two officers. Moving together, they turned the corner, where they found a bloody man backed into a corner, hands up, guarded by a ferocious-looking Charlie.

Della called her dog to her. The instant Charlie left his post, the intruder stood up. "I demand you arrest her," he said. "Her dog attacked me."

"Inside of her own home," Max pointed out, throttling the urge to put his hands around this man's throat the way he'd clearly done to Della. "I'm guessing you must be Hal?"

Though surprise flickered across the other man's face, he slowly nodded.

"Della?" Without turning to look at her, Max kept his gaze and his gun trained on Hal. "Please tell us exactly what happened here."

"Charlie's hurt," she said. "That man—Hal—followed me again. This time, I didn't notice him right away. After he blocked me in my own driveway, he broke my car window with his bat. He dragged me out of the car, choked me and forced me into the house." She took a deep, shaky breath. "But he didn't count on Charlie. I was able to get this baseball bat away from him, but not before he used it on my dog."

Tears streaming down her face, she knelt and began gently running her hands over Charlie's thick black fur. Tail wagging, he licked her face. He didn't yelp, not once.

Max inclined his head toward the police officers. "Go ahead and arrest him."

"For what?" Hal asked, his defiant expression aligned with his suddenly combative posture. "She invited me in here and then set her dog on me. If anyone should be arrested, I'd think it'd be her."

Ignoring this, one of the policemen began reading Hal his rights, while the other one cuffed him.

Hal began shouting curses, calling Della every vile

name he could. Shaking his head, the officer turned and marched Hal out the door, with the stalker cursing at Della the entire time he was led away.

"Is Charlie okay?" Max knelt down next to the two of them.

"I don't know," she replied, still silently crying. "I want to take him into the vet just to make sure. Will you call Ruby and see if she can fit him in?"

"Give me a minute," Max said. Instead of calling, he sent his cousin a text asking if he could call her. Ruby responded almost immediately, saying she'd just finished with a patient and yes, he could, if he made it quick.

Once she answered and he explained what had happened, Ruby asked to speak to Della. Passing the phone over, he listened while Della answered a few questions.

"Hold on," Della finally said. "Let me try." She stood and moved toward the door. "Charlie, do you want to go outside?"

Though the dog briefly struggled to get up, once he did, he didn't appear to be limping. Della relayed this information to Ruby. Then thanked her and ended the call.

"She said to bring him in. She'll squeeze him in for an appointment."

"Let's go," he said immediately. "I'll drive you. We can't take your Jeep with all the glass inside."

"You're right and thank you." She nodded, wiping at her eyes with her hands. "Do you mind lifting him into your truck? She doesn't want him jumping."

"I don't mind at all." He went to her and pulled her in for a hug. "And after we get Charlie taken care of, you need to have someone look at your throat."

Though she started to protest, something in his expression stopped her. "I'll think about it," she finally said. "Now let's go get my dog checked out."

Chapter 10

Never in her life had Della known such stark and outright terror as when she'd watched Hal swing that bat at Charlie. Roaring her outrage, she'd launched herself at him then, determined to protect her dog at all costs.

Hal had appeared equally determined to cause serious canine injury.

But, focused on defending her, Charlie had won out. He'd pounced on the intruder, teeth bared. While Hal tried to protect himself from the onslaught of both of them, Della had been able to wrest the bat away. Only then had she called Charlie off. She didn't want her dog to kill the man, after all.

"Are you all right?" Max asked again, while he drove. She appreciated that he not only tried to hurry but made sure Charlie wasn't thrown around in the back seat. Della was sitting back there with him, needing to be with her dog.

Instead of answering, Della spoke another truth. "I'd rather have been the one to have gotten hurt a million times over. I don't know how I'll live with myself if I allowed that bastard to cause Charlie serious injury."

Max nodded. "I get that. But go easy on yourself. From what I can tell, Charlie did his best to defend you too. I think you both did an amazing job protecting each other. And I know Ruby will get Charlie fixed up as quickly as she can."

Blinking back more tears, Della continued to stroke her beloved dog's soft fur. Charlie was panting more than he usually did, which she knew could be a sign of pain or distress.

Once they reached the vet clinic, Max parked. He came around to the back door and reached inside. But before he lifted Charlie, he eyed Della. "Do you want me to carry him inside or would you rather see if he can walk?"

She swallowed hard. "Carry him, please. I don't want him to hurt anything else."

Once inside, one of the vet technicians named Maria stood waiting. "Ruby told me you were on your way. Come with me," she said, showing them to an exam room.

Max placed Charlie gently on the metal table. Charlie lifted his head, wagged his tail, but made no effort to sit up. The already hard knot inside Della's stomach twisted. She brushed away more tears—stupid things—as she stroked her dog and promised him that he'd be all right.

The back door opened, and Ruby rushed in. "I'm between patients," she said. "I've informed them that we have an emergency."

Bending down, Ruby spoke softly to Charlie, letting him know that she was there to help him. After asking Della to describe exactly what happened, she listened quietly.

"That's horrible," she said, once Della finished. "I'm going to feel all over Charlie to see if he exhibits any pain or if anything seems broken. Is he walking okay?"

Again, Della felt tears threaten. "I'm not sure," she

replied, twisting her hands. "Everything happened so quickly."

"I see." Ruby looked to Maria, who'd remained in the room. "Please hold him while I perform the examination. Della, I'll need you to step back."

Though she wanted to argue, Della knew better. She moved a few feet away, far enough that she wouldn't interfere with the exam, but close enough that she could comfort Charlie if needed. Max moved closer and put his arm around her shoulders. Grateful, she leaned into him, glad of his strength.

Eyeing Della, Charlie lay still while Ruby gently ran her hands all over him. He grunted once and yelped when she touched his shoulder.

"I'd like to get some X-rays," Ruby said, once she'd finished her exam. "Honestly, I don't think anything is broken, but we won't know for certain without some images. Is that okay?"

"Of course," Della answered.

"I'd like to see him walk as well." Ruby looked at Maria, who nodded and then lifted Charlie off the table and placed him on the floor.

Still panting, Charlie shook himself and wagged his tail.

"Come on, you handsome boy," Maria crooned. Ruby watched intently as Charlie glanced back at Della as if needing her permission.

"Go, Charlie," Della told him. "I'll be right here when you get back."

Charlie blinked and then followed the vet tech out of the room.

"It looks like he's moving okay," Ruby commented. "We'll bring him back once we're done."

The minute the door closed behind them, Della turned her face into Max's chest and held on for dear life.

"You've got this," he said. "Charlie's got this."

With his muscular arms wrapped around her and his familiar scent filling her nostrils, Della managed to reach a feeling of calmness. Charlie hadn't seemed seriously injured, and when Hal had swung the metal bat at him, Charlie hadn't yelped.

A short while later, Ruby returned. "No broken bones," she said, smiling. "And all his vital organs appear intact. We did a sonogram also. He might have some bruising. He might be stiff or sore, so I'm giving you some meds he can take."

Maria appeared with Charlie. Tail wagging furiously, her good boy hurried over to Della, nudging her with his nose as if telling her he wanted to go home now.

"If anything changes, give me a call." With a friendly wave, Ruby went on to her next patient.

At the front desk, Della paid, and then the three of them left. When they reached Max's truck, Charlie jumped right in without any help. This made Della's heart happy.

Once in the truck, Max eyed her. "Now that we've gotten Charlie checked out, how about we do the same for you? I don't like the look of those bruises on your neck."

"I'm good." She waved away his concern. "They're just bruises, and they'll fade with time. He didn't hurt me anywhere else."

Though Max didn't appear entirely convinced, he

didn't argue with her, for which she was grateful. Instead, he took them home.

After they pulled up at her driveway, Della carefully kept Charlie away from all the broken glass. Inside, he went to the back door, signaling he needed to go out and do his business. Once she'd let him take care of that, he went straight to his favorite dog bed and curled up in it with a loud sigh.

Max watched him, grinning from ear to ear. "I'm so glad he's going to be all right."

"Me too." Suddenly exhausted, all Della wanted to do was go lie on her bed and sleep. But she needed to call Sebastian and let him know what had happened. She wouldn't be going back to work today. She needed to rest and try to get over the shock.

Before she could dial his cell, Sebastian called her. "I just talked to Ruby," he said. "She filled me in. Are you okay?"

"I'm fine," she sighed. "Physically. Mentally, I'm going to need a little bit of time to decompress. Max is with me, so I'm not alone. But there's no way I can come back to work this afternoon. If I were to attempt to work with any of the dogs, they'd sense what a mess I am."

"I agree," Sebastian answered. "Why don't you take a couple of days off? I can cover your classes tomorrow."

Though that sounded like heaven, she didn't want to foist all her work on her boss. "I appreciate the offer. We'll see how I feel tomorrow and go from there. I'll be in touch."

"Sounds good. Take care of yourself." Sebastian ended the call.

A wave of exhaustion hit her. She felt dizzy, not like

herself, and she guessed this must be a reaction to the trauma she'd suffered.

"Come here," Max said, pulling her close and steering her over toward the couch. "You look like you need to sit down."

Grateful, she dropped onto the cushions, with him right beside her. Laying her head on his shoulder, she closed her eyes.

Then she remembered her new outdoor furniture and sat up.

"What's wrong?" Max asked, concerned.

"I bought a couple of rocking chairs and a little table earlier. The store loaded them up in my Jeep for me, but with all the excitement…"

"I'll unload them for you," he said, pushing to his feet. "Where do you want them?"

Try as she might, she couldn't seem to summon the energy to join him. "Are you sure? They're pretty big and bulky. I was planning on putting them on my deck."

He smiled. "I can handle it. You just sit and rest."

Too tired to argue, she nodded and closed her eyes again.

She must have drifted off to sleep, because the next thing she knew, Charlie's barking startled her awake. She bolted up in a panic, once again feeling hands locked around her throat. Except she was alone. Even Charlie's barking had come from the backyard.

Wondering if Max had left and forgotten to let Charlie back in, she went to her sliding patio doors and opened them. Her new rocking chairs were in place on the deck, with the small table right in between them.

Spotting Max out in the yard playing with her dog

made her catch her breath. She watched silently while the two of them enjoyed each other's company, oblivious to her presence. She appreciated the way Max took care not to let Charlie do anything too strenuous. They simply walked the perimeter of the yard, Max talking and Charlie watching him, head cocked, as if listening intently.

She walked over to one of her new chairs and sat. Rocking back and forth, she felt a deep sense of contentment. While she knew it would take a while to recover from the trauma of being attacked, she also counted her blessings that she was still alive. Her cousin hadn't been so lucky.

This made her wonder. Had Hal been involved in any of the other women's murders?

"Hey!" Max waved as he noticed her. "I'll be right up."

Though there were steps outside leading up to the porch, Max brought Charlie into the house through the downstairs back door instead. A few minutes later, the two of them walked out through the slider and joined her.

"Nice chairs," Max said, grinning. He dropped into the one next to her. Charlie came over and sat at her feet, laying his head in her lap.

"Thanks," she replied. "I've been eyeing them for a good while. I finally bit the bullet and purchased them."

His grin widened. "They didn't tell you anything about who made them?"

"No. Just that it's a local." Perplexed, she gazed at him. "Do you know him or her?"

"I do." Still smiling, he nodded. "These are my chairs. I make them. Making furniture has been my hobby for years. It's how I relax. My family lets me keep all my tools and supplies in one of the outbuildings on the ranch."

Stunned, she stared. While they hadn't known each other very long, this completely surprised her. "You're very skilled," she finally said, meaning it. "I'm guessing you must come home to Owl Creek frequently, because the guy working in the store said these chairs sell well and he's constantly replenishing his stock."

"They do." He ran one hand down the arm of the chair, a pleased expression on his face. "I love making them as much as I love working for the FBI. Sometimes even more, I think. It's certainly less stressful."

They fell into a companionable silence, rocking slowly, with Charlie asleep and soaking up sunshine at Della's feet.

This, she realized. The longer she sat, the more her tension seeped away from her. She felt…safe. And happy. Being here with Max brought the kind of contentment one could only find with the right person.

Absently, she reached up and touched her throat. Wincing at the tenderness of her bruises, she thought of how differently that situation might have gone. "Thank you for everything," she said, her voice quiet. "The police got here quickly, but I was very glad to see you."

He met her gaze. "You did a good job protecting yourself."

Again, she thought of how close Charlie had come to getting injured. She shook her head. "Charlie did most of the work. I'm just relieved he's all right."

"Me too," he said.

She took a deep breath, aware she might be making

a big leap without any evidence but needing to get it off her chest.

"You know, ever since Hal attacked me, I've wondered if maybe he was involved in any of that mess up in the meadow."

"Me too."

This surprised her. "I'm glad I'm not the only one."

"You're not." He grimaced. "After I leave here, I plan to stop by the police station and have a word with him. Right now, we don't have anything to tie him to the murders, but I'm going to ask that they hold on to him as long as possible."

The thought of Hal being released made her shudder. "I bet they'll give me a restraining order now."

He nodded. "I'm sure they will. Though, honestly, since you've pressed charges, I plan to let Hal know we'll be watching every move he makes."

"The thing that bothers me the most," she said, "is that Hal now knows where I live. The thought of him hiding here waiting for me to get home…"

"You need an alarm system."

She didn't want to point out that she couldn't afford one. "Not here, not in Owl Creek. This isn't the kind of place where we need such things. Until recently, no one even locked their doors."

"I know. But times change." He checked his phone. "I have contacts. I'll take care of getting something installed."

"But…" she started to protest, but he cut her off with a quick kiss.

"Della, let me do this for you. Please."

Relenting, she agreed, aware she'd be paying him

back. "Nothing too expensive, okay? And the sooner, the better."

For an answer, he kissed her again.

Though he hated to go, Max knew he couldn't stay at Della's all day. After one final kiss, he got to his feet and looked at her, drinking in the beauty of her dozing in the sunshine in one of the chairs he'd made with his own hands.

He could get used to days like this. The thought no longer felt as shocking as it once would have. Which might mean he was ready for a change.

Seeing the furniture he'd made in the back of Della's Jeep had brought all kinds of tender feelings to the surface. On top of getting to her just in time to keep that man from seriously hurting her or her dog, the myriad of emotions felt almost too much for him. Working in law enforcement, he'd long ago learned how to remain detached and impartial. But not this time. Not when Della and Charlie were involved.

He wasn't sure he trusted himself to be around this Hal guy right now. Which was partly why he'd hung around Della's house. He needed to get a grip on his rage and regain his professional detachment.

Sometimes he wished he could build furniture for a living. Once, after a particularly disheartening case, he'd even run the numbers. He'd have to ramp up production and increase distribution to more than just Owl Creek, but it could be done. It was an option he always kept in the back of his mind.

But for right now, he needed to get his act together and question Hal.

After he'd called Owl Creek PD and heard the particulars on Hal, he'd gotten permission to come in and question the man himself. On the way, he'd phoned the team and given them and Theo the information. "Find out anything you can about this guy," he'd said. "See if there's anything that might tie him to those bodies in the meadow. And see if he's a member of the Ever After Church. My contact at the local PD says he's mentioned his church a few times."

"The what?" Theo had clearly never heard of them. Max had filled him in, saying he was operating off a hunch. One that might not even pan out.

"I'll get back to you," Theo had promised before ending the call.

Max parked outside the police station and walked inside. They'd already put Hal in one of the interrogation rooms in preparation for Max's arrival. He'd also been told, confidentially, that the judge was out on the golf course and couldn't be reached to come in and make a decision about Hal's bail. Any delay was a good thing, as far as Max was concerned.

Before turning the doorknob to enter, Max took several deep breaths. He needed to remain objective. Especially since every time he thought of this man with his hands around Della's throat, a red haze of rage clouded his vision.

Professional and detached, he reminded himself. Then he stepped into the room.

Looking up, Hal blanched when he saw Max. Wearing his street clothes, he sat in one of the hard plastic chairs behind a polished metal table. He didn't speak, just continued to stare sullenly.

"Good afternoon," Max said, pulling out the chair across from Hal and sitting in it. "I have a few questions for you."

"I want an attorney," Hal replied, sneering. "I've already told them I'm not answering anything without a lawyer present. You're wasting your time."

Staring at Hal, Max fought for control. The idea that this man had put his hands around Della's throat made Max see red. Despite his best efforts, fury pushed him back up out of the chair. "You..." He bit out the word. For the first time in his career, he teetered on the edge of acting unprofessionally. Somehow, he managed to rein himself in.

"Enjoy your stay," he said and let himself out.

All the way back to the ranch, he let his anger simmer. Though he kept telling himself that Hal would eventually pay, knowing how close he'd come to hurting Della made Max feel ill.

He'd just turned down the ranch drive when he slammed on the brakes. He didn't want to go home. Not now, with all these things bottled up inside of him. He couldn't talk to his dad or his brothers about what had happened today. They'd not only never understand, but they'd think Max had lost his mind.

Before he had time to rethink or reconsider, he made a U-turn and headed back the way he'd come.

The sun had begun to set, though it wasn't dark yet. The orange-and-red sky promised a warm day tomorrow. Gazing at it, he felt a sense of hope. As he neared his destination, his mood continued to lighten.

It wasn't until he'd pulled up in Della's driveway that he realized he should have called first. After all, she'd clearly been exhausted and the last thing he wanted to do was wake her.

This indecisiveness wasn't like him. Ever since he'd met Della, she'd occupied his thoughts constantly. He craved her, cared about her and quite honestly believed he could be falling in love with her.

The notion didn't terrify him the way it once might have.

Staring at her house, he realized she might not feel the same way. Or even close. They'd agreed to be friends, and even though they'd moved into the *with benefits* area, she'd given no sign of becoming emotionally entangled.

Which meant his unannounced arrival at her house might be problematic.

Calling himself a fool, he shook his head and decided he'd better leave.

Just as he put the truck in Reverse, the front door opened, the porch light turned on, and Della came flying down the sidewalk. He shifted into Park, killed the engine and opened his door. Jumping out, he met her halfway across the lawn. Grinning, feeling like he was in a greeting card commercial, he scooped her up in his arms and lifted her.

She clung to him, murmuring his name over and over. Then he kissed her, right there in her front yard, uncaring who might see.

Still locked together, they stumbled back toward her house, with Charlie barking happily.

Inside, Max kicked the door closed. She broke away, gazing up at him with wide eyes. "What are you doing here?" she asked, breathless. "You seem…unsettled."

His heart skipped a beat.

"I wanted to check on you and make sure you're all right."

Truth, but not all of it.

She seemed to sense this, because she continued to watch him, letting him work out what else he wanted to say.

"Plus, I went and saw Hal at the police station. He refused to speak without an attorney present." Swallowing, he gave her the rest of it. "Della, I almost lost it. When he eyed me with that smug smile, I wanted to come up out of my seat and make him pay for what he did to you."

She stared.

Pacing now, he dragged his hand through his hair. "If I'd acted on impulse, it would have been the end of my career. I'm an FBI agent. People in my position don't lose control like that."

"But you didn't." She touched his arm. "And Hal is still locked up. I'm pressing charges. I just hope they managed to delay getting a judge to agree to bail."

"They did." Smiling, he pulled her close again. "I was told the judge was playing eighteen holes of golf and couldn't be reached today. Which means he'll stay locked up for at least tonight."

"Oh, thank goodness." She sagged against him. "I appreciate you telling me that."

For a few heartbeats, they simply held each other. He breathed in the light vanilla-and-peach scent of her, marveling at how perfectly they fit together.

"Was that the only reason you came by?" she finally asked, her arms still wrapped tightly around him.

"No. I also came by because I missed you," he admitted, feeling she'd understand. "Were you asleep?"

"No." She shook her head. "I feel too restless for that. I was just about to get on the treadmill," she said.

Pulling back slightly, she reached up and kissed him again, the kind of lingering, deep kiss that promised more. "But now another kind of physical activity seems more likely."

The shiver of raw desire that went through him made him shudder. "You've got that right," he murmured.

Shedding their clothing as they went, they made it to her bedroom. Naked, they fell onto each other as if it had been weeks since they'd come together, even though it had just been days.

He couldn't get enough of her, it seemed. And she apparently felt the same way. Their lovemaking was fierce and wild, yet tenderness came through the passion.

After, neither seemed in a hurry to get out of her bed.

"You mentioned a treadmill," he said, drawing lazy circles with his finger on her bare arm. "Do you have one or do you go to the gym?"

"I have one." She sighed. "I usually only use it in bad weather. I like to run and try to get in a few miles every day if possible. When I don't run, I hike. Charlie enjoys going with me and that way we both get exercise."

Lost in thought, she looked down at her hands. "Though with the whole Hal thing, I don't feel safe. Which I hate. So I thought the treadmill would have to work for now."

"I run too," he said, though he hadn't for at least three months. "Or I used to. I've been meaning to get back in shape. Maybe we can go together, though you'll have to be patient with me."

Hope blossomed in her eyes. "That would be awesome," she breathed.

"You say that now," he teased. "You may not think so if I end up slowing you down."

Lightly, she punched his arm. "If you do, I'll whip you into shape in no time."

This made him laugh. "I bet you will."

Charlie barked, reminding them of his presence. Della grabbed a long T-shirt and shorts, slipped her feet into flip-flops and took her dog outside.

When she returned, she asked him if he wanted to watch a movie. Since he didn't want to leave her yet, he agreed.

Della handed him the remote and told him to pick something. She had all the streaming services, so he easily found an action-adventure flick he'd been wanting to see.

The scent of buttery popcorn filled the air, making him smile. "Movie night done right," she called from the kitchen.

"Do you need any help?" he asked.

"Nope. I'll be out in a moment."

Charlie emerged, tail wagging. He hopped up onto the couch and made a couple of circles before settling into what appeared to be his spot at one end.

This, he thought. If he'd been asked to describe the perfect domestic situation, this would rank up there at the top. Della, Charlie, a comfortable couch and a good movie. He couldn't think of anything better.

When Della returned, she had a huge bowl of popcorn and two bottles of cold beer. Setting everything down, she dropped onto the sofa next to him and eyed the TV.

"I've been wanting to see that," she said, smiling. "And

kudos to you for not sitting in Charlie's spot. Though I'm sure he would have let you know, he always sits there every night."

This made him smile. "I'll keep that in mind for next time."

She smiled back. Watching them, Charlie thumped his tail, as if he understood.

Max put his arm around her shoulders. She snuggled close. Clicking the remote, he started the movie. For the first time in years, he felt at home. His sterile apartment in Boise had always been simply a place to sleep, and despite growing up at the ranch, his lack of ranching ambition had always made him feel like an outsider.

Here, he felt like he could stay. Even if he knew he'd have to return to Boise once this case had closed, he decided to enjoy the feeling while he could.

Though the movie was entertaining, he found his attention straying to Della. Unaware, she ate popcorn while focusing on the TV.

Unable to help himself, he placed a soft kiss on the top of her head. Though she smiled, she barely looked away from the movie.

Debating whether to try harder to distract her, he couldn't suppress a groan when his cell phone rang. Though sorely tempted to ignore it, he didn't dare, since they were in the middle of an important case.

Shifting his weight away from her, he answered. An unfamiliar voice on the other end identified themselves as Officer Fuentes with the Owl Creek Police Department.

"We have an injured woman we are transporting to the hospital in Conners," the officer said. "Before she lost consciousness, she claimed she was kidnapped by a man who tried to strangle her. We're thinking there might be a tie to that serial killer case you're working."

Chapter 11

Della watched Max's expression change as he listened to his caller. Alert, she straightened and paused the movie, wishing she could hear the other end of the conversation. Somehow, she sensed the call might be related to Angela and the other women's cases.

"I'm on my way," Max said, ending the call. When he met Della's gaze, the stern FBI agent was back.

"What's going on?" she asked, her heart rate increasing.

"I'm heading to the hospital in Conners," he replied. "An injured woman was found who claimed she'd been kidnapped and strangled. Owl Creek PD thinks this might be tied to our serial killer." He took a deep breath. "Do you want to go with me?"

"Yes." She didn't even have to think before responding. Conners was a good forty-five-minute drive. Since Owl Creek didn't have an actual hospital, everyone had to travel to Conners. "Let me take Charlie out real quick and then we can head out."

After she'd taken care of her dog, she followed Max to his truck. He wasn't talking much, clearly lost in his own thoughts. Briefly, she considered asking him if he was sure he wanted her to go but decided against it. She really didn't want to give him the opportunity to change his mind.

Jaw set in a tight line, Max looked furious. Every choppy movement he made spoke to an inner anger that he seemed to be unable or unwilling to express.

"Are you okay?" she finally asked. "I'm a bit worried about you."

He glanced at her, a sharp slice of his gaze, before returning his attention back to the road. "Not really," he answered. "In fact, I'm pretty damn pissed that this guy got the opportunity to attack someone else."

"At least she survived," she pointed out. "It could have been worse."

"True. But he has to know we've discovered his burial place. Not only has everything been disturbed, but the news has been blasted all over the state. I figured he might lie low for a while. I'm actually surprised he attacked someone right now, with all the media attention on this case."

"But he failed," she said. "Luckily for this woman, and for us. She survived. And now she might be able to describe him, giving you the break in the case you needed to find and arrest this person."

"True," he replied, but he didn't sound convinced.

She thought of Hal, with his leering smile and his hands around her neck. "I was sure Hal had something to do with this. But I guess this latest development means it couldn't have been him, since he's still locked up."

"I thought the same thing," he admitted. "But I want to call Owl Creek PD and make sure he's still in custody. I didn't think to ask earlier."

Using his truck's Bluetooth, he placed a quick call

and learned that yes, Hal Murcheson was still a guest of the Owl Creek jail.

"Well, that settles that," he said, once he'd disconnected. "It couldn't have been Hal who attacked this woman." He glanced at her and the still-visible bruises on her neck. "Though I can't entirely rule him out on the others. Once he gets lawyered up, I'm going to put him through some pretty intense questioning. I've already got the team working on determining his whereabouts for the last couple years."

"Good thinking. But are you saying there might be two men going around and murdering women? Like a team?"

He shrugged. "Anything is possible and stranger things have happened. All we know for sure is that Hal didn't attack this one particular victim. I'm interested to get her description of her attacker. I hope she got a good look at him."

"Me too." Della nodded. "Did they say what kind of condition she's in?"

"No. Only that she gave a brief statement before she lost consciousness." He shot another quick glance her way, and then he kept his attention on the road. He drove competently and efficiently, although he couldn't help but exceed the speed limit. His rage seemed much less palpable, though she suspected it still simmered under the surface. She couldn't blame him. Every time she remembered how she'd felt, about to black out as Hal tried to choke the life from her, she alternated between terror and fury.

They made it to the Conners city limits in just under forty-three minutes. "Not bad," she remarked, itching with impatience. She could only hope this woman would survive. And that she'd be able to give a decent description of the man who'd attacked her.

"We haven't had any leads at all, until now," Max mused, pulling into the hospital parking lot. "If this case turns out to be related, this could be the information we've been waiting for."

"What do you mean, *if* this case is related?" Della glanced sideways at him, feeling queasy. "How can it not be?"

"You never know. Like I said, I felt pretty confident that Hal would turn out to be involved. And while we haven't entirely ruled him out, the fact that this latest attack happened while he's still in custody makes his involvement much less likely." He sighed. "And though it's entirely possible that there might have been two men killing these women, everything we know of serial killers tell us they operate alone."

"I'm still trying to wrap my head around all of this. Are you saying there's a possibility that the attack on this woman might not be tied to the murders in the meadow?"

He grunted. "There are so many variables. This—or Hal—could be an isolated incident. We need something to tie one of them to the murders."

"Like what? DNA?"

"I know Caroline would love to have some DNA to work with, other than the victims. But with the weather and wild animals, she said she was lucky to be able to identify the remains."

Della didn't bother to hide her frustration. "I'm still going to hope that this victim can tell us something that might help give you a break in the case. I need this killer to be caught. I want this over."

"I get that." He touched her shoulder. "But we want to make sure and put the right person behind bars."

"True." Refusing to allow her nervous energy to deflate, Della waited until he'd parked and killed the engine before jumping out of the truck. She kept close to Max's side as he strode into the hospital lobby. For whatever reason, she found herself continually checking over her shoulder, as if someone might be watching her.

At the information desk, he flashed his badge and was directed to the ER. There, the triage nurse smiled at him before pointing toward the back. "She's in ER room 8," she said.

After being buzzed through the double doors, they walked down the hallway, past the nurses' station. As they turned a corner, they encountered two uniformed Owl Creek police officers, standing outside of one of the rooms. Room 8.

Della recognized Officer Santis, the one who'd come to her aid at the gas station. He inclined his head in a nod when he saw her, but like his partner, he focused his attention on Max.

"What's the status?" Max asked, his voice stern.

"The doctor is with her now," Santis replied. "We've been told that she's stable, but still unconscious at the moment."

"Not critical condition, then?"

"Not that we've been told." Santis glanced at his partner, who nodded. "I got a quick look at her. She had a lot of blood. The bruises on her throat are pretty bad, but the doc says she has some internal injuries. He thinks she might have been beaten with something. They're getting some imaging done in a few minutes."

Hearing about the bruises, Della's hands involuntarily went to her own throat. And hearing this poor woman might have been beaten with something, she kept thinking about Hal and his metal baseball bat.

Seeing this, Max squeezed her arm. "We'll wait here with you," he said, offering her comfort.

The two officers nodded.

"Do you want her placed under guard twenty-four seven?" Santis asked. "We can call in reinforcements if you'd like. That way we can take shifts."

Max considered. "I'm not sure that's necessary, but let me think about it for the long term. For now, I'd like you to stay."

"We can do that." Officer Santis nodded. "I'd like to get my hands on the guy who did that to her. She looked pretty badly beat up."

Della swallowed hard. Her heart ached for this woman she didn't even know. Especially since she'd recently had a similar experience. It could very likely have been her who'd ended up in the ER.

The doctor came out of the room. Once again, Max flashed his FBI identification and asked for a word with him. The harried doc nodded but gestured at the two uniforms. "I've already shared everything I know with them. Maybe they can fill you in?"

"They have," Max replied. "I'll just ask you to update me once you have the imaging results."

"That I can do. Now, if you'll excuse me…" And the doctor rushed off.

As soon as the doctor left, a nurse appeared, directing

them to a small seating area between the nurses' station and the rooms. "If you'll wait here, I'll send the doctor to speak with you as soon as he knows anything."

They sat. Though the policemen eyed Della, they didn't question her presence. Which was good, since she didn't have any professional reason to be here. She didn't want to admit the truth—that she was only keeping Max company.

She badly wanted to ask Max the reason he felt this woman needed to be placed under guard, but figured it was something she'd need to wait to find out until they were alone.

Time dragged, as it always seemed to do inside a hospital. Della took to scrolling on her phone while Max stepped outside to make a phone call. The two police officers talked quietly among themselves, occasionally glancing at Della. Finally, Santis cleared his throat and addressed her.

"How are you holding up?" he asked. "I heard that guy who followed you to that gas station assaulted you."

"I'm doing okay," she said, realizing as she spoke that she actually was. "Just relieved he's still behind bars. I'm definitely pressing charges. Though all of this brings it all back up."

He gave her a sympathetic smile. "I imagine it does. I'm sorry."

Max returned and dropped back into the chair next to Della. "I filled my SAC in on what's happened," he said. "He definitely wants me to question this woman when she wakes up."

"Does this woman have a name?" Della asked softly,

directing her question to the policemen. "Do either of you know it?"

Officer Santis nodded. "Maisy," he replied, consulting his notes. "She didn't have any ID on her, so we weren't able to get a last name before she lost consciousness."

"Were you able to get any kind of a statement?" Max asked.

"Not yet. We did take one from the woman who brought her in. She happened to be driving by when Maisy came stumbling out of the woods, all bloody with torn clothing."

Again, he glanced at his notes. "The woman who brought her here is named Regina Quinten. She said that Maisy was able to tell her that she'd been attacked and that was it. Ms. Quinten asked her name, and Maisy got out that much before she went unresponsive."

"Did you get contact information for this Regina Quinten?" Max asked.

"We did." Officer Santis wrote something on a piece of paper and handed it to Max. "Here you go."

"Thanks."

"No problem." The officer closed his pad and sighed. "That's the extent of what we know."

"Thank you." Max looked thoughtful as he studied the sheet of paper.

A moment later, the doctor returned. Della saw him first, and since she met his gaze, he made a beeline over to her. Max looked up and stood, so of course Della did too.

"We've finished running her tests," the doctor said, his smile tired. "She has a couple of broken ribs, but that seems to be the extent of it. I took a quick peek at the

MRI, and though I still need a radiologist to evaluate it, there may be some soft-tissue injuries. She appears to have been severely beaten in addition to the nearly successful attempt to strangle her."

"Is she going to be all right?" Della asked.

The doctor nodded. "I believe so. She's conscious. We'll be admitting her so we can keep an eye on her, so she'll be transferring to a regular room." He looked at Max. "I know you have to question her, but please take it easy. I'll allow her to have one visitor, but you'll need to keep it short."

Without waiting for an answer, the doctor turned on his heel and hurried away.

Della looked up at Max. Again, his tight jaw and remote expression told her he'd retreated inside himself. She wanted to tug on his arm and whisper to him to please be gentle, but truthfully, there was no need. She knew he would.

Entering the small ER exam room, Max stopped just inside the doorway. Despite the fact that the medical staff had gotten Maisy cleaned up, the bruises on her face, throat and arms looked pretty horrific. The pale-blue-and-white hospital gown did little to hide how badly she'd been battered. Her short blond hair had bloody mats and appeared to have been hacked off with a dull pair of scissors or a pocketknife.

She looked up when he came in, her pale blue eyes clouded. Most likely she'd been given some medication to help with the pain. She attempted a smile, though her swelling must have made that painful, since it faltered and quickly turned into a grimace.

"I'm Special Agent Max Colton with the FBI," he said, approaching her bed and showing her his badge. "I know you are feeling pretty awful, but would it be okay if I ask you a few questions?"

She started to nod, but then apparently thought better of it. "Go ahead."

"Let's start with your full name."

"Maisy Pederson," she replied. "I'm twenty-two, and I work as a barista in a coffee shop in Boise while attending Boise State University."

Max noted this down. "Are you originally from Boise or somewhere else?"

"I grew up in Boise," she said. "I still live at home with my parents." For a moment, she appeared concerned. "Has anyone contacted them? I need to let them know that I'm all right."

"We'll have you do that in just a little bit," Max said. "First, can you tell me what happened?"

"I'm… It's all so weird. I've always sung in our church's choir. A week ago, after the service, a man approached me. He said I sang like an angel and asked me if I'd consider singing at his church. It had some weird name, which made me very uneasy."

"A church?" Keeping his expression impassive, Max struggled to contain his excitement.

A nurse interrupted, bringing a plastic pitcher of water and a plastic cup. "Here you go, sweetie," she said, setting them down on the tray near the bed. "You can have a little water now, but don't overdo it."

Once she'd gone, Max went over and poured half a glass for Maisy and handed it to her. She accepted it with shaky hands, took a few small sips and then put the cup back on her tray table.

"You can't remember the name of that church?" Max asked her. "It would be very helpful if you could try."

She sat still for a moment, her forehead wrinkled in thought. Finally, she sighed. "I'm sorry, but I can't."

"Was it the Ever After Church?" he asked, needing to know.

"Maybe," she replied. "But I can't be positive."

This time, Max had to work to hide his disappointment. He hadn't been able to shake the idea that the Ever After Church might be involved in all of this. He just needed some proof.

Maisy fell silent, apparently lost in her own thoughts. Max gave her a minute, aware she likely was in a lot of pain.

"Can you give me a description of this man?" Max asked, pen poised.

"He looked...ordinary," she finally said. "Brown hair, brown eyes, not too tall or too short. Just like someone you'd never take a second look at."

Max nodded. "Any idea of his age?"

"Older than me?" She grimaced and then blanched because apparently even that small movement hurt. "I'm bad at guessing age. I'd say mid to late forties. He seemed...nice. I was definitely wrong."

"How'd you go from being asked to sing in a church choir to being beaten and attacked?" he finally asked, as gently as he could.

Her gaze met his. She shuddered. "He told me I could think about it and asked if I would walk with him to his car, so he could get some literature about the church for me. I guess I'm too naive, because I did. He told me to go ahead and sit in the passenger seat while he put together some papers for me."

Hands shaking, she reached for the plastic cup of water and took another small sip. "I sat down, because it was windy and my skirt was blowing around. He got the papers together and sat in the driver's seat. Then he grabbed me by the back of the head and held something over my mouth and nose. I don't know what it was, but it made me pass out."

"Chloroform," he guessed.

"Probably." Her voice wavered. She swallowed and visibly struggled to compose herself. "Anyway, when I woke up again, he'd parked at the base of one of the hiking trailheads. My head was pounding and I felt nauseated. He told me we were going to go for a walk." She swallowed hard. "I knew if I walked up that trail with him, I'd never make it out alive."

Smart woman. Max nodded in approval.

"I thought about running," she continued, "but when I got out of the car, I could barely stand. He got behind me, prodding me with some kind of metal thing, like a police baton."

That was new. Thinking of Hal, with his metal bat, Max made a note. Coincidence? Maybe. Or maybe not.

"I played up my dizziness," Maisy explained. "Made it look like I was more out of it than I was. Stumbled and staggered and fell back toward him. It might have been reflex, but he caught me." Her eyes drifted closed.

Max coughed, hoping she could stay awake long enough to finish making her statement. "Then what happened?" he prodded.

Her lashes fluttered, but she finally reopened her eyes. "I grabbed the metal stick and swung." She slurred the last word as she fell back asleep.

The monotonous beeping of the machines was the only sound in the room. Max found them reassuring, because he knew if something had gone wrong, they would have sounded an alert. Aware he'd get nothing else from this woman for a while, he turned to make his way back to the waiting area. He wanted one of the uniformed officers stationed outside her room at all times.

When he reached the waiting room, he found Della sitting next to Officer Santis. "Where'd your partner go?" Max asked.

"Men's room. He'll be right back."

"Okay. Since you're here, you can take first shift. I need a guard posted outside Maisy Pederson's room twenty-four seven."

"I can do that." Santis pushed to his feet. "I take it you have reason to believe there's a credible threat?"

"I do. She wasn't able to give me much of a description. From what she told me, it's a miracle she made it out alive."

"I'll go do first shift starting right now."

"Thank you." Max passed Santis his card. "My cell is on there. Call me if you need anything."

Accepting it, Officer Santis nodded. "Will do."

"We'll wait for your partner and let him know what's going on. After that, Della and I are going to head out."

Watching while the young police officer went to take up his post outside ER room 8, Max turned to Della. "Are you ready to go?"

Expression pensive, she shrugged. "I really was hoping I'd get to talk to Maisy. Since I've recently been through something similar, even if it wasn't as bad, I really think I could get her to open up to me."

He considered. "She's out of it right now. How about we come back tomorrow morning, once she's been moved to her regular hospital room. I'm thinking once she gets some rest, she might have clearer memories. All she was able to give me so far was pretty vague."

"I'd like that," Della said. "And you're right—it is late. We could all use some sleep."

The other police officer appeared, looking remarkably alert. Once Max filled him in, he nodded and went down the hall to consult with Santis.

"Come on," Max said, taking Della's arm. "Let's go."

Walking outside into the well-lit parking lot, Max glanced up at the crescent moon. Here, the stars were still visible, though not as bright as they were someplace more remote, like the ranch. Or the campsite near the awful meadow where the killer had buried the bodies.

Just the thought brought a wave of exhaustion. He yawned, covering his mouth with his hand. "I'm more tired than I realized," he said.

They reached his truck. Once he'd unlocked it and they both got inside, Della touched his arm. "You're welcome to stay with me tonight," she offered. "I know it's a bit of a drive out to the ranch."

Touched, he nodded. "I'd like that."

"Me too." Her soft smile had him leaning over to kiss her cheek.

At her house, he parked behind her Jeep. "The insurance company gave me the number of a place to call to get my windows replaced," she said. "I just haven't had a chance to do it yet. It's some kind of mobile place, so they come out to your place of work. Which will be perfect."

Opening the front door, they were greeted by an ecstatic Charlie, bounding around them, tail wagging. Della made him sit before she began petting him. "You're such a good boy," she praised.

When she'd finished loving on him, Charlie came over to Max and nudged him with his nose. Max obliged, scratching the Lab behind his ears.

Satisfied, Charlie walked away and went to get a drink of water.

"Is he always this happy to see you?" Max asked, bemused, following Della into the kitchen.

"Yep. That's the thing with dogs. It doesn't matter if you've been gone a few minutes or an entire day. They greet you as if they haven't seen you in forever." She picked up Charlie's water bowl and carried it to the sink to rinse it out and refill it.

"I like that." Max came up behind her and wrapped her in his arms. "And I like you."

At his words, she went still. Then, shutting off the water, she turned to face him. "I like you too."

He kissed her then. Heat erupted between them, just as it always did. He took her hand, intending to lead her toward the bedroom. "Wait," she said. "Let me put Charlie's water bowl back down. I don't want him to get thirsty."

In that moment, he thought he couldn't love her more.

Later, as they cuddled together with the sheets still tangled around them, she sighed. "Do you think I'd be allowed to visit with Maisy tomorrow? I'd really like a chance to talk to her."

Curious, he nuzzled her neck. "If she's well enough, I can make that happen. Any particular reason why?"

"I can relate to what happened to her, in a way that no one else can. Not only did something similar happen to me, but my cousin lost her life at the hands of that same person."

Though he wanted to caution her about jumping to conclusions, he decided not to. While they didn't *know* with certainty that this incident was tied to the serial killer, it likely would turn out to be.

"Could we go first thing in the morning?" Della pressed. "I have to be at Crosswinds by nine."

"You're going back to work?" he asked.

"Of course. There are several dogs there waiting for me to work with them. Sebastian can't train his and mine. There aren't enough hours in the day."

"I get that," he told her. "But are you feeling well enough?"

His question made her laugh. "We just rather energetically made love. I'm surprised you even have to ask that."

She had a point.

"We'll run by the hospital first thing in the morning," he agreed. "I got a text that she's been moved to room 5128."

They fell asleep in each other's arms. Just before he drifted off, he realized he'd never been happier.

The delicious smell of coffee brewing woke Max. He stretched, momentarily disoriented. Then, realizing he'd spent the night with Della, he grinned.

She showered while he drank his coffee. When she emerged, dressed with her hair in a long braid, she walked over and kissed his cheek. "Your turn. I put a towel and washcloth on the bathroom counter for you."

Thanking her, he took a quick shower. Wishing he'd brought a change of clothes, he dressed in the ones he'd worn the day before. "We'll grab something for breakfast on the way to the hospital," he said.

They were out the door barely an hour after he'd first opened his eyes. He'd never known a woman able to get ready so fast. Including his sister.

Grabbing a couple of breakfast sandwiches on the way, they ate them as he drove. He pulled up to the hospital entrance and found a parking spot close to the door. Another bonus of arriving so early, he thought. Smiling at Della, he told her this meant today was going to be a good day. It had to be.

She seemed to share his buoyant mood. Linking her arm with his, she smiled broadly as they walked into the hospital lobby.

They barely made it past the information desk before the power went out, plunging the hospital into darkness.

Chapter 12

"Wait here." Jerking his hand free from hers, Max sprinted for the stairs.

Since there was no way Della intended to do that, she ignored him. The windows let in enough light that she could see. Though she hadn't been running in a few days, she was in excellent shape and easily caught up with him.

He shot her a look but kept going. So did she.

"The emergency generators should be kicking on," she said. "I don't understand why there's a delay."

Just then, the lights flickered on as if someone had heard her. They came on, went out and flickered a few times.

Despite the dark, Max located the door to the stairwell and wrenched it open. He'd gotten out his phone and used the flashlight on it to help him see. Taking the stairs two at a time, he barreled to the fifth floor. Della stayed right on his heels.

Meanwhile, the lights continued to flicker on and off.

"Backup generator problems," Max said. "They should have that fixed soon. Too many patients depend on electricity."

She nodded. "I wonder what happened."

"I'm betting this wasn't an accident." Barely out of

breath, he opened the door to floor 5. "Good thing I asked Owl Creek PD to place Maisy under a twenty-four seven guard."

Startled, she followed him down the hall. "You think this is related to her?"

"I do."

Though she still didn't fully understand, she stayed close as they rounded the nurses' station. The lights had now come on and remained steady.

They rounded the corner, and Max cursed as he spotted the empty chair in the hall outside of room 5128. "Where's her guard?"

As he started toward the room, a gunshot rang out. It sounded like it had come from inside.

Della froze.

"Get down!" Max said, drawing his gun. "Della, take cover."

Since she'd already instinctively ducked, she went all the way to the floor and crawled over to hide behind the nurses' station. Shaky, heart in her throat, she watched Max advance toward the room.

"FBI!" he called out. He entered the room with his weapon still drawn.

Della hated that she couldn't see him.

"Put the gun down," Max ordered. "Right now."

Shaky, Della tried to breathe. The gunman, still inside the room. Max in danger. Where were the police? Hands shaking, heart racing, she stayed down, on the other side of the counter. She hadn't expected this. She wondered if there was anything she could do to help, but she didn't want to get in the way.

Seconds ticked by. Only seconds, though they seemed like minutes.

Then another gunshot. Just one.

Who'd been shot? Max? The intruder? Agonizing over the uncertainty, she drew a ragged breath.

A uniformed police officer came tearing around the corner, focused on room 5128. He momentarily paused when he caught sight of her but drew his pistol and continued toward the room.

"Owl Creek police," he called out. "The hospital has been placed on lockdown. Come out with your hands up."

"All clear," Max said. "Max Colton with the FBI here. It's okay to come on in."

Relieved to hear his voice, Della got to her feet. Her legs were so weak it took her a moment to stand.

Another policeman ran up and joined the first one inside the room.

Slowly, people began to appear. First the nurses, three or four of them, cautiously gathering nearby. Several curious patients appeared in their doorways, peering down the hall but too afraid to leave their safe spaces.

One of the cops came out of the room and stood guard in the doorway. He shook his head as Della approached. "Ma'am, I'm going to have to ask you to stay back."

"I understand." Still, Della tried to see around him, needing to put her eyes on Max.

"Della, don't come in here," Max said, apparently having heard the officer. "The coroner is on the way. I'll be with you as soon as I can."

Stunned, Della stepped away. If they'd called the coroner instead of medical personnel, that meant someone hadn't survived. Who'd been killed? The shooter or Maisy? She didn't know. At least Max had spoken to her and let her know he was okay.

Though she had no business behind the nurses' station, Della found a chair and dropped into it. More people arrived, security people as well as police officers. The hallway near room 5128 got more crowded.

Time slowed to a crawl. And Max remained inside the room. She glanced at the wall clock and realized there was no way she'd be making it into work on time.

Resigned, she sent Sebastian a text, letting him know she was at the hospital and promising she'd be there as soon as she could.

Sebastian instantly texted back. Della! Are you okay?

After she explained she'd been visiting someone and would fill him in on the details later, he sent her a simple thumbs-up emoji.

Finally, Max emerged, disheveled. He appeared to have shut down. She understood. Sometimes closing off emotions was the only way to survive. He might be an experienced FBI agent, but shooting someone must have affected him. She could only hope the man he'd shot would survive.

"Are you all right?" she asked, her heart going out to him.

"Not really." Grim-faced, he took her hand. "Let me get you to work. I've called this in, but I still need to fill out a report. There's always a ton of paperwork."

Suspecting sympathy would be the last thing he'd want, she waited until they were inside the truck to ask him what had happened. She knew better than anyone how talking could help.

A muscle worked in Max's jaw. "The officer who

was supposed to be guarding the room went to investigate when the power cut out. The instant he left his post, the shooter saw his opportunity and slipped inside the room. We got there right after that, apparently. But we were too late."

"He killed Maisy?" she asked, aghast. "Did he also cause the power outage?"

"Yes, he did. Both things." Max backed out of the parking space and headed toward the exit. "She didn't deserve this. None of it. She survived a brutal attack only to be murdered in the one place she should have been safe."

"Oh no." Della covered her mouth as she blinked back tears. "I'm so sorry. But why? Why would anyone do such a thing?"

He glanced at her and grimaced. "Because now she won't be able to testify against the man who attacked her."

Shocked despite everything, she took a moment to process this. "That would mean the man who killed her had something to do with her attack."

"Most likely," Max responded.

Despite all the sadness, her heart skipped a beat at the thought her cousin's killer would be brought to justice. "What about the shooter? Is he in custody now?"

Max barely looked at her. "No. He's dead. He refused to drop his weapon. I had no choice but to take him out."

"He's dead?" She couldn't hide her shock.

"It was him or me." The clipped tone of Max's voice told her he wasn't good with the turn of events either. He hadn't just shot a man. He'd killed him.

Not sure how to comfort him, she went with the only

thing she could think of. She reached out and squeezed his shoulder. "I'm sorry."

Though he tensed, he didn't brush off her hand. "Me too."

Unsure what else to say, she swallowed. Appearing to sense this, Max turned up the radio, just loud enough to make conversation impossible.

Miserable for him, she got the message. When he pulled up in front of Crosswinds, he turned to her before she got out. "I'll talk to you later," he said.

The flinty look in his eyes made her heart squeeze. Aching for him, she kept her chin up. "I'll consider that a promise."

Then, before she could reconsider, she gave him a quick kiss before opening her door and getting out. He drove away without a backward glance. She stood watching until she could no longer see his truck.

Now the exhaustion from the trauma set in. Her legs very nearly buckled, but she held herself straight and managed to make it inside.

Sebastian took one look at her and motioned her to a chair. "Sit," he ordered.

Grateful, she dropped into the chair and put her head in her hands. She took several deep breaths, aware she needed to get a grip on herself. And she had no doubt she would. She was a fully trained search and rescue volunteer and knew how to react to stressful situations.

But what had happened today was gut-wrenchingly different. Immediate. More personal.

"I know you said you were visiting someone in the hospital." Sebastian knelt next to her. "But you honestly don't look good. Want to tell me what's going on?"

She made herself look up. More deep breathing. When she finally felt calm enough, she told him everything, though she left out the part about Max spending the night at her house.

Sebastian listened, one brow raised. When she finished, her voice finally trailing off, he shook his head. "What I don't understand is why Max Colton is involving you in any of this. He put you in danger by allowing you to accompany him to the hospital."

"He didn't *allow* me to do anything," she retorted. "I asked to speak with this woman. I thought I might help her, since I recently went through something similar."

Sebastian considered. "Of course you did," he finally said. "You have a huge heart. But the fact that Max asked for the police to guard the hospital room tells me he was worried there might have been trouble."

"There shouldn't have been." She tried not to think of how terrified she'd been that Max would get hurt or worse.

"Hey, does that mean the guy who attacked you was killed?" Sebastian asked.

"No. Hal is still locked up at Owl Creek PD. It wasn't him."

"Seriously?" Sebastian shook his head. "Then who was it?"

"Now, that I don't know. I'm guessing I'll find out soon enough."

Feeling slightly better, she pushed to her feet. "I'd better get to it. I've got a lot of work to do. Those dogs won't train themselves."

As she headed toward the kennels, Sebastian kept

pace with her. "How's George doing?" he asked. "Austin PD has been asking for a report."

Thinking of George, an incredibly smart Belgian Malinois, she grinned. "We're working on scent training," she said. "You're definitely welcome to stay and watch."

Sebastian smiled back, clearly relieved at her return to normalcy. "Usually, I'd love to. But I've got my own training to do. I have an appointment to take Clyde down to the fire station. We're working on noise desensitizing."

"Have fun." She gave him a cheery wave before grabbing a leash and collar and going to collect her first dog of the day.

Three hours and three dogs later, Della decided to take a break for lunch. Though she didn't have her car or anything to eat, she was hoping she could talk one of the women working the store into bringing her back something.

Luckily, Pepper was just about to leave for lunch. Della handed her a ten and asked her to bring her back something. Eyeing Della with concern, Pepper agreed and left.

Since it would be close to an hour before Pepper came back with food, Della decided she might as well go ahead and get in some training with her next dog. A young female German shepherd, Zsa Zsa had completed the first part of her training with Sebastian and was now ready to work with Della.

Responsive and eager, Zsa Zsa was an absolute joy to work with. Della took her around out back, where they'd set up an obstacle course of sorts. Della had continued Sebastian's work training the dog on hand signals, and today's task would be locating—and signaling—one particular item among various items Sebastian had buried. These things had been treated with various scents like lavender, lemon, peppermint and chamomile. Once Della let her know which scent she needed to locate, the dog set off. One at a time, Zsa Zsa made short work of finding each item. When she'd completed the work, in record time, Della gave her a piece of her favorite treat, a smelly liver bite, as reward.

Proud and tired, Zsa Zsa went back to her kennel run, where she immediately sprawled out for a nap, panting happily. Della watched her for a moment, and then returned to the office area. Pepper should be back any moment now with food.

Della opened a can of sparkling water and took a long drink. She considered texting Max but decided to leave him alone for now. In attempting to deal with the shooting, he'd retreated inside himself. She wished he'd let her help him, but she figured he'd reach out when he was ready. Since he hadn't said he'd be back to take her home, she wasn't sure if she'd need to find her own ride or not. She'd figure that out when the time came. Right now, she was doing her best to avoid thinking about what had happened at the hospital. If and when she allowed herself to break down, the only person she wanted to be around was Max.

Killing another human being had a way of shaking anyone the hell up, no matter how seasoned an FBI agent or police officer they might be. Even if doing so had been in self-defense.

After dropping Della off, Max released his iron grip

on his emotions. He hadn't wanted her to see him lose his composure. Hell, he didn't even want to look himself in the mirror right now. He'd gone over the scenario in his mind a hundred times and couldn't see any other possible result. It truly upset him that he hadn't been able to save Maisy. She hadn't deserved any of this. Once again, pure evil had won.

Even knowing all this, something had broken inside him and would take a while to heal. No matter how he spun it, a man had died by Max's hand. Pending ID, they'd be looking for something to tie the guy to the serial killings. If they didn't find anything, they'd be right back where they'd started, with no leads and nothing to go on.

He was in such a foul mood he actually contemplated making the two-hour drive to Boise, to deal with the paperwork in person. But that wouldn't make the tedious chore go by any faster and would add four hours of drive time to an already long day.

Instead, he found himself back at the ranch, glad his father and brothers were out working the land. The last thing he wanted would be to have to make nice with anyone, even his own family.

Especially his family. They were practical and down-to-earth. He suspected they'd never understand how shaken he felt. Taking a life wasn't something he or any other agent he knew took lightly. Even if he knew with certainty that man would have killed him if he hadn't taken the shot.

It had happened before, once. Judging by that experience, Max knew he just needed time to sort out his complicated emotions.

Except this time, he'd involved Della. The realization that he might have placed her in danger weighed equally on his mind. When she'd asked if she could speak with Maisy, he'd been touched by her desire to help. And while he'd asked the police to place a guard outside the room, he hadn't really thought anyone would try to harm a bedridden woman inside of a hospital. He should have known better.

It had all gone south and turned into one giant cluster. Right now, he couldn't stop blaming himself.

Grabbing a can of cola from the fridge, he sat down at the kitchen table and opened his laptop. Even on the best of days, he found doing the endless paperwork annoying, and today would be no exception. In fact, it would be worse. For the first time since this case had begun, they'd finally gotten a break. But young Maisy, who'd been lucky enough to get away, hadn't managed to make it out alive. Not only would she not be able to testify, or pick her assailant out of a lineup, but she wouldn't ever be able to enjoy all the life experiences that growing older brought.

Halfway through the multiple forms, Brian called. Max had left him a terse message on the drive home, filling him in on the details of what had happened.

"I've spoken with police chief Stanton," Brian said. "He wants to hold an immediate presser and announce that we've neutralized the serial killer. It will help all the citizens of Owl Creek—and the tourists—regain their sense of safety."

"But we don't know that guy actually was the serial killer," Max protested.

"Who else would he be?" Brian pointed out. "I mean,

come on. Why would this man murder the only woman who managed to escape the serial killer? He didn't want to be identified."

Max's gut twisted. "I really think we need to investigate this more. We need something that actually ties him to those women we found up in the mountains. Right now, we have nothing."

"I think it's enough." The finality in Brian's tone told Max his SAC's mind was made up. "You know we've been under a lot of pressure to wrap up this case."

"Does that mean you've agreed to do the press conference?" Max asked, though he already knew the answer.

"We've decided to let Owl Creek PD handle that," Brian answered. "They've been instructed not to release any information about you as the agent who took the killer down."

"Thanks." Jaw clenched, Max found himself rubbing the back of his neck. "If it's all the same to you, I'd prefer to quietly continue investigating. I honestly don't believe this was our guy."

Brian went quiet, which was never a good sign. "I'm sorry, Max," he finally said. "But I'm going to need you to stand down and head back to Boise. This investigation has been closed."

"I'm going to have to take some personal leave." Max surprised himself but kept going. "It's been a little rough dealing with shooting and killing someone."

"Understood. How long do you need? A couple of days?"

"Two weeks," Max answered. "I've got some vacation time built up that I'd like to use."

"I know what you're doing here," Brian warned. "And it's not a good idea."

"I don't know what you're talking about," Max replied, even though they both knew he did. "I'm just needing to spend a little time with my family here in Owl Creek."

Brian snorted. "Fine. Just stay away from that press conference. It's this evening at five thirty at the Owl Creek Police Department. They're timing it so it can go live on the local news at six."

Biting back a curse, Max promised to avoid city hall like the plague. Ending the call, he resisted the urge to throw his phone across the room.

They were closing the case. How in the hell did they think doing that without any conclusive evidence would bring justice to any of those poor murdered women?

He had no idea how he was going to tell Della.

Turning his attention back to the reports, he focused and worked with a savage intensity until he'd finished. Since he'd dropped Della off at Crosswinds and she didn't have her Jeep, he needed to find out what time she needed to be picked up.

He sent her a text before he made himself a sandwich. A few minutes passed before she texted back.

Sorry, I was eating lunch. You can pick me up if you want or I can try to find a ride home. I should be finished here around 4.

He sent a quick response, letting her know to expect him then.

Three dots appeared, indicating she was typing. Want

to grab dinner on the way home? I have to eat early, since I've got a Basic Manners class to teach at 7.

Yes! he sent back, liking the way he felt hearing her use the word *home* instead of *my place*. Since he knew Hal would likely be released on bond today, Max intended to go up to Crosswinds with Della. Though he doubted Hal would be foolish enough to try something so soon after being released, Max wanted to make sure to be there in case he did. And then he went to pack a bag, just in case she let him spend the night with her again. He really hoped she would.

He pulled up in front of Crosswinds promptly at four. Della must have been watching for him, because she came out the front door before he'd even had time to shut off the engine.

"Hey," she said, sliding into the passenger side and leaning over to kiss his cheek. "I don't know about you, but today feels like the longest day ever."

"Yes, it does." He studied her. Though she smiled, it didn't quite reach the seriousness in her gaze. "How are you holding up?" he asked.

Looking away, she shrugged. "Okay, I guess. As long as I keep busy, I haven't had time to think too much about it. How about you?"

Instead of answering directly, he told her about his conversation with Brian. "They're having a press conference at five thirty tonight to let the public know they're closing the case."

"Oh, I wish I could see it in person," she said. "But since I need to eat, let Charlie out and go back to work later, I'll have to settle for watching on TV."

Whatever reaction he'd expected from her, it hadn't

been that. "I'm going to keep digging," he said. "I promise you."

Tilting her head, she eyed him. "Why? You don't think the guy you shot was the serial killer?"

"It's possible he was, but there's an equal chance it could have been someone else."

"I get that." She sighed. "And I understand. I hope you're wrong, but I know that you have a job to do."

Though he probably should have shut up right then and there, he owed her the truth. "It's not my job any longer. The FBI considers this case to be closed."

"I see." Her voice wavered, just slightly. "Does this mean you'll be leaving Owl Creek and going back to Boise?"

"Eventually. But I'm taking a couple of weeks off. So you won't be getting rid of me for a little longer."

"That's good." Instead of looking at him, she began doing something on her phone. He couldn't tell if the idea of him leaving bothered her or not. It sure as hell did him. The idea of living two hours away from her gutted him.

They'd pulled into her driveway before he remembered she'd wanted to pick up something to eat. He parked but kept the engine running.

"It's okay," she said, when he reminded her. "I'll just order a pizza. Usually they can get it here in thirty minutes or so."

"Pizza sounds great," he said, killing the engine. "But only if you let me buy it."

Smiling, she shook her head. "I keep the app on my phone. I've already ordered. It will be here soon."

"Will you let me pay you back?"

"Nope." She hopped out of the truck. "But I'll let you pay next time."

Following her inside the house, he didn't comment.

As usual, Charlie greeted them enthusiastically. They all went outside so the Lab could roam around the backyard and take care of business.

"I'll be bringing him into work this evening," she said, still avoiding looking directly at Max. "He'll be doing some basic command demonstrations for the class. He loves that."

The stiffness of her posture told him something bothered her.

"Della?" He touched her arm.

Slowly, she turned her face to look at him. "Yes?"

"What's wrong?"

Instead of answering, she shook her head. "I just need a minute."

Not sure if it was delayed reaction to what had happened in the hospital or something else, he nodded. "Would you like a hug?"

"I would."

He wrapped her in his arms, loving the way she molded her body to his. She held on tightly, and some of the tension seemed to leach out of her.

"Do you want to talk about it?" he asked.

"Maybe later." She stepped away, brushing her hands off on her jeans. "Right now, I really just want to eat. I'm starving."

Once they'd gone back inside, it didn't take long before the doorbell rang, signaling the arrival of their pizza. When Della went to answer, Charlie stayed put. He wagged his tail and watched alertly, but he didn't bark.

A moment later, Della came back with the pizza. "Good boy, Charlie." Setting the box down on the table, she went to get some plates. "I hope you like pizza with everything on it," she said, with a wry smile. "I probably should have asked before I ordered a Supreme."

Suppressing the urge to kiss her, he dropped into a chair. "I'm pretty easygoing with pizza. I like all kinds. I'm particularly fond of Canadian bacon and pineapple."

"Eww." She made a face. "Pineapple does not belong on pizza."

"Have you ever tried it?" he asked.

Taking a seat before answering, she opened the box and pulled out a slice. "No. And I don't intend to. I know what I like."

He reached and got himself two. "So do I," he said, aware she didn't have a clue that he wasn't talking about pizza.

They ate in companionable silence for a few minutes. Then Della grabbed the remote and turned on the news.

Live at the Owl Creek Police Department was emblazoned across the top of the screen. The woman reporter spoke excitedly into her microphone. "We're here at a press conference just called by the Owl Creek police. Word has it that they're about to give us some news on the serial killer."

As if on cue, the camera cut to the Owl Creek police chief standing next to the mayor. For this one, Skipper Carlson had even put on a sports jacket, though he still wore his Wranglers and Western boots. Police chief Kevin Stanton was, as usual, in full uniform.

Struggling to contain his disbelief, Max listened while the events of earlier were described, starting with Maisy's rescue and ending with the killer being taken out by an un-named FBI agent. "While we are thrilled to have brought this case to a close, unfortunately the victim did not survive the shooting."

Following the statement, the reporters began asking questions. Max could hardly stand to listen when he knew damn well there had been no conclusive evidence to link the man who had shot Maisy to the other killings.

"What's wrong?" Della asked, turning the volume down on the TV. "You look kind of angry."

"I am." He shook his head. "I just want you to know I am going to keep investigating this case, even without the Bureau's blessing. I won't give up."

"Thank you," she said. "I'm certain that if anyone can find Angela's killer, it's you."

Chapter 13

Switching off the TV, Della told Max she needed to get ready for work. Instead of taking that statement as a hint to leave, he didn't move. "I hope you don't mind," he said. "But I'm going with you."

Touched, she shrugged. "That's up to you. Too bad you don't actually have a dog. If you did, I bet you'd learn a thing or two."

"I'm sure I will anyway," he replied. "You never know. Someday, I'll get a dog of my own. I'm partial to boxers."

This sent a flush of happiness through her and made her laugh. "Do your research before you get one. Those are a special breed for sure, but they're not for everyone."

"They seem like they'd make good emotional support animals," he said, surprising her. "For times like today, while I'm struggling to process how I feel about taking a life."

Stunned and relieved that he was finally opening up to her, she placed her hand lightly on his shoulder. "Do you want to talk about it?"

"Do you have time?" he asked. "Maybe we should discuss this later."

The rawness of his voice made her eyes sting. "I have an hour before my class starts. But if you'd like my undivided attention, which you definitely deserve, you're welcome to stay the night. That way we can take all the time we need."

Her use of the word *we* clearly didn't escape him. "You need to talk too, don't you?"

"Yes." She kept her answer short and sweet, not wanting to allow all the painful emotions to come flooding back. "But not before I have to teach this class. I can't let myself fall apart right now."

Gaze locked on her, he slowly nodded. "That makes sense. And yes, I'd love to spend the night. In fact, I packed a bag just in case you asked."

Joy knifed through her, both unexpected and welcome. At a loss for words, she simply nodded. Mumbling something about needing to get ready for work, she hurried down the hall.

Inside her bedroom, she closed the door and stared at herself in the mirror. Flushed, almost glowing, she shook her head at her own foolishness. She might as well enjoy Max while he was still in Owl Creek, because he'd made it plain he'd be going back to Boise. She sure as hell didn't plan to tell him how big her emptiness would feel once he'd gone.

She brushed her hair and put it up in a ponytail. The jeans, T-shirt and sneakers she'd put on that morning would be fine. She always looked forward to these classes. Watching that moment when owner and dog finally connected made her happy with her decision to teach.

When she returned to the other room, she stopped and stared. Max had taken a seat on the couch and Charlie had climbed up there next to him. Her dog had his big head in Max's lap, gazing up at him adoringly while

Max stroked his fur. She'd never seen Charlie act like that with anyone else, not even Sebastian. While he was a friendly dog and genuinely enjoyed being around people, he seemed to have taken a real shine to Max.

The sight made her chest ache. If ever anyone should have a dog of their own, Max should.

Catching sight of her, Max smiled. "Guess what? I got a text from Angus at Angus's Whatnots. He's sold out of my handmade patio furniture and wants me to deliver more ASAP."

Thrilled and proud, she grinned back. "I hope you have more made."

"I do. There are several pieces that are ready to go. And I've got more in various stages of production."

"Do you do all of the work yourself?" she asked, genuinely curious.

"I do." Expression pensive, he made a face. "I've realized that little hobby of mine has become something I can't live without." He gave Charlie one final pet, and then stood. Charlie jumped down as well. "Ready to go?"

"Yes." She clipped a working harness and lead on her dog, stifling a yawn with her hand. "You know, I'd like to watch you work sometime, if you don't mind."

On the way out to his truck, he didn't immediately respond. She opened the passenger door and moved the seat up, motioning for Charlie to get in the back. He hopped inside and sat patiently while she secured his harness to one of the seat belt receptacles.

Once she'd gotten Charlie situated, she moved her seat back and climbed in. When she glanced at Max, surprising an intense look of tenderness on his face, she found herself choking up. For no reason at all.

"What?" she asked, making her voice grumpy to hide her emotions.

"You're beautiful," he said softly. "And yes, I'd love for you to come to my workshop and watch how I work."

"Thanks." Buckling her seat belt, she gave herself a stern talking-to. Not only did she have a class to teach, but both she and Max had been through a lot in one day. No need to let things get too heavy.

Max started the engine. But instead of shifting into Reverse, he half turned in his seat so he faced her.

"You're the first person who's ever asked to see how I make furniture," he said, his voice gruff. "My brothers and father barely tolerate me taking space for my little hobby, as they call it. My sister, Lizzy, thinks I just use it as an excuse to have a man cave or something. Other than Angus, who has a vested interest since he gets a cut, no one else pays any attention to it."

"I can tell it's important to you," she said, touched. "Plus, you're so very good at it."

He laughed and finally shifted into Reverse. "Thanks."

They arrived at Crosswinds with fifteen minutes to spare before her class started. Though Della knew arriving with Max would cause a bit of a stir, she realized she didn't care. If her coworkers wanted to gossip about her, so be it. Max might have a reputation around town, but that man wasn't the same person as the man she'd come to know.

None of her class had arrived yet, which meant she'd get a few minutes to set up. With Charlie trotting proudly on her left side and Max flanking her on the right, she waved at the two women at the desk and continued to the working arena. For their part, they both stared. She was sure there'd be questions later.

Putting Charlie in a sit-stay, she started placing the partitions. With a full class, she liked to keep everyone in their own space until their turn came. She had them work their dog individually in the center of the ring so the others could watch and learn.

One by one, her students arrived. A few of the women eyed Max, who'd taken a chair and sat quietly in the corner. He looked big and brooding and handsome. Della truly couldn't blame them. It was all she could do to not stare at him herself. But in her SAR work, she'd long ago learned how to tune out distractions. She'd use every ounce of that training to pretend Max wasn't there.

"Today we are learning one of the most important commands," she told her class. "Recall. If you're going to teach your dog only one thing, this would be it."

Teaching interested students, both human and canine, gave Della a much-needed boost of energy. Charlie seemed to enjoy it too. Holding his tail high, he proudly put himself through his paces on command, demonstrating a perfect recall among other things.

By the time the class ended, she felt much better. Still a tiny bit shaky, but closer to normal than she had been all day.

A few people approached her with questions. She answered them with ease and gave each of their dogs some attention as well.

Finally, the last one left. She and Charlie headed over toward Max. He stood as they approached, the intensity in his gaze sending a shiver through her. Her body instantly responded. Dang, this man sure could get her wound up.

Normalcy, she reminded herself.

"Are you ready to go?" she asked.

"Sure." Cocking his head, he considered her. "Would you like to stop by the ranch and check out my workshop?"

Though he'd made the question sound casual, she knew how important this was to him. Plus, it secretly thrilled her that he'd asked.

"Why not?" she replied. "There's still plenty of daylight left. As long as no one minds if I bring Charlie."

"They won't even know. We'll avoid the house."

"Ah, I see," she teased, telling herself that this didn't sting. "Avoiding the family so they don't ask too many questions. I get it."

Expression serious, he shook his head. "That's not it at all. If you want to meet my dad, we can make a quick stop. You already met my two brothers at the dinner the other night."

Secretly mollified, she touched his arm. "It's not a big deal."

"Good. Because if we go inside, my dad will want to have a drink and talk, and that will easily eat up an hour or longer."

Now she understood. "I get it."

The drive north out to the Colton Ranch didn't take too long. Though Della had lived in the area for years, she mostly stuck to town and the mountain hiking paths. She found herself admiring the landscape, feeling like a tourist. Rolling pastures, herds of cattle and the occasional grove of trees made her feel almost as if she'd traveled to another state.

Finally, they turned off the main road and drove under an arched sign that read Colton Ranch.

"How much land does your family have?" she asked, noticing how the same color and type of fencing stretched as far as she could see.

"Eight hundred acres," he answered. "We farm and raise cattle. Or they do," he amended. "I got away from here as soon as I could. I knew at an early age that I wasn't cut out to be a rancher."

"I get that. While I never even thought about living anywhere else than Owl Creek, ever since I was a little girl, I knew I'd be working with dogs."

Expression curious, he glanced at her. "How'd you get started in all of that?"

"Lots of research on the internet. And I took classes. Some of them I had to travel a good distance for. I took one in Denver. Another in Orange County, California. I worked, I studied, I got my certifications. And I lucked out when Sebastian let me come work with him."

Max nodded. "He's well respected around here." He grinned. "And once he and Ruby marry, he'll be related."

"They're a good match."

"Look." He pointed. "There's the main house."

On a slight rise in the distance, she could see a large red structure. The closer they got, she realized it appeared to be a rustic house that had been made out of a renovated barn.

"It's been in the family for a long time," Max said. "See all those other odd-shaped additions? Those were all rooms that were built later. After my mother left, my dad put in a pool and a guesthouse. My oldest brother, Greg, lives in the guesthouse now."

She nodded. "I'm guessing your father and other brother live in the main house?"

"Yes. And I stay there when I'm in Owl Creek."

They drove slowly past the stately red house but didn't stop. She couldn't help but admire how, despite the bright color, the structure seemed to complement the landscape. The sun had started its journey toward the horizon, though darkness wouldn't come for another couple of hours. This time of day had long been one of her favorites. Backlit by the sun, the bright orange, shot through with pinks and reds, made the sky and the landscape seem to glow.

There were numerous other structures spread out over the rolling pastures.

"That's the guesthouse," Max said. "The main horse barn, and those are storage buildings. My workshop is there, attached to that one."

Enchanted, she waited until he'd parked and killed the engine before jumping out. Then, because she didn't want to seem too eager, she clasped her hands together until he joined her.

"It's not much," he explained as he unlocked the door. "A lot of woodworking tools, wood, paint and stain. I don't use this space for anything other than a workshop."

When he opened the door and turned on the light, he stepped aside so she could enter.

Inside, there were at least ten chairs, several settees and various other pieces in various stages of work. What caught her eye immediately was that he'd made different types of pieces. Some were rustic, like the ones she'd purchased. There were also a few made in a more modern, sleek style.

The area appeared well organized, at least to her untrained eyes. Woodworking machinery took up one entire space, and he'd made what looked like a small painting-booth-type area in the back corner. For a one-man operation, she thought it looked incredibly efficient.

"How long have you been doing this?" she asked, trailing her fingers across the back of one of his unpainted pieces.

"I started in high school," he replied. "Working with wood has always been a way to release tension. Of course, when I was in college, it was much more difficult to get back here and make time for this. Summers were always when I got the most done."

"Wow. That's amazing. These days, with you living in Boise and having such a time-consuming job, how do you find the time?"

Her question made him grimace. "I don't get to do it as much as I'd like. I have a smallish apartment in Boise, so it's not like I can move some of this there to work on."

"These are all so beautiful," she said, meaning it. "I bet you could make a living doing this if you wanted to."

He laughed. "Maybe so, but not much of one. Right now, it's a nice hobby that supplements my income. To make any serious money, I'd have to expand. I'd need more places willing to carry my pieces."

"Or you could rent space and open your own store," she pointed out. "Set up an online catalog and sell that way too."

"Shipping prices would be astronomical," he countered.

Liking the way he didn't entirely discount her idea, she nodded. "True. I'd guess there'd be some people willing to pay it, though. And we get a lot of tourists here, especially in ski season. Something to consider, for some day in the future."

"Maybe," he agreed. "But I like the way you think."

Chest aching, she smiled, wondering if he knew how she'd come to love him, and what the heck she was going to do about it.

Max had never brought a female inside his workshop, not even during high school, when the vast majority of his dating time seemed to consist of looking for private places to make out. Even then, he'd considered his workshop a sacred space. His brothers tended to avoid it, having no time for anything that didn't directly impact the ranch. And his father appeared to have largely forgotten about it, which suited Max just fine.

Now, watching Della as she roamed the small space, her hands caressing the wood, an expression of wonder lighting up her beautiful face, he realized she actually got it. No one in his family understood how happy working with the oak and pine and ash made him.

And her suggestions about growing his business had been spot-on. He'd often wondered what it would be like to have more time to build his furniture, but being an FBI agent didn't allow for him to cut his hours or adopt a flexible schedule. However, by living simply, he'd managed to amass a healthy savings account. More than enough to help him get started.

The fact that he was even considering such a thing would have shocked him any other time. But now…he wasn't sure.

Quite honestly, the thought of going back to Boise and

his empty, sterile apartment didn't sound even remotely appealing. And the fact that the Bureau wanted him to drop this case and pin the blame on someone without a single shred of evidence stuck in his craw.

He had two weeks to run his own investigation, as long as he was careful to stay under the radar. More than anything, he didn't want to let Della's cousin, or any of the women who'd lost their lives to this monster, down. If the man he'd shot actually turned out to be the serial killer, great. If not, Max wanted to make sure the right person was brought to justice.

Even more importantly, he needed to make sure no other woman suffered the same fate.

"Oh, I love this piece." Della's comment brought him out of his reverie. Blinking, he saw her crouching in front of one of his more experimental items. A small corner cabinet, whitewashed and made to look rustic. Inside, he'd placed two shelves.

"How much for this?" she asked, delight filling her gaze. "I absolutely love this, and I know just where I want it to go."

Looking at her, so filled with joy over something he'd made with his own hands, in that moment he knew he would have given her the world.

"It's yours," he said, managing to contain his emotion despite the roughness to his voice. "I'll load it up and get it to your place when I take you home."

She stared at him, her beautiful eyes wide. For a moment, he thought she might protest, but instead she pushed to her feet and rushed to him. Wrapping her arms around his waist, she hugged him tightly.

He never wanted to move again.

"Thank you," she muttered, face pressed against his chest. "How about we load it up and head out?"

"Okay." Kissing the top of her head, for the first time ever he realized he wanted to make love to her here, among all the things he valued. His body stirred and he shifted his stance so she wouldn't feel his growing arousal pressing against her.

As if she sensed this, she raised her head. "Not here. Let's go home."

Home.

Later, while Della showered, Max found himself on her back porch, sitting in one of the chairs he'd made, staring at the moon and stars, so bright in the night sky. Charlie had followed him outside and lay curled up at his feet. Max felt a sense of contentment and rightness that he hadn't ever felt before. As if he *belonged.*

Shaking his head at himself, he pulled out his phone. Though technically he was on leave, he went ahead and left a message for Caroline, asking her to call him when she was back at the office. Though he doubted the body of the shooter had been sent to her, he knew she maintained close connections with other forensic pathologists around the state. He wanted to find out if she'd heard anything about the man he'd shot.

Then he called his cousin Fletcher, who worked as a detective for Owl Creek PD. Despite the late hour, Fletcher picked up on the second ring.

"I figured you'd be calling," Fletcher drawled. "Let me save you some time. We're working on an ID for the shooter you took down. Since it's after hours and everyone has gone home for the night, I'm sure we'll know something tomorrow."

"Thank you." Relieved that Fletcher understood, Max took a deep breath. "I know everyone thinks this guy is the serial killer and considers the case closed. Including the Bureau. But I'm not so convinced. Once we find out this guy's identity, I want to work on a timeline of his whereabouts over the last couple of years."

"You do?" Fletcher sounded surprised. "I thought everyone was in agreement that you'd taken out our man."

Max coughed. "Everyone but me, I guess."

"I'm surprised the FBI is letting you continue to work on this case. From what I was told, they consider it closed. Hell, did you watch the press conference?"

"I did. And the FBI has closed the case." Max paused. "I've actually taken a couple weeks' PTO. I'm looking into this on my own."

"Wow." Fletcher let out a low whistle. "You're that unconvinced."

"Aren't you?" Max countered. "There's no other evidence. None."

"Not yet," Fletcher replied calmly. "But don't you think the fact that he killed the one woman who managed to escape him is pretty damning?"

"Possibly. But alone, it's not enough proof. This could have been an entirely separate, unrelated incident."

"Not everything has to be so complicated," Fletcher said. "You've worked in law enforcement long enough to understand that. Maybe this is exactly what it seems."

"I'd like nothing better." Max swallowed, aware he wasn't getting anywhere. "But would you mind giving me a holler once you have more info?"

"I don't mind at all. As soon as we learn more, I'll let you know."

Ending the call, Max sat for a moment, trying to think. He respected Fletcher's opinion. If Fletcher felt there might be a credible chance that the man Max had shot was the serial killer, it could be that Max was about to keep knocking himself out investigating nothing.

Still, he had to try. He'd long ago learned to trust his gut, and right now every instinct he possessed told him they were blaming the wrong man.

The sliding glass doors opened, and Della stepped outside, her hair still damp. "Hey," she said softly. "I wondered where the two of you had gotten off to."

Charlie wagged his tail but didn't raise his head. Shaking her head at her dog, Della stepped around him and took a seat in the chair next to Max.

"You look perturbed," she commented. "Is everything okay?"

"Just work stuff," he replied, not wanting to rehash the situation.

"I thought you were on leave."

He should have known she'd see right through him. He shrugged. "Just doing a little investigating on my own time. Even though I'm not going back to the office, I still want to be kept updated on the case."

"I get that." Running her hand down the arm of her chair, she stroked the wood. "These truly are beautiful pieces."

Watching her, all he could think about was how badly he wanted those hands on his skin.

As if she read his mind, she got up, took his hand and gave a tug. "Come on. Let's go inside."

The invitation in her voice made his body instantly respond. They barely made it to the couch.

As usual, their lovemaking was intense and tender.

The next morning, he woke up at sunrise. Leaving Della sleeping in the bed, with Charlie curled up at her feet, he headed for the bathroom to take a quick shower.

When he emerged, Della sat up and gave him a sleepy smile. "Morning."

The warmth in her gaze tempted him. But then Charlie barked and jumped down, trotting toward the back door.

"Would you mind letting him outside?" Della asked, yawning. "I'm going to jump in the shower."

"No problem," he said.

After he'd let Charlie out, Max made himself a cup of coffee with the intention of carrying it to the back porch. But before he could even take his first sip of coffee, Caroline returned his call from the night before.

"I hear congratulations are in order," she said by way of greeting. "You solved the case *and* took out the unsub. Way to go, Max."

Try as he might, he couldn't detect even a hint of sarcasm in her voice. He groaned. "Not you too?"

His question made her snort into the phone. "I know you have doubts, as do I, but sometimes these cases have a way of working themselves out. It seems this one did."

"Yeah, maybe so." This time, he knew better than to argue his point. Clearly, he was the only one who felt the case should remain open.

"Caroline, I called you because I need to know everything we know about the man I shot. His name, where he's from and if he has any ties to any local churches."

She went silent for a few seconds. "Are you okay, Max?"

"I'm fine. It's just bothering me that I had to kill him. I would have liked to question him, but..."

"I get that." She sighed. "You are aware that the autopsy will be done by the county, right? The local police resumed jurisdiction at our request."

"I heard," he said. "But I also know all forensic investigators talk. I'd really appreciate you filling me in on anything you might hear through the grapevine."

"You got it," Caroline responded. She hesitated a moment before continuing. "Max, I heard you were taking a short vacation. Is that true?"

He nearly groaned out loud. "Damn, news sure travels fast. Yes, I'm on a bit of PTO."

"We had a team briefing yesterday. That's how I knew," Caroline said. "Brian filled us all in on everything. He told us he didn't include you because you were off."

Which stung. Though Max couldn't really blame him. After all, it sounded as if Max had been the only one who objected to the case being closed so abruptly.

"I'm glad you're taking some time off," Caroline said softly. "Because I think this case might have become too personal to you. A little vacation away from all of this should be a good thing."

"Hopefully so." Before ending the call, he once again extracted a promise from her to call him with any information. "Even though I'm on PTO, I still want to stay informed."

She muttered something noncommittal and said goodbye.

A few minutes later, Della came strolling into the kitchen. "I need to feed Charlie," she said. "Where is he?"

"Outside." He smiled. "I left the slider cracked a bit. I assumed he'll push it all the way open when he's ready to come in."

She froze, then hurried toward the sliding door. "I

don't usually leave him out there unattended. I should have told you that."

Not understanding her concern since her backyard was completely fenced, he followed her out onto the porch.

"Charlie?" she called. "Time to eat. Charlie, come."

Nothing. A quick scan of the backyard revealed no black Lab anywhere in sight.

"Oh no." Della rushed down the outdoor stairs, moving so fast Max worried she'd fall. He hurried down after her, wondering what on earth he'd missed in the scenario.

"Charlie," she called again. "Charlie, come."

But the well-trained dog didn't respond.

A moment later, Max realized why. The side gate had blown open. And Charlie was nowhere to be found.

Chapter 14

No Charlie. Filled with an icy panic, Della found herself struggling to breathe. Panicking wouldn't help anything. If she was going to find her dog, she needed to remain cool, calm and collected.

When she caught sight of the open gate swinging in the morning breeze, she spun to face Max. "How long was he out here?" she asked, struggling to keep from sounding accusatory. "I'm just trying to figure out how far he might have gotten."

"Maybe fifteen, twenty minutes," he replied, looking worried and apologetic. "I'm so sorry. I didn't know. Hopefully, he didn't go far. Do you want to hop in the truck and go look for him?"

"Not just yet." Damned if she wasn't fighting back tears. She cleared her throat. Now was not the time to break down. "Charlie isn't the type of dog to just wander off. He's trained off lead. We also have an emergency recall command that's different than the usual one. I'm going to go out front and try that."

Striding through the open gate with Max right behind her, she looked both ways. Up and down her street. No sign of her beloved black Lab. For a moment, anguish closed her throat. She couldn't lose him. She simply couldn't.

"Della, it's going to be all right." Max touched her shoulder, his voice reassuring. "We'll find him. He can't have gone far."

For one second, she let her shoulders sag. Then she straightened, willing herself to calmness. "You're right. Let me try calling out his emergency command. If he's anywhere within hearing distance, that will bring him running."

She walked out into the middle of the street. Then, cupping her hands to her mouth to amplify her voice, she called out, "Charlie, URGENT! COME."

Certain this would bring her dog barreling toward her, she waited. When she still didn't see him, she took a deep breath and tried again, louder. "CHARLIE! URGENT! COME."

Her words seemed to echo off the deserted street. Still no sign of Charlie. If any of her neighbors were still sleeping, she knew she'd likely woken them.

Next door, the front door opened, and her uncle Alex stepped out. Catching sight of her and Max, he shook his head and went back inside without speaking. Neither he nor her aunt had spoken to Della in days. In fact, it seemed they'd gone out of their way to avoid her.

She was disappointed. But none of that mattered now. She had to find Charlie. "Let's drive around the neighborhood," she said. "If he didn't respond to the emergency recall command, he's got to be out of earshot."

"Come on." They ran for his truck. He started it remotely with his key fob before they were even inside. "Which way?" he asked, backing out of her driveway.

"Left." She pointed. "When we take walks, he likes to visit with a couple of the dogs out in their backyards."

Her voice broke halfway through, but she kept her chin up and her eyes peeled. Max drove slowly down the street. She had her window open, and she leaned out a little bit, scanning the bushes and the backyards for a sight of her dog.

"He's got to be around here somewhere," Max said. "Don't worry. We'll find him."

Instead of answering, she nodded. She didn't tell him it wasn't like Charlie to wander off. Of course, he'd never been tempted by a wide-open gate while unsupervised either.

Still, she couldn't blame Max. He hadn't known.

One time around the block, and still no sign of her boy. The dogs he usually interacted with were outside, standing by their chain-link fences, tails wagging.

"We need to broaden the search," Max announced. "We'll move out another block and go around."

Speechless with worry, she nodded. She had taken Charlie for walks that way as well. "There's a pet llama in a small pasture at the end of the next street. Charlie loves to visit with her."

"We'll stop by there," he said. Still driving slowly, they rounded the corner and headed up in the direction of the llama.

Della leaned out her window, scanning, searching, for even the slightest flash of black fur. Charlie couldn't have disappeared. Unless someone had grabbed him and taken him away in a vehicle.

No. She refused to let her thoughts skitter off in that direction. He'd turn up here soon. He had to.

As they approached the next corner, she saw the llama standing at the fence, staring down the street. Della looked in that direction but didn't see anything.

"Hey, there," she said, using that particular crooning tone the llama had always seemed to like. "Have you seen my Charlie?"

The animal cocked its head, listening.

"Too bad he can't talk," Max said.

They continued slowly past. At the next intersection, Max turned right. "Look!" He pointed.

Two blocks up, on the opposite side of the street, a man walked with a large black dog on a leash. Seeing this, Della felt her heart begin to race. "That looks like Charlie," she breathed.

Max sped up. As they drew closer, Della realized that man had her dog!

"Charlie!" Opening her door, she jumped out of the truck while it was still moving. As her boy fought the man with the leash, trying to get to her, she rushed over.

"Excuse me. That's my dog," she called out, sprinting toward them. The instant he heard her voice, Charlie began to struggle in earnest to break free. Clearly startled, the man let the leash go and took a step back.

With a glad bark, Charlie leaped for her. His entire body quivered, and his tail whipped furiously. Dropping to her knees on the sidewalk, she opened her arms and took her boy in. He was so happy to see her that he nearly knocked her backward with his enthusiastic greeting. He kept licking her face and making soft chuffing sounds as he tried to get as close to her as possible.

Overwhelmed with relief and joy, Della let the tears

fall freely. Charlie tried to lick them away, which made her laugh.

"What's going on here?" Catching up to them, Max addressed the stranger who'd had Charlie.

"I was out walking and found this dog," the man said, sounding bemused. "He came right to me when I called him. I used my belt and managed to get him leashed up. There's a vet's office a few blocks that way, so I was taking him in to see if he has a microchip. That's when you two drove up."

Arms around a still-wiggling Charlie, Della looked up and smiled. "Thank you from the bottom of my heart. The side gate blew open and he disappeared. I can't tell you how much he means to me."

"It looks like he feels the same way about you," the man replied, smiling back. He quickly put his belt back on, buckling it. "I'm just glad it all worked out." With that, he walked away.

Frowning, Max watched him go. "Good thing we came up on him before he made it to his vehicle."

"What do you mean?" Della asked. "He said he was out for a walk."

"Maybe so, but look. He's getting into that Toyota parked under that tree."

Looking up, she watched as the man drove off. "Wow. You're right. I wonder if he was trying to drag Charlie over to his car."

"Maybe so. But I guess it doesn't matter. We got him back."

"Thank goodness." She returned all her attention to her beloved dog.

"Again, I'm so sorry," Max said. "This happened on

my watch. I'd never have forgiven myself if anything had happened to Charlie."

"All's well that ends well. But still, I'm putting a lock on that gate," she vowed. "This can never happen again. Ever."

"I agree." Holding out his hand, Max helped her get up. "Let's head back to the house."

Throat tight, she nodded. As she moved toward the truck, Charlie kept himself close, always with part of him up against her leg.

Once they were all inside the truck, Max started it up and drove back to the house. Della glanced at the dashboard clock, surprised to realize that nearly an hour had passed. Still, they'd started so early that she wouldn't even be late for work.

Neither she nor Max spoke on the short drive back home. When they pulled up into the driveway, she opened the door and Charlie bounded out. She immediately headed around the side of the house toward the still-open gate. Charlie followed, close on her heels, apparently loath to let her out of his sight.

She waited until Max, who came right behind, had joined them before closing the gate. While she didn't have a lock just yet, she knew she could jam something into the hole in the gate handle so the gate couldn't be opened.

"Do you have a bolt and a nut?" Max asked. "That would work just as well as a lock."

She did. After fetching them from the garage, she rigged them up. "Perfect," she said, satisfied. "That gate will be a lot more secure now."

"Look." Max pointed. "Your dog is happy to be home."

Charlie rolled on his back in the grass, all four feet in the air, tongue hanging from his mouth. Noticing them watching him, he jumped up and shook himself, before trotting over to nudge Della's hand with his nose.

"He's definitely coming to work with me today," she said. "I'm not letting him out of my sight."

Smiling, Max nodded. "Do you have to work all day? I was planning to hike back up to that meadow and wondered if you and Charlie would like to go with me."

Though the prospect of going back to the scene where so many women had lost their lives made her stomach churn, an afternoon of hiking and fresh air with Max would be just what she and Charlie needed. She'd like nothing better. But even so…

"I'll have to see if I can shuffle things around," she replied, allowing regret to color her voice. "I've missed so much time already, and if I don't get back on schedule, the dogs I'm working with will get seriously behind." She thought for a moment. "I need to spend at least five hours at Crosswinds. If I get there at eight and skip lunch, I could be done around one."

"That'd work," he agreed, smiling. "And I can bring you something to eat on the drive up to the trailhead."

"Sounds perfect." Giving in to impulse, she kissed him. On the cheek this time, because she didn't want to get distracted by passion. "Now I just need a few minutes to get ready. Since you're picking me up later, would you mind dropping me off?"

"Not at all." He grinned. "Though you really do still need to get that broken window on your Jeep repaired."

"I know." Shaking her head, she led the way into the house. Charlie trotted along right after her, leaving Max to once again take up the rear. Della liked having him there. She felt like he was watching her back.

Pushing away her fanciful thoughts, Della excused herself and went to get ready. She dragged a brush through her now-dry hair and put it into a ponytail. Grabbing her backpack where she kept her hiking supplies, including sunscreen, she hurried back out into the living room, where Max and Charlie waited.

Max had taken a seat on the couch to wait, and Charlie had made himself at home next to him. The two of them huddled together, Charlie's head in Max's lap. Max was so engrossed in petting the dog that he didn't even realize Della had returned.

Only when Charlie spotted her and started wagging his tail did Max turn his head.

"Are you ready?" he asked, his gaze darkening as he looked at her.

Again, she felt that tug of attraction, aching to go to him and kiss him until they were both mindless with passion.

"Yep," she said instead, aware she sounded a bit breathless. "Let's get going. The sooner I can get to work, the better."

Calling Charlie to her, she clipped a lead on his collar. Usually, she just made him heel by her side on the way to her vehicle, but not after what had happened earlier. Right now, she couldn't bring herself to take any chances.

They made the short drive to Crosswinds in a companionable silence, Charlie sitting happily in the back seat. After the hellish way this day had started, this bit of comforting normalcy right now felt like a soothing balm on her nerves.

He pulled up to the front door to let her and Charlie out. "I'll see you around one," he said, leaning over to place a quick kiss on her cheek.

At the last moment, she turned her face, needing his lips on hers. He lingered a moment, before chuckling as they drew apart. The heat in his gaze made her body tingle.

"I'd better get going," she said, slightly breathless again. She grabbed Charlie's lead and waited while he jumped out of the truck. Suppressing the urge to blow Max a kiss, she turned and walked into the building without a backward glance.

With several hours to kill, Max went ahead and called Brian. Still slightly irritated that he'd been left out of the briefing, he figured he might as well get the details straight from his SAC's mouth.

"Max, good to hear from you," Brian said. "Caroline told me you'd called her earlier."

"I did," Max replied, slightly surprised. "She told me you had a team meeting yesterday to fill everyone in on the case. I'm wondering why you didn't include me."

"Because I'd already discussed it privately with you. The case is over, Max. We're considering it closed."

"I know, but I was hoping for more concrete evidence that the man I shot actually *is* the serial killer," Max said. "That's why I called Caroline. I am assigned to this case."

"Was," Brian corrected. "Past tense. Let me say this again." His tone became stern and clipped. "The case is closed. The Bureau will not waste any more time or resources on it. Do you understand?"

Max swallowed, his jaw tight. "Yes. I do."

"Which is why I asked you to drop it," Brian continued. "I know you mean well, but there was a lot of behind-the-scenes pressure on us from high-level government officials. Closed means closed." He took a deep breath. "That's an order."

It took every ounce of self-control Max possessed to not inform his boss that he could do whatever he wanted on his own time. "Understood."

After ending the call, Max allowed himself to seethe for a few minutes. Over the last several years, politics and bureaucracy had gotten worse. Sometimes, it seemed to be less about making wrongs right and more about surface appearances.

Hell, he knew better than to allow his feelings to get hurt. Once upon a time, he would have been able to shrug this off and get on with his life.

Except this time, Caroline was right. This case had become personal. Anytime he thought of Della's grief-stricken face when she'd realized her cousin had been killed, he wanted justice. More than justice. Vengeance.

How could he let this go? But Brian had made it abundantly clear that he had to, or risk losing his job.

Fuming, Max drove back to the ranch. He had a lot of serious thinking to do. And what better place to do it than in his workshop.

Thirty minutes later, after he'd vigorously sanded a new chair he'd built, most of his tension had left him. But he'd also reached a decision. He couldn't give up on the case. Especially since every gut instinct he possessed told him they were blaming the wrong guy. The killer had gone undetected for years, murdering his victims and burying them in shallow graves in a remote location. If he started up again, how long would it take for him to get noticed this time?

He'd decided to make a special batch of chairs to sell in town. Instead of his usual brown, white or black, he wanted to paint them bright colors. He'd bought yellow, red, orange, green and blue paint. Cheerful chairs, perfect for summer. He had a feeling they'd sell quickly.

Lost in his work, when he looked up to check the time, he found several hours had passed. Deciding to take a short break, he went up to the house to grab some water and use the bathroom. He'd have just about enough time to finish painting one more chair before he'd need to get cleaned up and head over to pick up Della.

Time flew, as it always seemed to when he worked on his hobby. Idly, he wondered if it would remain as joyful if it became his full-time job and only income. Somehow, he suspected it would.

His stomach growled, making him realize he'd need to stop so he'd have time to pick up lunch on the way to get Della.

Whistling a catchy little tune, Max quickly changed into his hiking gear. Grateful for the bright blue cloudless sky, he locked up and got in his truck, heading for Crosswinds. On the way there, he stopped by Burger Barn and picked up a couple of meals, including a special burger only on a bun for Charlie.

The prospect of a hike with Della and her dog felt like exactly what he should be doing on such a perfect afternoon. A trip to the meadow would definitely help him get his thinking straight. He'd been ordered to drop his investigation. Seeing the burial ground once again might help him decide if he could.

When he pulled up in front of Crosswinds, Della and Charlie came right out. Her bright smile immediately lightened his mood.

She let Charlie in first. The black Lab hopped into the back seat, clearly comfortable and relaxed. Della grinned and ruffled Charlie's fur. "Spoiled boy," she said, without a hint of regret in her voice. "Such a good dog."

Damn, she was beautiful. Max could barely tear his gaze away from her. Her smile widened again as she met his gaze. "Hey," she said, her voice soft.

When she got into the passenger seat, she leaned over and kissed him, a quick brush of her lips across his. Just that light touch had him instantly craving more.

To cover, he cleared his throat. "I brought lunch."

"That smells amazing," she said. "I'm starving."

"I hope you don't mind, but I got a plain burger for Charlie," he told her. "I don't know if you let him eat that kind of thing, but I thought he might like it."

"How thoughtful." She kissed him again, as if doing so was the most natural thing in the world. "I don't usually, but every once in a while, he can have a treat." Reaching into the back seat, she ruffled her dog's fur. "Is it okay if we eat on the way? I'm too hungry to wait until we get there."

"Sure." He felt tongue-tied, something he'd never been. "How about we chow down here? It'd be easier for me than trying to navigate some of those winding roads with a burger in one hand."

"Sounds good." With a shrug, she grabbed the food

bag. First, she handed him his burger and fries, then carefully unwrapped Charlie's. Breaking that burger into small pieces, she fed them to the eager dog, one at a time, placing each piece on one of the paper napkins. Only once Charlie had gobbled down his meal did she get her own.

Max ate quickly, barely tasting his food. He tried not to stare, but the way she practically inhaled her meal had him transfixed, somehow.

"What?" she finally asked, smiling slightly as she popped the last of her fries into her mouth. "I was hungry."

"Me too," he managed, using his thumb to gently brush a crumb from her lips.

"Thanks," she said, clearly oblivious to the way she affected him. "Let's go. I'm definitely ready to get up in the mountains."

"Are you?" he asked, starting the engine and shifting into Drive. "I worried it might be too much for you."

"Thanks." She thought for a moment. "While I confess I'm not sure how I'll handle seeing that field again, getting up in the higher altitude is always good for my soul."

"Me too."

Della seemed pensive as they drove. She looked out the side window, watching the landscape. Max managed to keep his gaze on the road.

When they turned into the trailhead parking area, there were only a couple of other cars there. He found them a spot and cut the engine. Charlie sat up in the back seat, tail wagging.

"That's the best part about going hiking on a random weekday afternoon," Della said. "I try to never come up here on the weekends." She grabbed her bag and changed out her sneakers for hiking shoes. Once she'd done this, she grabbed Charlie's leash and they got out of the truck. Max joined them, taking deep breaths of the clean mountain air.

"Let's do this!" Della offered him a high five. Then, side by side, the three of them set off on the trail leading up the mountain.

Every time he came out this way, the beauty of the Bitterroots struck him anew. He'd been troubled, and some of that tension hadn't entirely loosened its grip on him, but he suspected the fresh air and exercise would help.

"Do you want to talk about it?" Della asked, making him wonder if she'd been able to read his mind.

"Just work stuff," he replied. "Trying to figure out some things."

"Okay." She elbowed his side. "Put all of that away for now. It's a beautiful day. It'd be great if you'd enjoy it."

"I can take a hint." Giving in to temptation, he grabbed her free hand. This made her laugh and give his fingers a squeeze.

They kept their mood light almost all the way to the meadow. The sunshine felt good on his skin, but more than anything, he enjoyed being with Della. Charlie too.

As they reached the large rock outcropping that marked the last area for cell phone signal, they stopped. Della gently pulled her hand free. Charlie, still on lead, sat, waiting to see what they'd do next.

"Not too much farther." Expression pensive, Della gazed up at the rock.

He nodded, hoping she'd want to go with him but understanding why she might not. "Do you want to wait here while I hike up there?"

"Of course not. I want to go. It'll be a good training exercise refresher for Charlie. But I have to say, I'm kind of curious about what you might be hoping to find."

Since Max didn't know the answer to that himself, he wasn't sure how to respond. He finally settled on the truth. "I wanted to see it again."

"To see if it affects you the same way?" she asked.

"Not that." He made a movement with his hand. "It will still be disturbing to both of us. How could it not? It's just since we found the woman who escaped, I felt like we had our first actual lead to discovering his identity."

"Which is why he killed her," Della said.

"That's the general consensus."

"But you don't agree?" she asked. "Why else would that man go into a hospital, cut the power, enter a room that had a police guard and kill Maisy? It's only logical to think he was the killer, trying to cover up his tracks."

Pensive, he considered her words. Everyone, including his cousin Fletcher, thought the same way. He didn't understand why he appeared to be the lone holdout, steadfast in following his instincts. Maybe the time had come to admit he might be wrong?

Except what if he wasn't? That could be the kind of dilemma that kept him up at night.

Pushing the thoughts from his mind, he took a deep breath.

"Let's do this."

Because the terrain got rougher the rest of the way, they went single file, no longer holding hands. Della and

Charlie went first, and Max brought up the rear. The knowledge of where they were heading did little to dim the beauty of their surroundings.

When they reached the clearing where the team had pitched their tents, the remnants of the charred logs inside the fire circle had him remembering the first time he and Della had kissed. A quick glance at Della's pink cheeks told him she remembered it too.

Charlie, on the other hand, clearly wanted to surge forward. He stood at full alert, tail high, nose sniffing the air. Max supposed that only the fact that he'd been well trained kept him from pulling on the leash.

"He's ready to go," Della said, her attempt at a smile falling short.

"You don't have to do this," he told her, his voice quiet.

"I know." She grimaced. "But I've never been one to avoid doing hard things. I've revisited this meadow more than once in my dreams. Nothing here can hurt me anymore."

Aching with love for her, he started forward. Before, Della and Charlie had led the way, but now Max felt he had to go first. If Della were to change her mind, he didn't want to be in the way.

There, that small grove of trees. Around that, and the field stretched before him. Yellow crime scene tape fluttered in the breeze, still marking the place where so many innocent young women had met a violent end.

Max stopped, inhaling deeply as he took it all in. Della removed Charlie's leash, giving him a hand signal command that Max supposed meant the dog could roam freely.

"I asked him to go to work," Della said, her quiet voice matching the sadness in her eyes. "I know he's already checked and made sure there aren't any other buried remains, but he can always use the practice."

Side by side, they watched as Charlie checked out the area, nose to the ground. He made several circles, each one larger than the last.

"He's very thorough," Max commented.

"Yes."

Neither of them moved while the diligent canine continued searching. Finally, Charlie made it to the perimeter of the meadow, still intently searching.

"Do you call him back to you when you think he's done?" Max asked.

"I can. But in a situation like this one, where there's no danger and not a lot of other people and dogs, he'll return to me to let me know he hasn't found anything."

Sure enough, a few minutes later, Charlie came bounding back and sat in front of Della.

"Good boy," Della said, ruffling the dog's head. She glanced at Max. "I'm really glad he didn't find anything."

"Me too." Now Max forced himself to move forward, stopping to look at each area where the earth had been disturbed. His team had been careful to shovel the dirt back into each grave once the bones had been removed.

Once he'd viewed all of them, he stopped, conscious of Della watching him. Each and every woman who'd died here deserved justice. If the man Max had killed in that hospital room truly was the unsub, then they'd gotten it. If not, until more women were brutally murdered, no one would know the truth.

"Are you okay?" Della finally asked.

Returning to her, he met her gaze. "I'm thinking about leaving the FBI," he said, his heart pounding as he spoke his thoughts out loud. "I can't seem to reconcile myself with the way they're not allowing me to investigate this case. I have to know, beyond a shadow of a doubt, that this serial killer has been stopped. And right now, I don't feel comfortable with everyone believing he has."

Chapter 15

Hearing the anguish in his deep voice, Della's heart ached.

"I owe it to you," he continued. "You and your cousin and all the other victims." Gesturing around the field, he grimaced. "But without the Bureau's support, or that of the police, there's not a whole lot I can do."

She put Charlie in a stay, went to Max and took both his hands in hers. Standing on tiptoe, she kissed him. "You know what? There's no need to risk everything for my peace of mind. While I deeply appreciate you wanting to do that, I finally feel like it's going to be all right. Some questions never find their answer. Since you shot that man who killed Maisy, I can truly believe that Angela's killer is now dead and put my cousin to rest."

Max froze, his blue gaze locked on hers.

She watched several emotions flicker across his handsome face. For a stoic FBI agent, he wasn't all that great at hiding his thoughts, but maybe he only let down his guard when he was with her. The thought sent a rush of warmth through her.

"But…" he began, his brow furrowed.

"No buts." She kissed him again, lingering this time. "Let me have this. Please. It's what I want."

She felt the tension leave him. He pulled her close, slanting his mouth over hers. By the time he lifted his head, they were both breathless. Heaven help her, but she didn't know how she was going to survive once he returned to Boise. It would be like trying to breathe without air.

"Are you sure?" he asked, his voice raspy. "Because I promise I'll drop it if you're positive that's what you want."

"I am." She turned and eyed her beloved dog, who watched them both with his head cocked. "It's time to put this case to rest."

Slowly, he nodded. "Okay. Are you ready to head back down?"

What she really wanted to do was kiss him again. Instead, she ducked her head and murmured her assent. When she lifted her chin again, she realized she felt stronger and more at peace.

Charlie whined, as if to remind her she'd asked him to remain where he was. This made her smile.

"Charlie, *free*," she said, releasing him from his stay. Instantly, Charlie bounded over to her, tail wagging, tongue lolling. She clipped the leash on before glancing at Max. "Let's go."

The hike back down the trail went quickly. By the time they reached the parking area, Charlie had begun panting. She got her water bottle and poured some into the collapsible water bowl she always carried. While her dog drank, she took a few swigs herself. Next to her, Max did the same.

Then they got into his truck and drove back home. When they reached her house and Max parked, she wasn't sure if he planned to drop her off and leave or if he wanted to come in. As she opened her mouth to ask, he kissed her. "Would you like to have dinner with me?" he asked.

"Yes." She made no attempt to squelch the joy that flooded her at his question. "I can cook something if you'd like, or we can get takeout."

"I think we should go to a restaurant," he said, watching her closely, a teasing glint in his blue eyes. "Like a real date. That is, if you're not embarrassed to be seen out in public with me."

She started to protest but settled on a shrug instead. "Because of your reputation? Maybe, but I've always loved to live dangerously."

This made him laugh. "Me too. I'm in the mood for fajitas. Is Mexican food okay with you?"

"Definitely. Mexican food is always a good thing. So is a delicious frozen margarita." Hand on the door handle, she hesitated. "Would you like to come inside?"

"Of course I would, but I've got a few errands to run in town, plus I need to stop by the ranch and shower and change. I'll pick you up in a couple of hours. I'll text you when I'm on the way," he told her, his steady gaze filling her with the kind of warmth that made her long to seduce him.

Instead, she hid her disappointment with a quick nod. "Sounds good. See you soon." Opening the door for Charlie, she held his leash while he hopped out of the truck. Then she and her dog stood on her front porch and watched as Max drove away, taking a piece of her heart with him.

"Della?" Next door, her aunt Mary stepped outside

and walked slowly over, shuffling like a woman several decades older. The change in her appearance shocked Della. In the time since her aunt had learned of Angela's death, she'd seemed to age at least ten years. Sorrow had made deep lines around her eyes and mouth, and she no longer attempted to cover up the gray in her hair. Before, she'd always loved dressing in colorful Western outfits that she'd chosen carefully to match her jewelry. Today, she wore a faded T-shirt and wrinkled khaki capris with flip-flops. She had no jewelry on whatsoever.

Swallowing back the ache in her throat at the change, Della felt her smile wobble.

"Aunt Mary!" They hugged. Della couldn't help but notice how thin the older woman had become. "It's been a long time since I've seen you. How have you been?"

The instant she asked the question, she regretted it. Glancing down at her dog, she saw Charlie waiting patiently to be noticed, slowly wagging his tail.

"Not too well," Aunt Mary replied. "Alex and I are both trying to come to terms with knowing we'll never see Angela again. Knowing that the man who murdered her was shot and killed has helped a little, but not as much as I thought it would."

"That's helped me too," Della said. "But I'd really like to have some sort of celebration of Angela's life, if you and Uncle Alex are all right with that. Angela had a lot of friends here in Owl Creek."

Mary recoiled. "I don't think I can handle that. I know your uncle can't. Maybe after more time has passed. I don't know."

"I understand," Della said, even though she didn't.

"Just let me know whenever you're ready. I'll organize everything."

"I will, dear." Her aunt cocked her head. "I've noticed you've been seeing a lot of that Colton boy."

Hearing Max referred to that way made Della smile. "I have. He's a good guy."

"Is he? I'm sure quite a few other brokenhearted women here in Owl Creek thought the same thing. Please be careful, Della. You've been through a lot. Don't let him take advantage of that."

Unsure how to respond to this, Della managed a nod. "I won't. But for the record, he's not like that."

"For your sake, I hope you're right." Mary hugged her once more before turning and making her way back home. She never acknowledged Charlie's presence, not even once. This too wasn't like her. Her aunt had always fussed over Della's black Lab, even referring to him as her dog nephew.

Charlie dropped his head, his tail going still. Della ruffled his fur and dropped a kiss on his head. "It's okay, boy. She's still going through a lot."

As if he understood her words, Charlie licked her hand.

Della could only hope that someday, after the pain wore off, everything would return to a semblance of normalcy. Her aunt and uncle were the only family she had left, and she'd missed them more than she could express.

"Come on, Charlie. Let's go in."

Once inside her own house, after taking Charlie outside for a quick potty trip, Della jumped into the shower. Max's words, calling their dinner tonight an actual date, kept replaying in her head. She couldn't help but wonder if he'd begun to have the same kind of feelings for her as she had for him.

He'd mentioned quitting his job, which had stunned her. But then she'd realized he'd only said that because he wanted to continue working on the case and the FBI wouldn't let him. Not, as she might wish, because he didn't want to leave Owl Creek and her.

Shaking off her fanciful thoughts, she decided that she'd still make every effort to look her best tonight. She wanted to knock his boots off.

After drying her hair, she used her flat iron to straighten it. Then she sat down and carefully applied makeup. She rarely wore more than mascara, but for tonight she went all out. When she finished, she eyed herself in the mirror, feeling as if she looked like a completely different person. Someone beautiful and sophisticated, like the type of woman who would date a man considered a playboy.

Except in her heart, she didn't feel Max was that person anymore. Or maybe she was too naive to realize the truth. Either way, she knew better than to reveal her feelings. The last time she'd made an attempt to do so, Max had completely shut down. Which hurt, despite her going into this with full awareness that he wasn't the type of man who wanted commitment. Nor had he ever pretended to be.

Which was a shame, since he'd be so damn good at it.

She sighed. No matter what happened between them, even though she knew she'd likely see the last of him in two weeks when he returned to Boise, she was determined to enjoy the time they had left together. And in order to do that, she knew she wanted to knock his socks off on what seemed likely to be their one and only real date.

For tonight, she chose the green dress she'd bought earlier and flirty gold sandals. Long, dangly gold earrings and a few bracelets completed her look. Peering at herself in the mirror, she thought she almost looked like a completely different person. Someone glamorous, nearly beautiful. The kind of woman who would have absolutely no problem waving goodbye to a casual lover.

Even if deep inside her heart, she knew what had roared to life between them wasn't the slightest bit casual.

Shaking her head to clear it, she realized since she'd gotten herself ready, she needed to take care of her dog. Scooping out his usual amount of kibble, she turned to find him sitting and waiting in his usual place.

After she fed Charlie, she poured herself a glass of lemonade and carried it outside on the porch to drink. Charlie came with her, content to lie on the deck in the sun with his full belly.

Lowering herself into one of the chairs made by Max's own hands, she kicked off her shoes. In this moment, life felt good. She'd never been one to want anything other than the path she'd chosen, but right now she ached for a man she couldn't have. He'd return to his life in Boise and she, she'd stay here in Owl Creek, doing the things she loved.

Eventually, she realized she'd get over him. Maybe she'd meet someone else, someone who made her feel close to the same way. A man who'd welcome a simple life in the only home she'd ever known and would want to share it with her.

Except she suspected a part of her would always yearn for Max. That made her sad.

Not wanting to allow her mood to slip into melancholy, she slipped her sandals back on and pushed to her feet. Tonight, she'd allow herself to dwell only in the present. Worries about the future could come another day.

Though the summer days were long, the brightness of the day had begun to soften as the sun began its journey back toward the horizon. Since her backyard faced east, her patio stayed mostly in shadow, though long yellow fingers of sunlight made the green grass appear to glow.

Her phone chimed, letting her know she had a text. Max wanting to let her know he was on the way and would be there in twenty minutes. After sending back a message that she'd see him soon, she called Charlie and together they went inside the house. She finished her lemonade, touched up her lipstick and brushed her hair. She was as ready as she was going to be. Honestly, she didn't know why this felt like such a big deal. They'd eaten together before, even gone to the barbecue place with his entire family. Maybe because, for whatever reason, he'd made a point of calling this a date. A date. Despite the way both of them kept insisting they were only friends, she loved the idea of a date with him.

By the time his truck pulled up in the driveway, she'd managed to calm her racing heart. This was Max, after all, and she looked forward to enjoying some delicious fajitas with him.

She opened the front door, with Charlie beside her. Her dog stood at full alert, his tail wagging furiously.

Carrying a plastic-wrapped sheaf of flowers, Max

hurried up the sidewalk. When he saw her, he abruptly stopped moving and stared. "You look...amazing," he said, his voice husky, his eyes darkening.

As always when he looked at her like that, desire heated her blood. Hoping she wasn't blushing too badly, she tried for nonchalance. "Thanks."

Next to her, Charlie's entire body began to wiggle. He could scarcely contain his excitement. Her dog sure liked this man. Almost as much as she did. The thought made her smile since she considered Charlie an apt judge of character.

Meanwhile, Max continued to stare. Then, apparently remembering the flowers, he cleared his throat. He moved forward again, holding out the brightly colored bouquet. "These are for you."

Another first. There were carnations and roses, lilies and bright yellow daisies that complemented her dress.

"A summer bouquet, the florist said," Max told her. "I hope you like it."

"I do." Accepting the blooms, she motioned him inside. Then, while he bent down to greet Charlie, she took the flowers into the kitchen to put them in a vase.

Breathtaking. Even the flowers couldn't compete with Della. He had to make himself stop staring. Not wanting to gape at her as she left the room, Max crouched down and managed to focus all his attention on Charlie. All wiggles and tail wags, the big black Lab immediately rolled over for a belly rub. While Max gave it, Charlie's head lolled to one side, his tail still going, clearly over-the-moon happy.

"I know the feeling," Max told the dog. "Your mama

sure is something." He could have sworn Charlie winked at him.

The sound of Della's heels clicking on hardwood alerted him to her return.

"He's definitely a fan," she observed, standing in the kitchen doorway. The green dress made her skin appear to glow.

Still gobsmacked and trying not to show it, Max grinned and got to his feet. "The feeling is mutual. You've got a really special dog here."

"Yes. I do."

Again, he fought the urge to stare. "You look... amazing," he finally said. "Actually, you always do, but that dress..."

Her color deepened but she nodded. "Thanks." A hint of a smile played around her mouth. "I chose it because I wanted to knock your socks off."

"Well, it worked," he said, fervently. "If I wasn't starving for fajitas, we'd be staying in instead."

This had her chuckling. "You know, that would also work. But I could eat too."

"Later," he promised. "Are you ready to go?"

Smoothing down her dress, she lifted her chin and nodded. Brown eyes sparkling, she took his arm. As always, having her touch him made him realize they were meant to be together.

He couldn't leave her, wouldn't leave her. He could only hope she felt the same way about him as he did about her. She was everything a man could want in a woman. Tough and yet soft, confident and smart and funny. Not to mention, breathtakingly beautiful. All the different aspects of Della were reasons why he loved her.

That was right. *Loved.* More than he would have ever believed it was possible. At the age of thirty-four, he'd finally realized all the things he'd thought were important weren't. He'd faced the truth. About his lifestyle and career, everything really, but most especially Della and her place in his heart.

After they said their goodbyes to Charlie, he took her arm and escorted her to his truck. A slight movement at the house next door caught his eye and he looked over to see Della's aunt Mary watching from her front porch. Realizing he'd noticed her, she lifted her arm and waved. Smiling, he waved back.

When he got into the driver's seat, Della stared, wide-eyed. "My aunt waved at you."

"She did," he agreed, backing out of her driveway.

"I've been a little bit worried about her," Della admitted. "She and Uncle Alex took Angela's death really hard. I'm hoping now that the killer has been located and is dead, that might help them heal."

Located and dead. Maybe in time, he'd come to believe that as well.

Slowly, he nodded. "I hope so."

"And you're all right with this?" she asked.

"I've decided to let the case go," he replied, aware he wasn't actually answering her question. Since he didn't want her to notice, he kept his gaze on the road. "There doesn't seem to be any point in continuing to beat my head against the wall over something everyone views as over."

Would that be enough? He hoped so. Even though he seemed to be the only person in Idaho who believed the man he'd shot might not be the killer, he'd keep quiet about that and hope he was wrong. Whatever was necessary to bring Della and her family peace.

"Thank you," she murmured, lightly touching his arm. "Honestly, now that it's settled, my family and I can finally put Angela to rest. I'm hoping to talk my aunt into allowing some sort of service, a celebration of life maybe. I think Angela would have liked that."

Changing the subject, they talked about other things. She told him about some of the dogs she was training and the amazing jobs they would soon be headed to. "Law enforcement and other agencies come from all over the country to buy our dogs. Besides working search and rescue, helping these canines realize their full potential is my passion." She sighed.

He'd been that way about law enforcement once. When he'd been much younger. He wasn't sure when his job had started to become a grind or when he'd realized he hadn't made any sort of life for himself outside of work.

Well, all of that was about to change. Both excited and slightly nervous, he couldn't wait to discuss it with Della.

When they reached the restaurant, it looked like half the town had decided to go out for Mexican food. He lucked into a parking spot near the entrance. He hurried around to the passenger side of the truck and opened her door. Smiling, she let him help her out. As she emerged, she flashed a bit of her long, shapely legs, sending a jolt of raw desire through him.

Damned if she wasn't beautiful. Both inside and out.

"I'd like to eat on the patio if possible," she said, slipping her hand into his, sending another flash of heat to his core.

"Sounds good." He gave her fingers a light squeeze.

As luck would have it, there were several open spots on the outdoor patio. It seemed most people, despite the beautiful weather, wanted to wait to eat inside.

After a few minutes' wait, they were shown to a small table in a corner, underneath a large umbrella decorated with twinkling lights. The smell of homemade tortillas and sizzling fajitas filled the air, making his mouth water.

Max pulled out a chair for Della. "I like this," she said, smiling up at him as she sat.

"Me too." He lowered himself into a seat across from her. Being with her made him feel like the luckiest man in the world.

Someone brought them a basket of tortilla chips and two small bowls of salsa. The waitress took their drink orders—a large margarita for her and a Mexican beer with a lime for him—and handed them menus before taking off to help another table.

The only thing that could make this night any better would be learning Della felt the same way about him as he did about her.

"What's wrong?" she asked, tilting her head to look at him. "You seem awfully serious all of a sudden."

"I've been thinking about making some major life changes," he admitted, his heart rate increasing.

"Like what?" she asked.

"I've given the FBI one hundred percent of myself for a long time now," he explained haltingly. "I've shoved everything else to the back burner while I focused on what I thought I wanted."

Sitting quietly, she kept her gaze locked on his and listened. Tonight, in the soft moonlight with a flickering candle on their table, her skin seemed to glow. When he looked at her, he found it difficult to breathe from wanting her so badly.

"At least you love your job," she said, her tone light.

"Loved," he corrected. "Past tense."

She stared. "I'm not sure what you mean. I know you were disappointed when they asked you to drop this case, but…"

"That's only part of it." Heart pounding in his ears, he hoped like hell he hadn't misjudged her feelings. But even if he had, he wouldn't change his decision. He'd finally realized what mattered in life. "I'm ready for a change. Ever since we discussed it, I've been thinking a lot about starting my own handcrafted outdoor furniture business."

"Wow!" She took a sip of her margarita, her gaze never leaving his face. "Full-time? Instead of working for the FBI?"

Slowly, he nodded. "Yes."

The waitress chose that moment to appear, asking if they were ready to order. Startled, Max shrugged. "Beef fajitas, please. Corn tortillas, with refried beans."

"I'll have the same, except chicken instead of beef," Della said.

"Perfect." The waitress took their menus and sailed off toward the kitchen.

Max took a deep drink of his beer. "What do you think?" he asked, glad his voice remained steady.

"I'm surprised," she admitted. "You've always talked like you were super dedicated to your career."

He shrugged. "Now I'm ready to be dedicated to

something else." And *someone else*, though he let that go unsaid, at least for the moment.

Reaching for a chip, she nodded. "Good for you. I've always believed in following your passion. That's why I train dogs. For your furniture business, I know we talked about a few options. What's your plan?"

Trying not to be put off by her brisk, impersonal tone, he took a deep breath. "I've got quite a bit saved up and I'm going to look into opening my own store."

"Oh, really? Where?"

"Here in Owl Creek. I've been looking and there's a perfect place for rent off Main Street. It has space downstairs for both a workshop and a showroom, and there's even an apartment upstairs where I can live."

Were those tears in her beautiful eyes?

"Please tell me the idea of having me around all the time doesn't make you cry," he said, only half joking.

Sniffing, she shook her head. "Actually, it's the opposite. I honestly didn't know what I was going to do once you went back to Boise."

A tentative hope made him catch his breath. "Are you saying you would have missed me?"

"Yes." The simple word carried a weight of emotion. "More than I can say."

Now. Instinct had him leaning forward, reaching for her hand. "Della, I—"

"Here we are!" Their food had arrived. Max let go of Della's hand and sat back, while the waitress placed everything on the table. "Does anyone need another drink?"

"Not just yet," Max managed, gulping beer and trying to regain his equilibrium.

The moment, if that was what it had been, had vanished. They both eyed each other across the table, and then she shrugged and dug into her food. A moment later, he went ahead and did the same. Gradually, his heart rate returned to normal, though he still wasn't sure what to think.

He let her try some of his steak and she shared her chicken. He felt as if they were back on familiar ground.

As they ate the delicious meal, his mood lightened. Her smile, no longer so tentative, lit up her face.

Finally, she leaned back in her chair. "I'm too full to finish. I'll get a to-go box and take the rest of this home."

Eyeing his nearly empty plate, he laughed. "Unfortunately, I demolished mine. I'm guessing you don't have room for dessert?"

She groaned and shook her head. "Heck no. But you go ahead."

Just because he'd been craving them, he ordered the house specialty, a plate of light and fluffy sopaipillas with honey. Even though Della said she was full, she smiled and reached over to spear a couple with her fork. "I can't resist sampling these," she said, transferring them to her plate.

He loved watching her eat. Even full, she approached the dessert with passion, savoring every bite. There was something sensual in watching the way she licked her fork, getting every bit of the sweetness off it.

Once he'd paid the check, he took her arm, and they walked side by side to his truck. Driving home, he made small talk, commenting on the weather, the meal and the moonlight.

"I wonder if anyone will be gossiping about seeing

us together," she mused. "Being that you're the playboy of Owl Creek and all."

The description made him wince. "Former," he corrected. "I *was* that once. Not any longer."

They pulled up to her house just then. He walked her to her door, hoping she'd invite him inside. As she unlocked the door, she turned to face him. For one breathless moment, he thought she meant to kiss him good-night and say goodbye.

Instead, she smiled up at him. "Would you like to come in?"

Relief nearly made his knees sag. "Yes."

The instant the door opened, Charlie came barreling over to greet them. He went from Della to Max and back again, his tail wagging furiously. Della dropped to her knees and gathered her dog to her, murmuring nonsensical sweet talk to him. Max almost dug out his phone, wanting to capture the moment. Instead, he simply watched, grinning like a fool and more aware than ever of where he belonged.

"Charlie needs to go out," Della said. "Would you like to sit on the porch with me, in one of those amazing chairs that you made?"

"Lead the way."

She grabbed them both a couple of bottled waters and they settled in under the stars and full moon. A yellow porch light by the door provided additional lighting, attracting a few fluttering moths. Charlie ran down the steps, spent a few minutes taking care of his business, before coming back up to lie at their feet.

Max sipped on his water and tried to figure out the right words. He might have once been considered a playboy, but back then he'd specialized in avoiding commitment. Now he wanted nothing more.

"What do you think about my plan?" he asked, attempting to sound casual.

"You've got to follow your heart. I'm glad you decided to stay in Owl Creek," she said, the moonlight casting a soft glow on her features. "It'll be nice having you around."

"Are you sure?" he teased, aching to tell her how he felt.

"Positive."

"That's good," he said, smiling. "Because I'm planning to turn in my notice tomorrow morning."

Her eyes widened. "Have you truly thought this through?"

"I have."

Gaze never leaving his face, she nodded. "Then I guess you'd better get busy building those chairs."

Right then, he could have detailed all the various pieces he planned to make, in addition to the chairs. He could have pulled up photos on his phone, shown her the sectionals, the loungers and swings. But there'd be plenty of time for all of that later. Right now, he knew he had more important things to discuss with the woman he loved.

Leaning over, he took her hands. "Exploring a new career isn't the only reason I want to stay in Owl Creek."

"It's not?"

"Nope." Taking a deep breath, he squeezed her fingers. "In fact, pursuing self-employment is secondary. I don't want to leave you, Della. I feel we have a very real chance of making a life together, you and me."

Her cheeks turned pink as she stared at him. Was that confusion he saw in her eyes?

It felt like an eternity passed while he waited for her to respond. Heart thudding in his chest, he began to wonder if he'd misjudged her. Maybe she didn't feel the same way about him.

"Well?" he finally asked, feeling desperate. "Aren't you going to say something? Anything?"

"I..." She pulled her hands free. Which wasn't a good thing. "I wondered if there was anything else you wanted to say. To...you know, clarify things."

Now he was the one confused. "What do you mean?"

"You say you can see us making a life together," she said, leaning forward. "As what? Friends?"

"Friends?" he sputtered. Then he saw the twinkle in her brown eyes. All the tension inside him vanished, replaced with a warm glow. He took her hands again, glad she let him. "I'm following my heart, as you aptly directed. I love you, Della Winslow. Is that specific enough?"

Her laugh made his heart light.

"I love you too, Max Colton. And yes, I definitely will enjoy having you around."

He kissed her then, as best he could from the deep seat of his chair. "I need to make you a love seat," he muttered, once they broke apart. "That way we both can sit together and make out under the stars."

She laughed again. "I have a better idea. How about we go inside and truly celebrate?"

"You don't need to ask me twice," he responded. "I'm already more than ready."

* * * * *

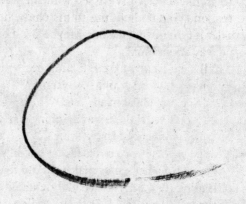